Lora Leigh's novels are:

"TITILLATING."
—*Publishers Weekly*

"SIZZLING HOT."
—*Fresh Fiction*

"INTENSE AND BLAZING HOT."
—*RRTErotic*

"WONDERFULLY DELICIOUS . . . TRULY DECADENT."
—*Romance Junkies*

D0189830

LORA LEIGH
AND
VERONICA CHADWICK

strong, silent cowboy

St. Martin's Paperbacks

NOTE: If you purchased this book without a cover you should be aware that this book is stolen property. It was reported as "unsold and destroyed" to the publisher, and neither the author nor the publisher has received any payment for this "stripped book."

This is a work of fiction. All of the characters, organizations, and events portrayed in this novel are either products of the author's imagination or are used fictitiously.

First published in the United States by St. Martin's Paperbacks, an imprint of St. Martin's Publishing Group.

STRONG, SILENT COWBOY

Copyright © 2021 by Lora Leigh and Veronica Chadwick.

All rights reserved.

For information, address St. Martin's Publishing Group, 120 Broadway, New York, NY 10271.

www.stmartins.com

ISBN: 978-1-250-22009-7

Our books may be purchased in bulk for promotional, educational, or business use. Please contact your local bookseller or the Macmillan Corporate and Premium Sales Department at 1-800-221-7945, ext. 5442, or by email at MacmillanSpecialMarkets@macmillan.com.

Printed in the United States of America

St. Martin's Paperbacks edition 2021

10 9 8 7 6 5 4 3 2 1

IN PRECIOUS MEMORY

We lost our beloved Veronica Chadwick on August 21, 2019, to metastatic colorectal cancer before we knew how to process the fact that she was leaving. Before I could process it or accept it. Now a wound has been left inside us forever, one that will never heal. A missing part of our hearts, forever loved and missed.

No words can express, no amount of tears can heal the wound your absence has left inside us. I miss you, sis. So very much.

FROM HER HUSBAND, PAUL
To my first love, my best friend, my companion, cheerleader, my fragile flower. I love you and miss you every day. You were a friend to all you met. Your contagious smile will be forever embedded in my mind.

FROM HER SON, NATHANIEL
Your love and influence will be felt by and through those you've known until the end of time.

FROM HER DAUGHTER, MARY LUE
Hey, Momma, I miss you so much. It's hard being here without you.
I hope you're having fun up there. Don't get into too much trouble.

FROM THE SISTER SHE CHOSE, SHADOE
My best friend. My sister.
I'm lost in the dark.

When my soul cried out.
When the darkness surrounded me.
You were there.
A friend. A heart I'll forever treasure.
Because you cared. You understood.
And you didn't leave me alone.

Love is just a word
Until someone gives it meaning
Doesn't matter the heartbreak
The love is worth the wait.

prologue

Jake.

It had been three years. Three long, lonely, heart-broken years since he'd disappeared one snowy after-noon in Sweden.

Three years, two of which had been spent running, terrified, certain that death lurked around every corner. Now, relocated to another state, another town, another name, and the past was staring at her as though she had never existed before this moment.

"Jacob, I'd like you to meet the new manager for Dill-erman's Feed and Supply, Sallie Hamblen. Sallie, one of our most eligible ranchers, Jacob Donovan . . ."

Who made the introduction, she had no clue. All she knew was the man who stood in front of her, hand ex-tended, one of those distant little curves to his lips that people gave someone they didn't know and weren't cer-tain they wanted to know.

She fought to swallow, to speak. What came out of her mouth was polite enough.

"Nice to meet you." The sound was strangled to her ears. Too rough.

She barely allowed her hand to touch his before pulling back from him. If he saw it as rude, then so be it. She couldn't make herself do more, give more. Not now. Not with this man.

He didn't know who she was.

The three years had been hard ones, but the stress and worry hadn't yet marked her features. She was the same woman he'd spent three days in a bed with, three days marking her soul in ways she still hadn't recovered from, in ways her heart couldn't forget.

But his name was different as well.

"Where you from, Miss Hamblen?" His tone didn't show disinterest, but there was zero familiarity.

He didn't remember her.

The pain, the humiliation was almost overwhelming. It burned through her mind, into her chest, and struck at her heart. She'd found him after three years of searching, only to learn his name hadn't actually been Jake Rossiter as he'd claimed, but Jacob Donovan. He was a rancher rather than attached to an embassy. But she recognized him. She'd seen him the moment he entered the room, just as he'd seen her. Their eyes had met, and then he'd turned away as though he hadn't spent three days making her scream with pleasure. That he hadn't disappeared from her life as though he had never truly existed.

"Miss Hamblen, are you okay?" her new assistant Tara queried in concern.

Was she okay? She was dying inside. Okay was not an option.

"I think I'm just tired." Sallie turned to the other woman, fighting to hide her desperation to escape. "And it's rather warm in here. I believe I'll return to my hotel if you don't mind, Tara."

She ignored Jacob. She had no choice. Pain was ripping at her chest, tears threatened to fill her eyes. Oh now, wasn't this just wonderful? She'd spent three years agonizing over him, two years of that time she'd spent running for her life. And now, he was here, staring at her, watching her curiously, but he didn't know her. She'd mattered so little that he didn't even remember her.

"I can take you back. Let me get my bag." The other woman rushed off before Sallie could tell her that was okay, she'd make her own way back.

"It was nice to meet you, Mr. Donovan." She barely forced the words past her lips. "If you'll excuse me."

"Of course." A polite smile, a narrowing of his eyes, but he didn't say anything more and allowed her to turn and walk away from him.

She pressed a hand to her stomach, wondering if it were possible to hold back the emotions tearing through her now.

This wasn't what she'd expected to find in the small town of Deer Haven. A place to hide. Time to give her stepfather to figure out who was stalking her and why. That was all she'd hoped for when he'd deposited her in her hotel two weeks ago. Stanley Dillerman had arrived the next day and given her the manager's position at his feed and ranching supply store, and Sallie had fought to just get through each day until she found her balance here.

Found her balance.

Yeah, that wasn't happening now. There wasn't a chance.

Because Jacob Donovan was here. And the weekend she'd spent with him was still a brutal, pain-filled reminder of everything she'd lost since. Everything. Especially the man and the dreams she'd once allowed herself to believe in.

chapter one

Three Years Later

Some men should be outlawed for the sake of all women worldwide. Especially tall, dark-haired, dark-eyed cowboys like Jacob Donovan.

And some women should know better than to allow themselves around them.

Most especially a woman who knew he couldn't be trusted. One who knew exactly how dangerous he could be to her heart and to the defenses she'd built around it.

She was insane to be here, knowing he would be as well. He'd hurt her once already, and she was tempting fate, giving him a second chance to do what he'd done to her the first time around.

And she couldn't help herself.

For three years she'd managed to stay away from him, no matter the temptation or her need. She hadn't even meant enough to him to remember her. But she'd never been able to forget him.

His face drew the eye, commanded attention, and warned a woman she was dealing with a true alpha male.

Sun-bronzed and savagely hewn, that face didn't betray any emotion that he didn't willingly allow it to show, nor did the whisky brown of his gaze. Thick brown hair framed his face carelessly, falling just a little long and tempting a woman to run her fingers through it. It was warm, slightly coarse, and she'd once loved the feel and weight of it against her fingers, her breasts, between her thighs . . .

Broad shoulders and obviously tight abs were covered with a black cotton shirt that did nothing to hide the fact that he was truly built. Long, powerful legs were encased in denim, a wide belt cinching hips a woman would love to wrap her legs around. She'd definitely loved wrapping her legs around them.

And he wore cowboy boots.

What was it about cowboy boots that made a man look so damned sexy?

And he was sexy as hell.

The fact that he was the most desirable male in the bar wasn't debatable.

Why didn't he recognize her?

It had been more than a few years, and her looks had changed. In ways, everything about her, who and what she had been and was now, was completely different. She wasn't the eighteen-year-old he'd charmed on a cold winter's night in a foreign land. But he wasn't the twenty-five-year-old man she'd so been fascinated with anymore either. He'd known her as Kyra, not Sallie. The man who had bound a part of her with his kiss, his touch, and three days and nights of the most incredible passion a woman could ever know, and he'd forgotten all about her when he'd left her.

Sallie drew in a long, slow breath and forced her attention from the man leaning relaxed against the bar as he talked to another rancher.

His friend was an irritant. Pride Culpepper had done everything but offer her his brothers' ranch if she'd just go to dinner with him. The oldest brother, Justice, had actually offered the ranch, then grinned and took it back.

Lifting her beer, she took another sip of the warming drink and barely held back a grimace.

She wasn't particularly fond of beer, or of bars. So why the hell had she allowed herself to be convinced to come to this one again? She could have just hung around the house, washed clothes, painted her nails. Or something. Instead, she was hiding in the corner of a rowdy, country music bar filled with men on the make and women pretending they weren't there for the same thing.

Even her friends, as much as she liked them and enjoyed their company, were consumed with the search for that perfect man. And what made them think this was the place to find him, she wasn't certain.

She had known Jacob would be there, though. He was often there with his friends. He rarely danced, never brought in a lover or chose a lover from the bar. He drank a few beers, chatted with friends, sometimes flirted with the women who came up to him, then left alone. Just as Sallie did.

She should have left when she realized he lived in the area. She should have definitely left when it was apparent he didn't recognize her. Sallie Hamblen was nothing to the rancher who lived in Deer Haven, California, all his life. But for a moment in time, long, long ago, she'd believed she could mean something him.

She'd been introduced to him as Kyra Bannon, he'd been introduced to her as Jake Rossiter. And for one incredible weekend, she'd lived a young woman's most passionate dream.

Her lips quirked at that thought. And like most dreams, it had been over far too quickly. He'd disappeared with a promise to return in a few hours. A promise he'd broken. He'd never returned. No one had known who he was when she asked, and her life had gone on.

Or had it?

Her gaze moved over the dance floor from where she sat in the shadowed corner, wondering if she could possibly escape while her friends were occupied. She should have never agreed to meet them. Not again. Not knowing that he'd be there, and the sight of him would torment her with memories better left forgotten.

God, she should just leave right now. Now, before her wants, her needs, overcame her good sense. It was obvious he didn't recognize her, and even if he did, what good would it do?

Yeah, it was time she left before she made a complete fool of herself. Before years of anger, hurt, and betrayal drove her to do something completely irrational.

She'd driven herself, and she'd barely had half a beer. Getting home wouldn't be a problem. Except she was certain her friends would give her hell over it.

She had promised to go out with them and have fun, after all.

This just wasn't her idea of fun.

Come tomorrow they'd shake their heads at the fact Sallie had once again left alone, hadn't danced, hadn't flirted, or even tried to meet any of the eligible men there.

Because that was what she always did, she went home alone. She slept alone. It was safer. And it would keep her away from Jacob Donovan. And perhaps it would keep her friends and Jacob safe.

Setting the beer on the table, she restrained another sigh, caught sight of her friends, Lily and Shay, and decided they'd probably never miss her. When she got to the car, she'd text her goodbyes and let them know she'd given up on the "fun" part of the night and gone home.

It was probably what they expected anyway.

A second later, her gaze moved back to Jacob and she found herself caught, snared, her gaze held by his, and he didn't seem in a hurry to release her. Her heartbeat sped up, and her breathing became heavier. A flush heated her face, her body, and her thighs tightened in reaction.

Her breasts felt heavier, her nipples hard and more sensitive as a heated warmth curled in the pit of her stomach and worked its way lower. She was suddenly aware of her own body in a way she never had been before. It was crazy. This hadn't even happened the first time they'd met. Not like this, so deep and intense.

Sweet mercy, that look had her toes curling with pleasure. With memories that haunted even her dreams.

With a certainty that Jacob Donovan had ruined her for another man's touch, and she wanted more.

In the years since that single weekend she'd spent with him, the power of that look only affected her more. She knew the pleasure he could give her now, knew his touch and his possession. Six years hadn't been long enough for her to forget.

But would there ever be a time she would forget?

Yep, she should go home before she managed to get herself caught in a mess that would have only one outcome.

Sallie's broken heart.

Looking out over the dance floor one last time, she saw Lily and her sister still dancing and knew it would be a while before she was missed. They'd just have to be upset with her. She was not going to allow herself to become fascinated with the one man every woman lusted for, and it seemed, none of them had possessed.

She didn't need the angst. She damned sure didn't need to torture herself with a man she couldn't have, even for a night. Because God knew, she could only become a problem. What followed her wouldn't tolerate anyone standing in the way when she was found.

As she began to push her chair back, a broad, strong male hand placed another beer next to the half-full bottle she'd been sipping from. And beside it, a short glass, half full of what she was certain was whisky.

And oh, how she could use the false courage it might bring her.

Sallie stared at the bottle, damp droplets of icy water easing down the neck. She was all too aware of the man taking the chair next to her and leaning back, relaxed, watching her. From the corner of her eye she watched as he lifted his own bottle to his lips and drank, his gaze never leaving her.

This was a really bad idea.

Still, she turned her head and gazed back at him, fascinated by the hint of gold she glimpsed in the whisky depths of his eyes. And the fact that he watched her with a complete lack of familiarity but a hell of a lot of lust.

How easy it had been to forget her, evidently. He'd spent three days and nights in her bed doing things to her she'd never imagined a man could do to a woman. And he didn't even know who she was.

It was almost laughable.

"The bartender told me that was your favorite." He nodded to the beer. "But you didn't seem too interested in the one you were nursing, so I brought a backup."

Before she could stop herself, her tongue swiped over her lower lip, and the way his gaze narrowed and his expression tightened told her she'd betrayed far more than she wished with that action.

She cleared her throat before saying, "I was just leaving."

"Alone?" The question was asked almost absently as his gaze lifted from her lips to her eyes.

Sallie swallowed, wishing she could breathe in enough to actually get some oxygen to her suddenly dumbfounded brain. He might not recognize her, but he wanted her. She knew the look of hunger, of lust on his face, and it only made her need him more.

"That would probably be best." But instead of getting

up and doing just that, what did she do? She lifted the glass and brought it to her lips before sipping the liquid, all the while holding his gaze.

And it was a hell of a lot better than the beer.

The whisky was a wash of sensual heat traveling from her tongue to her belly and warming her insides in a way beer could just never do. But it came nowhere close to how Jacob could warm her or the heat his look alone could send traveling through her body.

Placing the glass next to the bottle, she stared at it for a moment, knowing she should have just left.

She should just leave now.

"Do you always do what's best?" He leaned forward, bracing one arm on the table as he turned to her, the other resting on the back of her chair as a hint of amusement lit his gaze.

She always did what was best. It was ingrained in her. Survival instinct. Doing what was best was the only way to protect herself. But now, all but surrounded by him, she wanted nothing more than to lean in closer, to feel his body heat wrapping around her once again.

"Usually." Because she damned sure wasn't doing what was best now.

This man was dangerous, and she knew it. Something about him warned her that he rarely played, but when he did, he played to win.

She'd lived there for three years, knowing who he was, remembering that single night far too often, and allowing herself to be tormented by it. And now, here he was, plying her with some damned fine whisky and watching her with no small amount of hunger in his hard features.

"And now?" His brow arched, arrogant certainty so much a part of him that there was no disguising it.

What was she going to do now?

She lifted the glass and finished her drink, the tingling warmth washing through her, reminding her of the warmth he'd once filled her with. Only reminding her of it, though. Jacob had the power to burn her alive and she knew it.

She didn't dare gaze around now, certain every eye was on them, too curious, too intent. Most people in the community knew each other, or at the very least had heard of one another. And she knew Jacob did not take women home from bars, and he hadn't been known to take a lover from the community in over six years.

"Doesn't look like it." She sighed, turning her gaze back to him.

She didn't play games, unfortunately, and she wasn't much of a flirt. She was too straightforward, too mouthy her friends sometimes said. She wasn't going to start now.

"Did you drive yourself?" Was his voice a little rougher, darker?

God, she'd orgasm before he ever touched her if it got any deeper.

She nodded at the question.

"Your place, or a hotel? My place is simply too damned far away." There was nothing arrogant, or superior in the way he asked the question.

His expression seemed, perhaps not softer, but not so hard either.

"My place," she all but whispered.

Her bed.

If she was going to do this, and it appeared she was going to, then she wanted him in her bed where his scent would linger once he left. Where she could remember, torment herself, and ache more than ever.

She was a fool and she knew it, yet couldn't resist the need for just one more night.

He rose to his feet, extending his hand out to her, his gaze still holding hers. An irresistible invitation.

Just for tonight, she told herself. Just for this night.

"I'll have your car brought around later," he told her as she laid her hand in his. "We'll take my truck."

And she didn't argue.

This was crazy. It was insane.

As she let him lead her through the bar, she kept trying to tell herself what a huge mistake this was, but that inner part of her, the part that ached in the dead of the night for his touch, refused to listen.

She was going to end up kicking herself in the nights to come, and she knew it. If she was incredibly lucky, then her memories of that long-ago night were just a young woman's illusions. If she was very lucky, it had been nothing more, and once this night was over, so would be her fascination for him.

As they left the bar and the night wrapped around them, the chill of the early fall night slipped past the narrow gray skirt and short-sleeved blouse she wore. She would have thought reality would return. And it might have had a chance if his arm hadn't slipped around her, his palm lying at her hip as he led her through the parking lot.

If the hard-muscled warmth of him didn't feel as

though it were wrapping around her, cocooning her from reality and giving her this one fantasy.

She was insane, that was all there was to it. Crazy to leave like this with him when she knew he didn't remember her. She'd meant nothing to him before, and this night would probably mean little more.

She hadn't pleased him their first time together, a little voice reminded her, what made her think she could please him now? She was no more experienced now than she had been then. Sexually, she had only that weekend to draw on, nothing more.

She'd disappointed him then. What in God's name made her think this time would be any different?

"I can drive myself." The words slipped past her lips as fear and uncertainty began to take hold of her. "I don't live far from here. You could follow me."

She could take a moment to think, to be certain that this was what she wanted to do. That the risk wouldn't be too great.

There was an electronic beep of a door unlocking as he drew to a stop and a second later, he'd opened the passenger side of a truck. Before Sallie could completely process what he was doing, he turned her to him, one hand sliding into the hair at the back of her head, long fingers clenching sensually to drag her head back, and he destroyed her with a kiss.

A kiss hotter, more explosive than even those she remembered.

She was only distantly aware of her fingers clenching at his powerful shoulders, her lips parting for his tongue, her body becoming too warm, too sensitive as she arched to him. Need swept through her with the force of a hurricane, tearing down barriers, washing away fear.

It was fiery, sending heat sweeping through her, inside her. It was better than the finest whisky, and a damned sight more intoxicating. So intoxicating that when he lifted her closer and she felt his erection against her lower stomach, she moaned in need.

He was so hard. She knew his shaft was large, the crest wide and capable of giving the most ecstatic pleasure.

Her arms curled around his neck as he held her between his hard body and the truck behind her. Poised on the four-inch heels she'd worn, she strained to get closer, desperate to feel more of him.

One large, callused hand gripped her hip now, holding her in place as his lips moved on hers, nipped, licked and a moan whispered from her lips. At the sound, the hand at her hip moved to her waist and the drag of her blouse from the band of her skirt had anticipation searing her.

When his hand touched the bare skin of her waist, Sallie curled her fingers into his neck, the rasp of his palm awakened every nerve ending in her body as it slid to the lace-covered mound of her breast.

She couldn't stop the whimper that left her lips or the way her body pressed closer, silently begging for more.

Oh God, she needed more.

His lips released hers, and before Sallie knew it, he'd lifted her, placing her in the seat of the truck and turning her to face forward before closing the door firmly.

Sallie fought to breathe, to make sense of what had

just happened, of why this one man's touch could sweep away years of doubts and fears.

Jacob slid into the driver's side seat, closed the door behind him and started the vehicle with a push of the auto-start but he didn't put the vehicle in gear immediately.

"If you're going to say no, do it now." The growl in his voice had her fingers curling where they lay in her lap. "Because I'll be honest, this goes much further, and I'll have a hell of a time pulling back."

Turning her head, she stared back at him and knew she wouldn't be saying no at any point.

She held his stare with her own. "It was too late to say no when I stepped out of the door of the bar. My house is about five miles from here, just outside town."

He gave a short nod. "The old Hanover place." The truck reversed from the parking lot. "I know where you live."

And that should have surprised her. She was certain she'd be surprised later, once she had a chance to think about it. Once the cold light of day revealed all the mistakes she was certain she was getting ready to make.

"Jacob Donovan," she murmured as he pulled from the parking lot and headed for her house. "You've just broken a major rule as I understand it. You've never been known to leave that bar, or any other, with a woman."

There was no sense of triumph in her tone, if anything, she sounded slightly put out.

"I'm not the only one," he reminded her quietly, glancing over at her. "Three years and not a single date. They probably have a betting pool somewhere on both of us."

He didn't know the half of it.

"As I understand it, yours somehow ended up with the Ladies Auxiliary, according to my friends. I'm rather scared to know where mine's located."

He shot her a look of surprise. "Ladies Auxiliary? Hell, my grandmother's on the auxiliary. That can't be true. Someone's lying to you."

She almost laughed at the confusion and denial in his voice.

"You seem to be a local legend in sheer self-control when it comes to the hometown women," she pointed out. "Which in hindsight, perhaps we should have been more discreet."

Or perhaps she should have given this more thought.

The need for touch was something she dealt with by ignoring it. If she hugged her pillow a little tighter at night and fought back the inner fury that her body was betraying her, then so be it.

"Discreet doesn't happen in this town," he told her. "Might as well show 'em you don't give a damn to begin with."

"I don't give a damn." She frowned at the thought. "But I'm not from here and I don't have a betting sheet with the Ladies Auxiliary."

"Think that matters?" he drawled, and the sound of his voice sent another pulsing surge of heat rushing through her body.

Her nipples ached now, her panties were wet, and she wanted him in a way that would frighten her later. She could feel her feminine moisture as it eased from her body, slickening her, preparing her for him.

She'd made her decision tonight, and she would stick

to it. And she'd make memories she hoped would keep her warm once she had to run again. She couldn't stay and she knew it. Sooner or later she'd be forced to run again. And she didn't want the broken heart she was certain to have when he was finished with her.

It was far better to take a single night, to save it within her memories and hold it to her when the nights became cold.

She'd been here for three years, far longer than she'd expected to be when she first arrived. With a lot of luck, she'd finally managed to escape whoever had chased her since the night four years ago when she'd been forced to run from home.

Four years, she thought, staring into the darkness beyond the truck's lights. She was only twenty-four, and sometimes, she felt eons older. Her life was being stolen, taken from her, one year at a time, and what had she missed the most?

She'd missed Jacob's touch.

chapter two

Be bold.
 Be daring.
Her mother's advice went through Sallie's mind as she watched the headlights cut through the dark on the empty country road. When Sallie moved to Deer Haven, Megan Dougal had smiled coolly and told Sallie to find happiness for a change. To be bold and daring and perhaps it would find her.

Bold.

Daring.

She released her seat belt, aware of his glance and the dark sensuality that lit his expression as she turned toward him. She moved closer.

"Start and I'll end up fucking you on the side of the road," he warned her, lifting his hand from the steering wheel as she moved in closer.

"No, you won't," she said, her voice low. "You're

renowned for your self-control under pressure. You'll make it to the house."

And if he didn't, then she'd know she broke that control. If he pulled the truck over to take her rather than allowing her to take him, then at least she'd know she could still affect him.

His expression hardened when she gripped his belt buckle and released it, then loosened the metal tab and zipper straining over the heavy erection beneath.

Grimacing, he glanced at her, then back to the road as she drew the straining flesh free, trepidation building inside her at the wide, steel-hard flesh revealed.

The broad, mushroomed crest throbbed in her hand as she fisted it for a moment, the shaft straining as her grip slid over it, loving every single inch.

"Sallie, sweetheart, you're playing a very dangerous game." That warning slid through her senses. It was a challenge, a dare she wasn't about to turn down. "You put your mouth on my dick, and you'll find out how dangerous it can get."

"Don't hold my head," she warned him, knowing it was more a dare. "If you do, it's over."

"You get my dick in that hot little mouth of yours and all bets are off, baby." His body was tight with tension, with self-control. "So, take your chances."

She wanted to. She wanted his flesh in her mouth again, wanted to taste him, to tease him.

"No," she retorted. "You'll take yours."

Turning to him, she lowered her head between his body and the steering wheel, her tongue peeking out to taste him first.

And whatever dark hunger had gripped her in the bar surged forward with a force she was helpless against. A need she couldn't deny herself.

He tasted like a storm and of midnight beneath her curious tongue. Clean and intoxicating. Her lips parted, spreading over the wide crest, a moan slipping past her lips as she gave herself to the twisting, shadowed needs she'd never realized were lying in wait for a moment's weakness.

For a man as dark as the hunger that tormented her in the deepest parts of the night. A hunger he'd taught her to crave.

As the heavy crest filled her mouth, she was only dimly aware of Jacob's hand smoothing down her back, tugging at her hip, urging her into a kneeling position. Once he had her where he wanted her, his cock moving between her lips as she knelt in the seat, his hand bunched in her skirt, tugging it to her hips.

"Fuck!" The exclamation was a rasp of dangerous desire, stroking over her senses as he pushed his hand beneath the band of her panties. "That's good, baby. So fucking good."

A second later she couldn't halt her cry as her panties were torn from her, fragile lace rending and being tossed away. Her head lifted, nearly clearing the iron-hard flesh she held in her mouth.

"Don't you dare stop," he demanded, his hand smoothing over her rear. "Or I won't do this."

Broad fingers slid through the crevice of her rear to the silky glide of feminine juices coating the bare flesh below.

The stroke of his fingers between the swollen folds of flesh was incredible. Flares of heat and exquisite sensation raced over her clit, circled it, tightened it.

"That's it, sweetheart." He groaned. "Suck me deep and I'll see if I can make you feel real good too."

She hadn't anticipated that. The way his fingers rimmed the entrance to her sex, stroked, urging more of the moisture free. His fingers played over the swollen folds, petted, slid through the thickening layer of natural lubrication, and teased around the hardened bud of her clit.

"Ah hell, your sweet mouth." His voice was low, sensual need pulsing in the tone as she moved her mouth over the hardened flesh, her tongue licking with sensual delight as another moan slipped past her throat.

Jacob fought to keep his eyes on the road and from crossing at same time as Sallie's mouth tightened on the head of his cock and her moan vibrated over the sensitive flesh. And it shouldn't be so damned erotic that it threatened the control he'd never had a problem with before.

His balls were tight with the need to come, the shaft pulsing beneath her delicate hand as her mouth worked over the sensitive head. She sucked, licked, drew the crest nearly to her throat, and moaned with desperate need.

She was hungry. Hungry to touch, to be touched. He could feel the heat in her rising with each stroke of his fingers on the slick, heated folds of her pussy. Fine tremors washed through her delicate body each time his fingers neared the clenched, snug entrance and with each moment the tension building in her heightened. And so did his.

She'd come so damned easy.

One thrust of his fingers inside the heated grip of her sex and she'd explode for him.

And it was tempting. So damned tempting.

Just to feel her shuddering, to hear her cries . . .

Perhaps if he did, the pressure on his cock would ease, he thought desperately as she sucked him like a favored treat. Her mouth was slow and easy, then hungry, suckling him deeper. She knew just where to lick, to stroke, to take him deeper than he'd imagined she'd do. She did it slowly, as though she knew exactly what he liked. Exactly how he liked it. As though she'd stepped out of his fantasies and come to life.

That thought had his cock pulsing, spilling a short, violent spurt of his release before he managed to pull her head free of him and twist the steering wheel to turn into the paved driveway of her home. He came to a hard stop at the side of the house and threw the vehicle into park.

Reaching across the seat he flipped the glove box open and pulled a condom free of the box he kept there.

There was no waiting until he could get to her bed. Still, it seemed to take forever to roll the condom over his erection.

She'd never gone parking in her life. The odd thought went through Sallie's mind as Jacob lifted her, pulling her legs over his denim-covered thighs and holding her in place, poised above the erection rising from between his thighs.

"I can't wait." Deep, dark, his voice rasped through her senses as the buttons of her blouse gave way beneath his hand, revealing the lacy bra she wore beneath.

The clasp gave way a second later and the cups pushed back from the sensitive flesh.

Sallie's head tipped back, a cry tearing from her lips as her hands jerked to his head, burying in the long hair as his mouth covered a tight, too-sensitive nipple and sucked it in. At the same moment, the blunt head of his cock pressed slowly inside her.

The thick intrusion was both pleasure and pain. A slow, stretching penetration that had her crying out, uncertain if she could bear the sensations. His mouth at her breasts, first one then the other, wasn't easy either. But easy wasn't what she needed. She needed to feel, the lash of sensual intensity, rising ecstasy. Teeth and tongue, his mouth sucking, drawing on her with hunger. His cock, forging inside her in short, hard strokes, sending arcs of sensation through flesh long unused and rarely thought about.

"Jacob . . ." she gasped his name as she took more, agony and ecstasy merging until she didn't know which she wanted more.

But she knew she needed more.

Panting for air, she undulated against each thrust, taking more of him as she swore flames were igniting inside her.

"Hold on, baby." His voice was hoarse, a low rasp of male lust that only made her need more, made her juices spill faster, slicker, to ease his way.

She felt his thighs bunch, his body tense, and a second later, his cock thrust fully inside her, buried completely as Sallie felt the world dissolve in such an explosion of ecstasy so brilliant, so white hot it bordered on terrifying.

She thought she cried out his name as lashing pleasure tore through her, jerking her body as he held her in place and groaned her name. She was only distantly aware of the fact that he was finding his release as well. The violent tension, the ripple of a tremor racing through his body, and the hard flex of his cock inside her assured her he'd found pleasure with her.

"Damn, sweetheart, I don't know if my legs are going to work." Amusement threaded his voice, but what shocked Sallie the most was the way his hands caressed her back, his lips brushing over her temple.

Was he petting her?

She couldn't remember a time when she'd been stroked, touched since Jacob. And when his hands cupped her shoulders and smoothed the flesh of her upper arms, she wanted to purr in sheer contented pleasure.

"We have to move." His lips touched her neck as she lay against his chest, her head resting on his shoulder. "I'm not finished with you yet, sugar."

He wasn't . . . finished with her?

"Come on, baby." He helped her off him, his hands tightening on her waist as she moaned at the feel of his still hard cock pulling from inside her. "Damn. Not enough room in this truck."

In less than a minute he moved her, fixed his jeans, and pushed open the door. Stepping out, he turned back to her as she slid to the edge of the seat.

"My shoes." She turned to search for the heels when she found herself suddenly lifted into his arms.

"Got your keys?" The timber of his voice was darkening again, that sound of male lust causing her womb to clench, her inner flesh to spasm with her own renewed desire.

"My pocket," she answered him, looping her arms around his neck. "You didn't have to carry me."

But he wanted to. And that was dangerous.

Jacob ignored the voice of caution. There was something about carrying her and stroking her as she eased down from her orgasm that gave him a sense of satisfaction.

He was always protective of the women he fucked, always made certain they found pleasure, that he did more than simply get them off. Women's bodies were soft, delicate, and he wanted to give them affection during sex.

It was different with Sallie.

She was different.

Taking the keys from her, Jacob managed to unlock the door and open it without putting her down. Once inside he kicked the door closed, slid the lock back into place, and glanced around the shadowed rooms.

He took in the dark wood floors, firmly closed curtains, and spotless living room and kitchen. A light tan sectional was positioned in front of a screened fireplace with a low light burning on an end table.

The kitchen was open and airy with light oak cabinets and marble countertops. A bar, two barstools, and a gas island stove. The kitchen flowed into the dining room and there a short hallway led the way to a dimly lit bedroom.

He glimpsed a few pictures in the living room. A

young couple with a child and a stern, older man. There were no pictures of Sallie and only a few items that appeared to be mementos.

The bedroom held a king-sized walnut sleigh bed with an old quilt draped over the footboard. Matching walnut furniture, thick rugs. He'd check it all out later, he promised himself as he placed Sallie on the bed and followed her down, his lips catching hers in a deep, hungry kiss.

He hadn't had a chance to touch her, to watch her face flush with her need, see her swollen, hard-tipped breasts, or eat that soft pussy in the truck. Something he intended to rectify before he took her again.

"Jacob." There was a soft protest in her voice as his lips lifted from hers. Her thick, blonde lashes lifted languorously. Her face flushed a pretty soft pink, and her pale blue eyes darkened, revealing a dark gray border he'd not noticed before at the bar.

"We need to get these clothes off." He groaned. "I intend to kiss every inch of your pretty body. Can't do that with all these clothes in the way."

Some emotion—surprise—flared in her expression before her flush deepened.

Sitting on the edge of the bed, Jacob pulled his boots and socks from his feet. Standing, he turned, undid the few remaining buttons left on his shirt, and shrugged it from his powerful shoulders. As he undressed, he watched Sallie shed her torn blouse and bra.

Taking off his jeans, he gripped his straining dick, grimacing at the tightness in his balls as Sallie lifted her hips and pulled off her skirt.

Have mercy.

Jacob nearly groaned the words aloud as his gaze centered at her thighs and the feminine sweetness gleaming on the delicate flesh there.

"Spread your legs." How daring would she get for him?

Pale, slender thighs parted and he nearly demanded she tease him, touch herself for him, but that shadowed need he kept glimpsing in her expression and the memory of her reaction when he touched her in the truck drifted through his lust-clouded brain.

"You're beautiful," he told her instead, his gaze going over her firm, hard-tipped breasts, slightly rounded tummy, and—damn—the silken, so wet flesh between her thighs. "So fuckin' pretty I could come just looking at you."

"Don't." A little shake of her head had something in his heart clenching. "You don't have to say that. Just touch me again. Please."

Placing his knee on the side of the bed, Jacob lowered his head, lips brushing over hers as he stretched out beside her, rather than moving immediately between her thighs.

She'd expected that. She should have known better. Jacob liked to linger, to stroke and tease and drive her to the edge of reason before allowing her release.

She didn't want to spoil this, didn't want to destroy the illusion his touch and the pleasure weaved around her. She'd give him whatever he wanted as long as she could feel his callused hands on her flesh, his kiss, and his erection moving inside her again.

Staring up at him, she lifted her hands to touch him,

only to have him catch her wrists with one broad hand and draw them over her head, restraining them.

He didn't like her touch?

Her fingers curled into loose fists, hoping it would be enough to remind her not to try. She couldn't guess what he wanted. With her hands restrained, she had no way of pleasuring him. If she didn't pleasure him, he wouldn't pleasure . . .

The thought scattered, disintegrated as his head lowered and his lips moved to the opposite side of her neck. Bending her head, resting it on his shoulder, Sallie fought to breathe. Her lips parted, a moan breaking free as she felt his teeth against the sensitive column of her neck, his free hand stroked her side, her belly.

It was so good.

Her body jerked involuntarily as he began to explore her neck with teeth, lips, and tongue. Gentle kisses changed to rougher, heated caresses. By time he made his way to her shoulder, she was a shuddering mass of sensation, and all she could do was crave more.

"Let me touch you." She gasped as the backs of his fingers drifted over her hard nipples and those diabolical kisses began moving lower.

"Later." The demand, the dominance in his tone spiked with lust wasn't threatening or a warning. "Let me taste you, baby. All over. The taste of you goes to my head."

Her taste went to his head?

Her lips parted again and pressed to the hard, sunbronzed shoulder as her tongue peeked out and licked at him, tasting him. He tasted like a lightning-charged storm, salt, and something that teased at her taste buds, drawing her back for another taste. And another.

With each taste, she needed more. Lost in the knowledge that his breathing was growing more ragged, his body tensing against hers, she was jerked from the exploration by the feel of her nipple exploding with sensation.

She lifted to him. Her head went back, neck arching as a cry tore from her lips. White hot, wicked forks of sensation raced toward her womb as it clenched with desperate pleasure. Heated moisture spilled from her vagina onto the naked folds. Her hips lifted, thighs bunching as she fought the need building inside her.

"Oh God, Jacob, more . . . more . . ." Harder, like he had in the truck.

Her head twisted on the pillow, perspiration slickened her flesh.

"More?" His voice was a hungry growl. "Tell me what you need, baby. Harder?" His mouth drew on the tip, his teeth raked it, but for a second. "Or lighter?" He licked, curled his tongue around the tip.

"No," she cried, desperate now. "Harder. Like you did before. Oh God, please."

Jacob drew in a hard, ragged breath as his tongue licked delicately at her nipple. He could feel the tension gathering in her belly, her thighs, as he stroked her with his free hand. She was going to come from his mouth at her nipples, he could sense it. She was humming with the need, poised so delicately close to the edge of orgasm.

Damn her. He'd never make it to her pussy with his mouth if she got off from the hard, hungry pull of his mouth on her nipple.

And he wanted to give it her.

Feel her.

His mouth covered a pebble-hard tip and drew it in, and he didn't just suckle her, he let himself consume her. Nips, draws of his mouth, his tongue lashing at it.

She tasted damn good. She tasted like something out of his dreams. Sunshine, sugar, and heat and she was making his balls ache with the need to come again. At the same time, the need to taste the sweet flesh between her thighs was killing him.

Releasing her nipple, he kissed and nipped his way down her body, taking lingering tastes of her flesh as he moved ever lower. He released her hands and stroked down her sides, lost in the feel of her silken flesh and the treat awaiting him below.

"Jacob . . ." she moaned as he pushed her thighs apart, the breathy sound washing over him with a sense of déjà vu.

He was close to panting as his lips moved over her thigh while he lifted her leg and braced her foot at his shoulder, leaving her open to him, those soft, broken little moans reminding him of far too many dreams. With her thighs spread wide he was able to glimpse the pretty bare lips of her pussy. They glistened with her cream, made him crave the taste of her. Parting the soft flesh, he let his fingers rub and play. He circled her straining little clit with one, not really touching it, teasing it as her gasping breaths became moans of need.

Dipping a finger lower he drew the slick honey spilling from her to cover it. He rimmed the narrow little opening then slowly, so slowly pushed inside her.

His teeth clenched at her sharp cry, the jerk of her hips as she lifted to him and he knew he was riding a razor's edge where his control was concerned. Easing his finger back, he relished the tight grip of her sheath, the little fluttering ripples of it.

He wanted to go slow, to eat her like a rare, precious treat, and he was damned if he knew why. The control for it wasn't there, though. The second he lowered his head and sent his tongue tunneling inside her, he was lost to her.

Her taste was exquisite. Sweet, a little spicy, like a fantasy. The hunger for her had his normally tightly leashed control surging free. His tongue stabbed inside her responsive little sheath, licked, flickered around the opening, and caught the fresh wave of sweetness that spilled onto his tongue.

She was addictive. Something he'd hungered for without knowing exactly what it was or how or where to find it. Now he had her. And she was hot and sweet. Like ambrosia.

He was dying for her.

As he tasted her, he used a thumb to circle her clit, play with it, brush against it. He could feel the surging sensations gathering inside her, taste it against his tongue. And when he felt her orgasm race over her, he nearly lost control of his own.

He'd be damned if he was going to come on the sheets instead of inside the sweet heat of her pussy.

Rising to his knees, he pushed her thighs apart, moved between them, the painfully engorged flesh of his dick pounding in need. Positioning himself at the entrance, he began pushing inside her.

She couldn't take all of him at once.

So fucking tight, clenching the head of his dick, milking it, pulling at the seed in his painfully tight balls. And fuck him. No condom. Son of a bitch.

He looked down at her, a question in his eyes.

She looked back up at him and nodded.

"I need to hear it," he said, his voice hoarse.

"Yes. Yes, please," she said, breathless.

The clench and release of her vagina bit around the head of his cock with ever increasing waves of sensation.

She was climbing for him again.

As he began penetrating the fist-tight grip of her body, she began climbing to the next orgasm. And he'd feel it when she came. It would kill him. Not spilling inside her might give him a stroke, but he'd feel her. Naked and hot against the oversensitive head of his dick, her flesh stretched so tight around him, he'd feel every ripple, every contraction of her orgasm.

Coming over her, his lips caressed her breast, a hard, little nipple, stroked to her neck where he caressed the sensitive flesh as her nails dug into his back. With a groan he surged completely inside her, pulled back, and thrust again. Each hard impalement dragged a cry from her lips as her body began to vibrate with the need to explode around him again.

He held her there, poised on that razor edge, each thrust different, short, then filling her until she screamed that he do it again.

"Sweet baby," he groaned. "You gonna come for me again, honey? Come around my dick, Sallie. Let me feel you fly."

He thrusted inside her hard and deep then, again,

powerful thrusts that pushed past the clenched flesh stretching it, stroking inside her, giving her that striking border of pleasure and pain.

"Jacob . . ." His name tore past her lips. "Oh God, Jacob. Hold me. Please hold me."

He increased the tempo of his thrusts as his arms went around her, holding her, keeping her close to him. He felt her when it hit her. Her body tightened until the tension sang through her flesh. A wail parted her lips, breathless, gasping and the heated depths of her pussy locked down on his cock in a sensual vise.

Fuck.

Her come rained over the throbbing head of his dick, causing his balls to clench dangerously.

He'd never come inside a woman . . . Hell, he'd never fucked one bare like this. A violent pulse of pleasure shot up his spine as wracking shudders tore through Sallie. Her pussy sucked at his erection from base to crest, pushing him closer. Too fucking close.

His hips jerked back, the head of his cock barely clearing the ecstatic grip of her pussy before his seed shot across her thighs. Jacob moaned at the sight.

Goddamn. He was going to fuck her bare again. It was too damned good, too fucking hot. He wanted to bury himself deep and mark her with his release, spill inside her and . . .

He was fucking insane.

chapter three

Sallie pulled the collar of her blouse a little higher against her neck and tried to tell herself no one was going to see what Jacob had done to her the night before. She wondered if he was able to hide what she'd done to him.

Pushing through the back entrance of Dillerman's, she ducked her head, avoiding the gazes of the men working on the loading dock and hurried up the stairs to her office.

If she stayed at her desk today, kept her head down, and didn't make her usual rounds, then she might actually manage to keep anyone from knowing for certain that she'd slept with the town's local legend. The love bites he'd left on her neck would proclaim her a liar, though.

Closing the office door behind her, Sallie leaned against it and blew out a hard breath.

She'd tried countless times to tell herself the marks

weren't really as bad as she thought they were. She'd never had a love bite before, so of course that would make the marks seem worse, she reasoned. Wouldn't it?

She knew better. Even with the makeup she'd tried to apply, the fact that Jacob Donovan was a wild man in bed showed itself on her flesh.

Something he hadn't done that first time. He hadn't marked her skin, just her heart, her passions. Somehow, he'd managed to imprint his touch on her in a way she'd never been able to forget.

After he'd taken her the second time, he'd all but jumped from the bed and run to escape. As she watched him in silence, he'd dressed, his expression closed and hard, pulled on his socks and boots, and simply walked out. She still didn't know why. She had no idea what she'd done wrong, or what he wanted that she hadn't provided.

She should have never left the bar with him. She should have just told him to meet her at the house and hide his truck in the back so no one could see it. Then, she'd never have to face the fact that she'd failed to satisfy Deer Haven's legend. Again. Or that he was more lover than she'd known how to handle. Shaking her head at the futility of even trying to guess at what she'd done wrong, Sallie pushed away from the door and strode to her desk. Collapsing in the leather chair behind it, she propped her elbows on the smooth wood and buried her face in them.

Jacob had been her only lover, despite the facsimile of a marriage she'd endured for nearly a year. Her lover had left her and not come back, her own husband hadn't wanted to touch her, and once finished, this time, Jacob had run even faster than he had the first time.

At this rate, she may as well just stamp "failure" on her forehead and be done with it.

An abrupt knock on the door had her lifting her head, her hand falling to the collar of her shirt to make certain it was in place as the door pushed open and her assistant strode in.

Tara Danner placed Sallie's morning cup of coffee on her desk, stepped back, and crossed her arms under her breasts and stared down at her reprovingly. She was several inches taller than Sallie with short black hair and vivid blue eyes. She'd been a life saver when Sallie had first moved to Deer Haven. The woman knew everyone, and her insights into the customers and possible problems had been invaluable.

"What?" Sallie demanded as Tara continued to frown at her.

"We have gossip," Tara informed her as though it were some kind of store emergency. "Something about you and Jacob Donovan leaving a bar together and his truck being seen at your house?"

Sallie widened her eyes in mock shock. "Seriously? I believe I may have spoken to him in the bar."

Yeah, that one wasn't going to fly.

Especially when Tara pulled her smartphone free, pulled up a picture, and showed it to Sallie.

Yep, that was her house, and that was Jacob's truck.

"Wanna try again?" Tara's lips twitched in amusement.

"Amazing what technology can do nowadays." Sallie looked closer, as though amazed.

"And that mark on your neck is a technological marvel as well," Tara suddenly said wryly, the laughter in her eyes unmistakable. "Oh my God, Sallie. That's a hell of a hickey."

"Is not." Sallie slapped her hand over her neck to hide the mark. "Go away, Tara. And I'm not in for the rest of the day. I have work to do."

Tara continued to stare at her, her lips parted, blue eyes wide.

Tara scoffed, planting her hands on her hips and staring down at her imperiously. "You're dreaming. I heard about you leaving the bar with him last night. Before I woke up this morning, I had a dozen messages concerning the two of you. I know you knew better. You know how every woman in this damned county is focused on that man. He comes into town and he just about has a mob watching what he's doing and who he's talking to."

Sallie groaned in abject defeat and buried her face in her hands once again. Oh God, she'd made a mess of this. There was no way to fix it.

"And you will never, not in a million years, hide those hickeys on your neck. Wow." Her voice dropped to amazed disbelief. "You lucky bitch. That man made a meal of you last night."

In ways she couldn't have imagined. What he'd done to her body had destroyed her senses and left her shaking with her orgasms. It was all she could do to restrain shivering at the memory of his touch and the incredible pleasure.

"I know you have work to do," Sallie all but whimpered behind her hands to hide the heat searing her face. "Close the door on your way out."

She knew Tara, and she knew that wasn't going to work even before the desperate demand slipped from her lips.

"Not until we make you presentable," Tara declared. "Hang on. Let me get my bag."

Sallie peeked through her fingers and watched the other woman reenter the room moments later carrying the large leather bag she brought to work every day. Lowering her hands, she would have groaned if Tara hadn't surprised her by coming around the desk and gripping Sallie's forearm.

"Bathroom. We don't have a lot of time before folks begin dropping in to be nosy. Ignore them and the gossip gets worse. Ignore innuendos, meet outright questions with that wide-eyed innocent look you give everyone. He gave you a ride home and left a while later. Don't give times or details." The door closed behind them. "Now, let's see . . ."

Over an hour later, with a light, hand-painted scarf tied around her neck and tucked stylishly into the vee of her blouse, Sallie was back at her desk, and as Tara predicted, fielding phone calls as well as supposed business visits.

Tara took care of the business meeting requests and many of the calls, leaving Sallie to complete as much work as possible. Not that concentrating was easy. It was impossible. No one else could see the marks on her neck but she knew they were there. And she couldn't forget the wild hunger that had drove Jacob to leave those marks.

He'd wanted her enough to mark her, so why had he left so quickly, as though he couldn't wait to get out of the house?

She'd never known that kind of lust, either from herself or anyone else. Experienced she wasn't.

So really, she couldn't be surprised that Jacob had elected not to stay. He hadn't come back that first time after taking her virginity, and her ex-husband had been less than interested in being in her bed. Why he'd married her, she'd never really understood.

She should have never gone to that damned bar.

She avoided it whenever possible, but Lily and Shay invited her so often, urged her to go with them, and always seemed hurt when she refused. Perhaps this fiasco would convince them that Sallie and bars did not go well together.

She rubbed at that infernal ghostly ache just below her arms. It hadn't been there when she'd been with Jacob. She hadn't felt that hunger for touch, or the need for warmth, and that was damned dangerous. Because after last night, it was pretty clear he wouldn't be around again.

Forgetting what happened would be impossible, but Sallie forced herself to work in an attempt distract herself until later. If she kept going over it, kept thinking about it, she might end up crying.

And crying hadn't helped the first time. It damned sure wouldn't help this time.

A quick knock at her door a half hour before closing had her looking up from the projected sales report she was supposed to be working on, to see Tara step in and quickly close the door behind her.

"We have a little problem." Tara was at the very least

a little nervous, and it was rare to see Tara in any way flustered or uncertain.

"A little problem?" Sallie asked, a hint of trepidation tightening her stomach.

"Well, six feet three inches of Justice Culpepper might be more than a little problem, and he's waiting to discuss the Culpepper Ranch account with you." Tara stared back at her with a hint of laughter in her gaze as she fanned one hand at the side of her face briefly. "Damn, that man is hot." She frowned briefly. "Do we have a Culpepper Ranch account?"

No, and she really hadn't wanted one.

Sallie shook her head slowly, searching frantically for a way out of this.

Then, her gaze narrowed, the memory of Pride Culpepper standing at the bar with Jacob the night before coming into focus.

Justice Culpepper had tried several times to get her to go out with him. He was always charming, always good-natured, but he wasn't above making outrageous bribes. No doubt, after learning she'd left with someone else the night before, he'd think he had a chance now.

Asshole.

Sitting back in her chair, Sallie smiled slowly. "We always love new accounts, now don't we, Tara?" she said. "Please do show Mr. Culpepper in."

Tara gave her a doubtful look, but turned and left the office to show the rancher in.

Justice Culpepper was the eldest of the three Culpepper brothers. Justice, Rancor, and Pride. And no one laughed over those names, she was once told. Though she snickered over them often.

The office door reopened and Justice walked in, clad in jeans, riding chaps, and motorcycle boots. He couldn't decide if he was a rancher or a motorcycle gang member. Thick, black hair framed the face of a fallen angel, while gray-blue eyes watched the world with an amused forbearance.

Several tattoos marked both his arms, and she'd heard his entire back was marked as well. He was the least typical rancher she had ever met. And she had met a few.

"Mr. Culpepper." She rose to her feet and extended her hand for a firm handshake before she gestured to the leather chairs in front of her desk. "Please, have a seat. Tara said you're interested in moving your account to Dillerman's?"

She resumed her seat as Justice took his. Leaning back in the chair, he lifted one big booted foot to the opposite knee and gave her a slow, amused smile. That smile could mean anything and everything, she'd learned. The fact that women claimed they orgasmed to that smile was lost on her.

"I am." He nodded. "I've been using Prader's in the neighboring county but thought it was time to buy local."

Prader's had also been slowly raising prices for the past few years, she knew, especially in regard to building materials and feed.

"I'm certain we can accommodate your ranching needs." She sat back in her chair and smiled coolly. "Tara can set up an account for you whenever you like."

He tapped his fingers against his knee, a movement Sallie knew couldn't mean anything good.

"Ours would be a large account," he stated, an amused grin tugging at his lips. "I'd of course expect a discount."

There was the arrogance, and he wasn't even bothering to hide it.

"A discount?" she mused thoughtfully. "I'd say Dillerman's prices, compared to Prader's, could be considered a discount. There's also no delivery fee on larger orders. I know that isn't their policy."

He simply stared at her.

She was certain that stare ensured he rarely heard the word no; unfortunately for him, she loved saying no.

Silence stretched between them for long seconds, and this wasn't a game she enjoyed playing.

"As I said, Tara can help you set up the account if you like," she reminded him, injecting enough disinterest in her voice that he should get the hint. "Dillerman's welcomes the business."

His brow arched. "I'll let you know." He rose to his feet and turned to leave.

Oh, she just bet he'd let her know.

"I'm certain if you call Prader's and inform them you're considering moving your accounts, then they may give you quite a discount." She smiled when he turned back. "If you're lucky, it won't be much higher than what you'd pay here."

A chuckle rumbled in his chest. "You're a tough little thing, aren't you? No wonder Jacob broke his number one rule for you. I'd have broken it too if I were him."

He obviously expected her to say something. She simply stared back at him.

He stepped closer to the desk, glanced at her neck,

then met her gaze once again. "You don't have to say anything. I saw his neck. And I can guess what that scarf is hiding on yours. When he's finished with you, give me a call."

Heat seared her face.

She came to her feet, anger boiling inside her.

"Keep your account, Culpepper," she told him with icy disdain. "Dillerman's doesn't need it."

Surprise showed on his face. "Does Dillerman know that?" He all but laughed at her.

"Inform him," she suggested as she moved from behind the desk and stalked to the door, opening it with a quick jerk. "And he'll tell you the same thing I am. I make the rules here, and I decide who to accept accounts from. Keep your money. I don't want it. Good day."

He nodded slowly and left the office. "Damn, tough little thing." He chuckled again. "I'll be seeing you around, Miss Hamblen."

He nodded to Tara as he passed her desk, and Sallie caught the grin on his lips.

The bastard. He'd never meant to give her that account to begin with. He was just there to rub her nose in the fact that he knew Jacob had spent at least some time in her bed. He'd seen the marks on Jacob's neck, had he?

And what the hell had Jacob said about them?

Striding back to her desk, Sallie pulled her purse from beneath it, found her car keys, and left the office.

"Close up," she told Tara, barely holding back her anger. "I'm going home."

She had a bottle of wine in the fridge and she was sure she could find a movie to watch. She wasn't answering the phones and she damned sure wasn't going to answer the door if anyone came knocking.

She hated cowboys.

Cowboys, Culpeppers, and arrogant, sexy-as-hell Jacob Donovan.

This was all their fault.

Sleep wasn't happening, Jacob finally admitted hours after he'd returned to the ranch. Sleep, clear thinking, rationality. It had all gone out the fucking window from the minute he'd decided he was going to have Sallie for the night.

He'd only thought in terms of one night. He didn't do relationships, especially not with a woman from Deer Haven. God knew he was probably related to more than half of them.

Forcing himself from the bed and into the shower, he felt as petulant as a two-year-old. He should have stayed with her, he told himself, not for the first time. But fuck. He'd been so damned close to coming inside that tight little pussy and to hell with the consequences, that it had shocked the crap out of him. And if that hadn't been enough, for a moment, just a moment, the misty image of a dream lover and Sallie Hamblen had suddenly merged into one in way that threw him completely off-balance.

The laughter, soft, whispering over his senses, feminine moans, shocked pleasure in her voice as she cried his name. He woke often to a vision, a fantasy that had him spilling his come to his fingers as the features of her face eluded him. But last night, that fantasy image had been Sallie; the moans, Sallie's moans. And the sweet taste of her hunger all too familiar.

Where the hell had that vision come from and why was she tormenting the hell out of him? It had been five years since she'd first appeared, at a time when he'd been engaged to another woman, certain he knew what he wanted in his life. She'd begun showing up in his dreams, whispering his name, her pleasure tightening his body, hardening his cock in ways his fiancée never had.

And now, for the first time in all the years he'd been haunted by the image, for one brief moment, her features had been those of Sallie's. And that sure as hell didn't make sense.

"Good morning, Jacob." Amusement and curiosity filled the older feminine voice as Jacob stepped into the main part of his house.

He paused at the kitchen entrance to see his grandmother at her usual place at the kitchen table, coffee by her side, her attention lifting from the smartphone she held in one hand.

Social media and his grandmother were like longstanding, intimate friends. And her smartphone was her lifeline.

Goddammit, he didn't need this.

"Gram." He greeted her warily as he made his way to the coffee pot.

Hell, how had he managed to forget about Gram, her infernal social media addiction, and friends lists? This wasn't going to be comfortable in the least.

He was aware of her gaze following him, her bright blue eyes twinkling, her expression telling him that he was about to be on the receiving end of one of her little inquisitions.

Hell, he should have never conceded and let her move in with him. He was a bachelor, set in his ways. He valued his privacy and this tiny, older version of the mother he'd lost so many years ago found far too much amusement in certain areas of his life.

Sipping at the fresh coffee in his cup, Jacob took a chair across from her and steeled himself for the coming inquisition. A plate of cinnamon rolls sat in the center of the table. A bribe no doubt, he thought glumly, reaching for one.

He'd just swallowed the first bite when she struck.

"It would appear Miss Hamblen snacked a bit on your neck, dear. Aren't you a little old for hickeys?" She was on the verge of openly laughing at him now.

Jacob resisted reaching up to cover the side of his neck with one hand, mostly because he was damned if he would act ashamed of them. And he knew the marks Sallie carried on her neck . . .

"Of course, I understand the scarf she's wearing covers quite a few hickeys on her own neck. Perhaps you should have taken her to dinner before taking her home," Gram remarked before turning back to her phone and using her thumbs to type quickly on the screen.

Laying the roll carefully on a napkin, Jacob decided to wait to eat. His gram had a talent for causing others to choke.

Her words circled in his mind, though. Whatever she was doing to cover the marks he'd left on her obviously hadn't worked. Good, he thought fiercely. Every bastard in the county would know she was his.

"You'd think Justice would be man enough and friend

enough to observe the fact that you marked her." Gram shrugged without glancing up from the phone. "It would seem he visited her office and offered her the Culpepper account." She shook her head. "Of course, the boy was only playing with her. When she told him to go to hell, he told her that when you were finished with her, to give him a call. So very rude of him, don't you think? His aunt is quite put out with him."

Jacob stilled, fighting back the surge of rage that snapped inside him. He made a silent promise to show Justice the error of his ways.

He should have known better than to stop by the Culpepper ranch that morning before heading home to try to sleep. Both Justice and Pride had looked at the marks on his neck and shook their heads while hiding their grins. He was going to bust those damned heads.

"I'm sure she was able to deal with Justice just fine, Gram." He forced the words past his lips.

It didn't matter if she was able to deal with the other rancher. Jacob knew he'd be dealing with the man himself.

"Told him to go to hell and take his offer with him." Gram grinned then tilted her head to the side and watched him questioningly. "Should you invite Miss Hamblen to dinner, sweetie? I mean, the two of you are marking each other like mates or something. I'd like to meet her before you marry her."

Jacob lifted his coffee mug for a drink, took a mouthful.

"Or you knock her up," Gram came back with precise, deadly timing.

The coffee went down, hot as hell as his hand jerked,

spilling several hot drops on the table as he struggled to swallow without choking.

He smacked the cup down, jerked a napkin from the small pile next to the plate of rolls, and wiped the coffee up before rising to his feet and taking the cup to the sink.

He should be breaking out in a panicked sweat, at the very least. He should be worried about the fact that he'd taken Sallie without protection. But there was no sweat, no panic. Just an unfamiliar ache that made no sense whatsoever.

"Gram, this subject is closed," he warned her.

Rinsing the cup and placing it on the rack, he tried to convince himself he was going to panic later. It would just have to fully register in his brain first. That was all.

"You *do* use condoms, right? A man can never be too careful these days . . ." his gram pointed out sweetly. "Of course, a few babies wouldn't be amiss around here."

Babies? No one said anything about babies.

"Enough, Gram." He could feel the desperation to escape tighten the back of his neck. "Subject change. Now."

Silence met his demand.

Turning back to the table, he met the pure mischief in Gram's gaze.

"I do believe I need to attend the next Ladies Auxiliary meeting." She smiled a little too innocently. "I'm feeling lucky."

That damned betting sheet. Jacob simply stared back at her.

"Gram, I'm beginning to question your taste in friends." He grunted. It was highly disconcerting to learn his grandmother was involved in such antics. "And just how long have I been on these betting sheets?"

He still couldn't quite get used to that piece of information.

"Oh, you aren't alone," she assured him, all but laughing at him. "There are Culpepper sheets, of course. Especially young Rancor. That boy's going to definitely be a challenge."

Rancor would be a hell of lot more than a challenge, Jacob thought, but he'd be damned if he'd tell his grandmother that. God only knew what she'd do with the information.

What in the hell had happened to his sweet, little grandmother?

"Really, Jacob, you seem surprised." She was definitely laughing at him now. "All the women on the auxiliary are either mothers or grandmothers. We're concerned, you know. If you don't settle down soon, I won't get my great-grandchildren before I die."

Rubbing at the back of his neck he could only stare at her, uncertain how to respond at this point. Hell, he didn't even want to respond. This was his grandmother.

"I'm leaving, Gram." He was escaping, pure and damned simple. "Torture someone else today."

"Invite Sallie over, dear," she called out to him. "Before I do it."

God forbid.

He was out the back door, a sigh of relief escaping him as he rubbed at the back of his neck again and tried to tell himself Gram really couldn't live by herself. She was getting on in years. She could fall or something.

Or one of these days he was going to gag her for his

own piece of mind. Since she'd moved into his ranch house with him, she'd decided he needed a wife, and that she needed great-grandkids. She'd informed him a month into the move that his house was too big, too quiet, and he had to fill it with love, laughter, and babies before it died of neglect.

And until now, he'd been ignoring her advice just fine. At least, that was what he told himself until that morning. Until he'd nearly spilled himself inside Sallie.

He told himself he'd escaped while escaping was possible that morning, but if that was truly how he felt, why was it all he could do not to drive into town and climb back into Sallie's bed?

And why was it her face he now saw when he thought of the woman who haunted his dreams and left him feeling helpless rage?

Who the hell was Sallie Hamblen and why was the need to touch her again driving him crazy?

He was losing his mind, he decided. Midlife crisis or something, though he thought thirty-one might be a little young for a crisis of any kind. Especially one that involved a woman.

Then he remembered the taste of her kiss, the silken skin he'd caressed and her breathy little moans. The feel of her sucking his cock like a favorite treat and the snug heat of her sheath. What he'd felt with her, the pleasure of her touch, the pleasure he found in touching her, was unique. Unexplainable.

And the unexplainable could be dangerous, he reminded himself.

The reminder wasn't going to stop him. It just made him more cautious.

Maybe.

He almost grinned at the thought. It probably wouldn't. For the first time in his life a woman had his complete attention and he wanted to know why. He was determined to find out.

chapter four

Sallie was halfway home before she remembered she was supposed to stop at the grocery store for dinner. She had wine and the beer she kept for Lily and Shay in the fridge, and a bag of ice in the freezer. Her choices were to starve that night, stop at the grocery, or order out.

It was going to be a pizza night, she decided as she drove past the crowded parking lot of the only decent-sized grocery store in the area. She was damned if she was going to go in there and feel the stares on her.

She touched the scarf Tara had wrapped around her neck earlier, her body weakening at the memory of Jacob's mouth, his teeth, the rasp of his shadow of a beard. She didn't regret the experience, didn't regret the marks, but the shaming knowledge that he'd rushed from her bed would take a while to recover from.

At least he'd bothered to make it as far as actually fucking her. Her ex-husband hadn't done that much. It hadn't exactly been ego boosting, and when he'd returned that last day, packed his few belongings, and told her to get a divorce, she hadn't exactly been surprised.

John was handsome and successful He could have had his pick of the women. It had never made sense that he'd married her.

The same night he'd left someone had broken into her home and put a knife to her throat as she slept, demanding to know where he was.

"Where is he?" her knife-wielding assailant had demanded. "Protecting him will just get you killed."

Terror had nearly choked her as she stared up at him, certain she'd die that night. If her stepfather, Rance Dougal, and mother hadn't called out to her from downstairs, she was certain he would have killed her. Instead, he'd run, crashing into Rance and nearly knocking her mother down.

Sallie had been nearly hysterical. Her mother had helped her pack some clothes to leave that night and her stepfather had called the police, but there was no finding who it was, or even who he wanted. John had disappeared after leaving, his cell phone no longer active, and the investigators her father hired had been unable to find him.

When someone had tried to break into Rance's home two weeks later, he and her mother had decided she needed to hide until John could be found. Nearly a year later, she'd been found and threatened again. When a neighbor had heard her screams and broke into her apartment to help her, he'd nearly died in his attempt.

Rance had demanded she leave the state then, take a new identity, and give his investigators time to find John.

That had been three years ago. She hadn't even been able to go home when her mother died of a stroke two years later. Instead, she'd hid in her house and grieved, nearly broken over the loss.

She and her mother hadn't been close. But Sallie loved her, and she knew her mother cared for her. Her mother had loved her enough to be frightened for her, to demand that Rance do something to protect her. And Rance had sworn that he'd continue to protect her.

Three years after the first attack and, still, John hadn't been found and the investigators still didn't have a clue as to why someone was after Sallie.

She'd begun thinking that whoever it was had stopped looking. She'd entertained the idea of returning to Oklahoma, but her mother was gone, she had no other family, and by then she'd already made friends, settled into Deer Haven. And she knew Jacob was here.

Her fascination with him was not going to end well, she told herself. Not well at all.

But that was beside the fact. She was still waiting for those investigators to learn something. Anything.

Yeah, waiting was a hell of a good time, wasn't it? John was still eluding capture, and his enemies might still searching be for her. And she was tired. So very tired of the fear, of being alone, of aching for a man who didn't remember her and likely hadn't wanted to remember her.

Dragging herself into the house, Sallie pulled the scarf from her neck, and tucked it in her purse before placing the bag on a small shelf just inside the coat closet. Dimly lit, because she usually didn't make it home until after dark, the house wasn't any more welcoming, but she hated the dark. A holdover from that first attack, one she hadn't been able to put behind her.

It was dark outside by time she finished a glass of wine, showered, and dressed in one of the lounging sets she preferred. The black cotton bottoms and camisole top were loose enough to give her freedom of movement without the need for a robe.

Pouring another glass of wine, she ordered a pizza. Minutes later she heard her cell phone ring, but after a quick glance that told her it wasn't the pizza place calling her back, she let it go to voice mail.

When she glanced at the screen, she groaned at the number of messages. Even Pride Culpepper called. What the hell did he want?

Disappointment filled her as she continued to scroll through her phone. Jacob hadn't called. Not that she'd expected him to.

Shrugging, Sallie tossed the phone on the kitchen counter. Grabbing her wine glass, she padded into the living room to wait for her dinner to arrive. She'd ordered enough to last the rest of the weekend while she was at it. She didn't want company; she didn't want questions. She wanted to find just a few moments to forget the fact that once again, she'd failed where most women seemed to excel.

It wasn't something she normally let herself dwell on. She'd gotten used to being alone.

At least, that was what she told herself. What she told others.

At that moment, she wanted nothing more than that touch, the rasp of broad callused hands, the hungry kisses from a man she should have known better than to let back into her bed.

It had been six years. Six long, cold years that she'd ached for his touch.

Once she'd learned the small town her stepfather had sent her to was also Jacob's hometown, she'd had a moment of panic before she'd remembered Rance Dougal had no idea she'd spent the night with Jacob that long-ago weekend in Switzerland. And if he had, he would have told her Jacob was there. Just in case the worst happened and she needed help. Or if things went to hell in a handbasket and her ex-husband's enemies found her.

The melodic chime of the doorbell floated through the house, announcing the arrival of dinner. Well, at least she wouldn't starve, she thought, collecting the cash she'd placed on the coffee table and wondering if she was even in the mood to eat now.

It was sheer luck, Jacob decided as he slipped from the back of Sallie's house to see the delivery car pull into the driveway. Catching the young man before he reached the door, Jacob paid for the pizza, adding a generous tip to the kid before striding to her front door.

Contrary woman wasn't answering her phone. He hadn't used his cell to call, but Pride's instead, thinking she'd be more apt to answer. In hindsight, after Justice's little visit to her office earlier, that might not have been the best idea. But according to his cousin, Tara, she likely wasn't answering anyone's calls.

Waiting until the car backed out of the driveway, Jacob leaned against the side of the house and pressed the doorbell. Seconds later the door opened, and before Sallie could do more than squeak in surprise, he slid past her, pizza box in hand, and pushed the door closed behind him.

"Big pizza for such a little thing." He grinned at her frowning expression. "Wanna share?"

"Wanna go to hell?" she said, her answering smile all teeth.

Jacob was certain a lesser man would have winced or at least be wary. Was he? Hell no. His dick was spike hard and he was damned if his interest level hadn't just rocketed out of the safe zone where his control was concerned.

"Been there." Turning, he strode into the house and placed the pizza box on the coffee table. "Lily and Shay leave any beer here?"

Sallie followed, slowly, her arms crossed over her breasts, her jaw clenched so hard he thought she might be cracking molars.

"What would make you think they would leave beer here?" That tone was pure anger, barely hidden by a thin veil of civility.

"Third cousins," he told her, heading for the kitchen. "They spend a lot of time here, so I know they leave beer."

Opening the fridge door, he grinned at the sight of the dark bottles. His cousins might have to buy more. Hell, he'd get them more himself. On second thought, this wouldn't be his last night here.

Grabbing two bottles, he made his way back to the living room and took a seat on the middle of the couch and opened the pizza box.

"Come eat. You're going to need your energy later."

Glancing up at her, his gaze fell to her neck and satisfaction all but drowned him.

Yeah, he'd marked her good and he was glad he had after hearing how Justice reacted. His friend was damned peevish over the fact that Miss Hamblen had chosen a lover, and that it had been Jacob.

Jacob wasn't a stupid man, though, he'd known he'd probably pissed her off last night, leaving as he had. But when a man starts thinking things like he'd been thinking when it came to a woman then it was time to get the hell out and consider what he was doing.

"It doesn't take much energy to sleep," she assured him with false sweetness.

He lifted his shoulders negligently. "We'll see."

Something clenched in his chest at the sudden flash of vulnerability he saw in her gaze. He hadn't just made her mad. He'd hurt her and that was the last thing he'd wanted to do. Sallie hadn't had a lover in the three years she'd been there, and according to her cousins, at some point, her heart had been broken. To know he'd hurt her after that didn't sit well with him. But he took comfort in the fact that she hadn't shot him yet, as Tara had predicted Sallie would do.

Moving slowly, warily, she sat in the chair next to the couch and simply watched as he pulled a piece of the loaded dough free and took a healthy bite.

It was from the best pizza joint around.

She wasn't eating, though, she just watched him as though she didn't quite know what to do with him. And that glimmer of hurt she wasn't hiding as well as she thought she was, was pricking at a conscience he hadn't known he possessed.

It was bad enough he was craving the taste of her like a man addicted to something sweet, but he was doing something he'd never done, allowing himself to use his training to decipher those minute expressions to see beyond the anger.

He was going to have to stop that shit, he thought irritably. Hell, he thought he had stopped doing that when he'd left the agency.

"Why are you here?" Cool, short, and to the point.

His survival instincts perked up in interest.

Finishing the slice of pizza, he pulled another free, placed it on a napkin that came with the delivery and extended it to her.

She looked at it then back to him with a go-fuck-yourself look.

Damn, he just might end up liking this woman far more than he'd first thought.

"Come on, eat with me, then I might leave you in peace." Though he sincerely doubted it.

"In peace?" Her smile was deadly. "What makes you think you can bargain with my peace? Or with my pizza?"

He turned the slice back and took a bite of it before eating it with relish.

She might call the sheriff on him to have him thrown out. Thankfully, he knew the sheriff pretty well.

"Good pizza," he assured her, lifting the cold beer and taking a long pull as he watched her.

He couldn't help but let his gaze slip to her neck. His cock throbbed at the sight of the whisker burn and the love bites he'd left there. Maybe he should be more careful of her delicate skin, he thought. Or place the marks in a less conspicuous place.

Maybe.

But then, everyone who saw those marks would know who she belonged to.

He frowned, taking another bite of the pizza. She'd covered her marks while she was at the store, hiding them beneath Tara's scarf.

"Finish it and leave." She rose, slapped the box closed, and picked it up as she strode to the kitchen as though she wasn't just as hot for him as he was hard for her.

He glimpsed those tight little nipples beneath her cotton top. She wasn't wearing a bra. Was she wearing panties? He couldn't tell for certain with the loose fit of the cotton pajama bottoms. And damned if she didn't have a nice ass. It curved just the way it was supposed to and tempted a man to take a bite . . . He could swear he could feel sweat forming on his brow at the thought of playing with that fine little ass.

He finished the slice of pizza, used a napkin she'd left him to wipe his lips, then finished the beer. Jacob rose to his feet and followed Sallie to the kitchen, watching as she pushed the pizza, box and all, into a nearly empty refrigerator. Dropping the beer bottle into the trash, he moved to her and let his hands settle on her bare shoulders as she closed the appliance door.

She froze.

Not in fear, nor in denial. From where he stood, he glimpsed her profile, watched her lashes drift to her cheeks and hunger flash across her expression.

"You need to leave." Her voice was just as firm as

ever, though she didn't move from beneath his touch. "Now."

Stroking her arms, feeling the delicacy of her, the silk of her flesh, he couldn't imagine leaving without another taste of her.

"I should have made an effort to protect your privacy last night," he said softly, his lips lowering to the shell of her ear. "I should have thought about how folks would react and taken the effort to hide the fact that I was here."

Brushing her hair from the back of her neck, Jacob couldn't help but rake his teeth over the nape of her neck before laying several kisses against the sensitive flesh. The shiver that worked through her body at least gave him hope that maybe she wasn't actually going to throw him out.

"And I'm sorry you felt you had to leave so abruptly." She all but tore herself from the grip he had on her shoulders. "Trust me, I won't be any better tonight than I was last night. Find someone else to amuse yourself with."

She thought he'd left because she hadn't pleased him? Hell.

He should have thought about this, but he'd been so damned screwed up with the thought of marking her and by spilling himself inside her that he hadn't been able to get past it.

"You do know I didn't wear a condom that last time?" he reminded her, watching her expression closely.

A small frown pulled at her brow and a bit of surprise showed on her face before she shrugged. "I was protected, and I haven't been with anyone in six years. And you don't seem the type of man to forget to protect yourself."

Protect himself?

"I protect my lovers first and foremost," he growled, the thought of being able to spill inside her drawing his balls tight in exquisite lust. "I don't forget condoms, Sallie. I don't forget that it's a responsibility I take for a lover. Forgetting and realizing I didn't bring any in with me slapped me upside the head with the fact that you stripped me down to my last thread of control. Not an easy thing for me to accept."

She rubbed at her arms, and he realized he'd watched her do that at the bar as she watched the dancers, and again as she'd watched him.

Stepping to where she stood in front of the center island, he let his palms touch her shoulders again, run down her arms and back up again. What he suspected wasn't something he was comfortable with. His stubborn, proud Sallie ached for touch. It was there in her expression as it softened, in the response he glimpsed in the darkening of her pale blue eyes.

Pride and hunger warred inside her, and he couldn't even blame her. He'd made her an object of interest and of gossip because of his own lust and refusal to consider what she'd face that morning. It wasn't a mistake he'd make again. Because he did see it as his responsibility to protect the women he slept with. Whether against pregnancy or against gossip, and he'd failed to protect Sallie.

Her chin lifted, pride flashing in her expression. "I don't need pretty lies, Jacob."

"Damned good thing. Pretty lies aren't exactly my forte. I'm not an easy lover," he warned her as he'd never warned another woman. "I'm an even harder man. No woman in her right mind wants to ever fall in love with me. But I'd make you a hell of lover while it lasted. You wouldn't have to worry about ever getting cold if I'm in the bed with you."

She was always cold, Sallie thought. Except when she'd been in his arms. How hard would it be to let that go when he decided their time together was over? It wasn't that she believed in happily-ever-afters or any version of the concept. She'd learned better, and those lessons weren't ones she was about to forget.

She could still be hurt, though, and she knew it. Last night had proven it. She could be sliced clear to her soul with the belief that she'd disappointed him as a lover. How would she feel when she became used to being warm, used to the pleasure, and it was suddenly gone?

She shook her head slowly, stepping back, needing to escape his touch.

"I can't afford what being your lover would do to me." Regret sliced nearly as deep as the hurt had the night before. "I may not believe in love, but that doesn't mean I can't be hurt. I'd rather just accept a one-night stand and leave it there."

She couldn't allow herself to believe in love; then she'd have to accept that out of all the women in the world, she would be one of those unlucky ones to have never known so much as the illusion of it.

He nodded slowly, watching her closely, his brown and gold eyes looking far too predatory at the moment.

"Can you forget it, Sallie?" he asked her then, step-ping closer, but thankfully, not touching her. "How hot it was? How hard I felt inside you? Stretching you like the snuggest little glove?"

Her inner flesh clenched, wept. God no, she couldn't forget, and she wouldn't stop aching for it, needing it.

"I didn't know forgetting was a requirement to a one-night stand," she tried to quip, to come off mocking and without concern. What she felt was another story. She wanted to grab hold of him and beg him, to plead for just one more night.

If that was what she wanted after just that one night, how much worse could it be after weeks or months? Like an addict in withdrawal, she feared.

His expression stilled, the gold in his eyes darker, deeper, and it seemed that was her only warning.

Before she could move, before she could evade him, his head lowered, his lips slanting over hers. He didn't grab her, didn't restrain her or hold her in any way except with his lips.

Her lips parted, allowing the kiss to deepen, to send pleasure racing through her with the force of a tidal wave. Sensual, erotic, his tongue danced with hers, tasted her, held her mesmerized.

Just his kiss.

Until she reached for him. Her hands gripped the fine cotton of his shirt, fisting in it, holding on to him as she went to her tiptoes to get closer, to take the heat, the sheer hunger he sent washing over her senses.

His arms came around her then, enfolding her in the warmth and power she'd never known a man could possess. He didn't just pull her against his body. His arms surrounded her, enfolded her, sheltered her. Sallie knew she was lost. She was a wimp. She was weak. She needed his touch, ached for it, and she feared, she'd possibly already become addicted to him, because she couldn't make herself turn away. He was going to break her heart, and there was no doubt about that. She might not believe in love, but she was still a woman, a woman who knew she'd never find with another man what she found in Jacob's arms.

Just as her senses were sinking completely beneath the onslaught of sensual pleasure, a heavy pounding at her back door had Jacob's head jerking up, the kiss broken as quickly as it had begun.

"Jacob!" A hard, male voice called out imperatively as the fist landed repeatedly on the door again. "This is important, man!"

Sallie stepped back quickly, bemused, shocked at the interruption as Jacob stepped quickly to the door, unlocked it, and opened it as though he lived there rather tricking his way in.

Pride Culpepper glanced at her quickly, grimacing and then turning back to Jacob. "Your foreman's been trying to reach you. There's a problem at the ranch. You need to get back there. Now."

No goodbye, no see you later. Jacob pushed through the door into the night, and just that quickly, he was gone.

"I'm sorry, Sallie," Pride lingered uncomfortably in the doorway, his expression heavy with regret. "It's an emergency."

Of course it was an emergency, she thought wearily. She was certain it just couldn't be anything else.

"It's for the best," she told Pride quietly. "No apology

needed. Please, ask him not to bother coming back. It wouldn't be good for either of us." It definitely wouldn't be good for her. "Goodbye, Pride."

Stepping to the door, she gripped it as he moved back, a muttered curse slipping past his lips.

"He'll be back," he assured, his gaze slipping to her neck before he sighed heavily. "You can bet on it."

"It would be best if he didn't." Closing the door, she locked it and turned back to the empty house.

Touching her lips, Sallie fought back the heaviness in her chest and the saddened knowledge that she was, once again, alone.

And just as before, it was for the best.

Rage gathered just beneath the false calm Jacob forced into his expression and demeanor as he came to a hard stop in front of the ranch house. The entire grounds were lit up, the house, stables and barns. More than a dozen ranch hands, mostly former military, armed and ready, stood protectively outside the residence, their expressions hard and suspicious.

"What the fuck happened?" he demanded as the foreman, John Grange, strode quickly toward him.

The other man's icy hazel eyes gleamed with anger beyond heavy black lashes as a muscle ticked beneath his jaw.

"Some bastard managed to get in the house on Gram and she unloaded a barrel of buckshot into him as he went out the front window," the other man snarled as they headed quickly up the walk. "She's fine. Hell, I think she enjoyed it. That woman's gonna give us a stroke, Jacob."

Jacob barely managed to keep from rubbing the back of his neck as he stepped into the house.

There was Gram, in her favorite chair in the living room, a cup of tea on the table next to her as one of her favorite "boys," as she called the ranch hands, squatted next to the chair and checked her blood pressure.

"I think your blood pressure is better than mine, Mrs. Donovan," he quipped as he removed the cuff from her arm and rose to his feet, shaking head. "At this rate, you're gonna drive the rest of us crazy while you sip your tea."

"Gram?" Jacob moved across the room in a few strides, hunkering down next to her chair and letting his gaze go over her quickly. "You okay?"

"I'm fine Jacob," she told him, her blue eyes filled with excitement. "But I doubt that intruder is fairing real well right now. I know some of that buckshot hit his back before he went through your window. It may have even popped his backside."

Jacob glanced at the window in question. Jagged pieces of glass still held on to the frame in places, though it appeared the majority of it had fallen outside the house.

"I heard the alarms deactivate and knew it couldn't be you," his grandmother continued. "So, I grabbed your granddaddy's shotgun. I was just coming into the living room when I saw him." A frown pulled at her brow. "He must have realized he was at the wrong place, though, because he asked where someone named Kyra was. Then he called me a bitch. Do you know a Kyra, Jacob?"

Kyra. He knew he didn't know anyone named Kyra, but still, something teased at his memories, whispered across his mind with a discomfiting feeling he was missing something.

He shook his head and turned back to her.

"What happened then?" he asked her.

"Well, that's when I raised the shotgun, dear, and took aim," she stated as though he should already know that. "He had on a mask and called me a vile name. He should have been a bit more polite."

Several chuckles, barely smothered from the hands behind him, were ignored.

"That's all he said?" he pressed her.

"Well, if there had been more, I'd tell you." She lifted her tea and took a sip, her hand as steady as a surgeon's as she blinked back at him innocently. "Really, Jacob, I don't have a problem with my memory yet."

No, she damned sure didn't.

"I know that, Gram." He let his gaze go over her once again as she set the cup back on the saucer and folded her hands atop the blanket one of the ranch hands must have given her before he arrived. "I'm just worried, that's all."

He was pissed the hell off.

No one should have been able to get into the house with the security system activated, yet somehow, they'd managed it. It was his system, set up and programed by him, as unique as any could be and it was meant to be tamper proof. Yet someone had managed to get past it.

"I'm more worried about that Kyra, whoever she is." Concern touched Gram's face as a frown worried at her brow. "He might have been wearing a mask, but I saw his eyes, Jacob. And he had mean eyes. He means to hurt her."

Kyra.

Jacob barely controlled a flinch and had no idea why. It was a distinctive name, one not easily forgotten once heard. Yet, he couldn't remember a time when he'd ever met anyone who used it.

"I'll look into it, Gram, make sure no one around here goes by that name," he promised her as he bent and kissed her brow. "Finish your tea. I'll be back in a few minutes."

It wasn't someone named Kyra that flashed across his mind as he stared at the broken window moments later from outside the house. It was Sallie, her eyes still glazed with passion, with need as she stared up at him, and that flash of regret in her face as he left.

"Bastard got clean away," Grange muttered as he moved to Jacob's side. "He was on foot, but not far away there's signs of a dirt bike. Must have been modified because we didn't hear anything. I sent a message to the Culpeppers anyway. Justice said he'd be on the lookout and he'd put out a notice to the doctors and medical facilities in the area."

Jacob nodded, his eyes narrowing as he let his gaze sweep out over the darkened forests beyond the now well-lit ranch yard.

"You know anyone named Kyra?" he asked the foreman.

"Not at present," Grange assured him. "And I think I know pretty much all the women in the area. None of the ranch hands recognized the name either."

That pretty much canceled out the idea that anyone named Kyra lived in, or had lived in, the county or most of the surrounding counties. Ranch hands, especially Jacob's and the Culpepper employees, tended to get around, going from county to county, bar to bar, each weekend. And as Grange said, most of the women would be at least recognizable to them.

He'd have to talk to Justice, see if he had any ideas.

Kyra.

The name tugged at him, tightened his chest and had his jaw clenching. And it shouldn't. Because he knew for a fact that he didn't know anyone named Kyra.

Didn't he?

chapter five

Several days later the marks on Sallie's neck hadn't faded away, but they were easier to hide with makeup and life had returned to normal. She had washed her sheets, eliminating all traces of Jacob's scent.

Justice Culpepper had somehow convinced Tara to set up that account for him, and Sallie ignored it instead of canceling it. She'd noticed a new account for Jacob's ranch as well. The Rocking D Ranch was considered a coup by the floor manager. Several smaller ranches had set up accounts the same day, causing Sallie to finally accept the fact that Dillerman's was going to end up making a profit for the year, no matter her efforts to the contrary.

Wouldn't Stanley Dillerman, the arrogant little squid of an owner, be rubbing his greedy little hands together in glee, she thought as she put away the paperwork and gathered everything together so she could leave.

The floor manager, Roger Oakley, oversaw everything on the weekends and did so gladly. Sallie knew if she let him handle things daily, he'd do an excellent job.

"Sallie, why don't you join Lily, Shay, and I at the restaurant?" Tara asked as Sallie stepped from her office. "A good steak never hurt anyone."

"Maybe next time, Tara," Sallie said regretfully. "Unfortunately, I have a meeting with Mrs. Foley and her sidekick, Chet Morris."

Rhonda Foley, head of the Chamber of Commerce, and the bank president, Chet Morris, had insisted on a business dinner rather than meeting in one of their offices.

"Eww." Tara grimaced. "Watch those two. They absolutely delight in finding new ways to make the businesses in town jump to their tune. And the annual Ranchers Barbeque is coming up in a few months. Those two are in charge of getting as many of the businesses as possible involved. As well as the heads of those businesses. Of which you are one."

Sallie shrugged. "Another year, another request," she reminded her assistant. "I'll be sure to send them your way."

Every year Sallie promised to participate, and every year, she sent Tara in her place. The other woman delighted in attending, whereas Sallie enjoyed watching from a distance.

Throwing her assistant a little wave, Sallie made her way to the exit and walked down the stairs to the warehouse and out the back door.

"See you Monday, Miss Hamblen." The dock manager

nodded to her with his normal friendliness, his craggy features wreathed in a smile.

"Have a nice weekend, Daniel." She waved in return, made her way down the short flight of steps, and hurried to her car.

There was no way out of the dinner. She'd already tried several times. Rhonda Foley and her brother-in-law, Chet Morris, were like hounds on the scent of prey once they got an idea into their heads. It was the same every year, and they couldn't just tell her what she needed to have Tara do at the festival. That would be too easy. They had to go through the same song and dance.

"Sallie, now you have to promise this year you'll at least help Tara," Rhonda said chidingly as Sallie glanced up from the grilled chicken and salad she was picking at.

Nearing sixty, but looking years younger, her thick auburn hair was arranged into an artfully messy updo and her hazel eyes were always warm and filled with good humor. Slender, dressed in a neat, blue silk sheath, she was the epitome of genteel elegance.

"Of course, I will." Sallie sat back in her chair and gave Rhonda a look of wide-eyed innocence. "I told you, there was that emergency at the store last year."

To her right, Chet snickered. "You've had an emergency every year, Sallie. Perhaps we should give you a partner, to make things easier, of course."

"Oh, Chet, what a wonderful idea!" Rhonda proclaimed, her hands coming together in a silent clap. "Why, I should have thought of that."

Chet smiled benignly. His cherubic features were

rather kind for a bank president, Sallie always thought. Deep brown eyes and thinning brown hair completed the appearance.

And just that quickly, Sallie realized the setup. She should have seen it coming, she thought in resignation.

Looking behind her, Chet's eyes widened and the expression of such obviously fake surprise had her glancing in Rhonda's direction in time to catch the woman's smile of smug satisfaction.

"Justice, fancy meeting you here. Rhonda and I were just getting ready to discuss this year's event with Miss Hamblen." His expression turned suddenly serious as Justice Culpepper stepped to the empty chair. "Hell, man, what happened to your face?"

Sallie looked up at the rancher to see one side of his handsome face bruised, his eye swollen. Someone blacked his eye good. No doubt he deserved it.

"Another fight with your brothers, dear?" Rhonda asked sympathetically as Justice took his seat and glanced at Sallie, his lips quirking as though amused.

"Not this time," he drawled. "It was a disagreement with a friend, I'm afraid."

Rhonda and Chet turned their gazes on her.

"I didn't hit him," she informed them, frowning.

Chet wiped his hand over his lower face, hiding a smile while Rhonda didn't even bother.

"Did we get you into trouble, dear?" Rhonda asked, regret shimmering in her voice.

His lips only twitched as he lifted a brow, meeting Sallie's gaze with mockery.

"Justice got himself into trouble, Rhonda," Jacob spoke behind Sallie, his deep voice causing a shaft of sensation to strike her belly and a flush to wash over her. "You know he likes to rile people. He riled the wrong man."

Clasping her hands in her lap, Sallie was aware of the three at the table with her, as well as several people close by, watching her and Jacob with far too much interest. Pushing back embarrassment, emotion, anger, she stared across the table at Chet and watched as several beads of sweat began to dot his forehead.

Enough was enough. Sallie had spent a week avoiding Jacob, his friends, as well as innuendos and downright snide remarks from several women. They were upset because the local legend and most wanted stud in the county wasn't deigning to share any of his attention with them. As far as she was concerned, they could have her part.

Pacing the floors at night, waking, certain he was there, craving his touch like an addict needing a fix? She didn't need it. She just wanted it to go away. She wanted to feel normal again . . . didn't she?

"Miss Hamblen." His hands settled on her shoulders while she remained still and silent. But when he brushed a kiss across the top of her head, she jerked so hard with surprise, she hit the table, nearly overturning her water.

Rhonda and Chet blinked at him in shock.

Releasing her shoulders, Jacob took the seat Justice was vacating at her side and sat down with lazy grace. He was like a satisfied cat, she decided, playing with his prey.

"I believe our meeting is over." She forced a smile as she turned to Rhonda and reached for her purse.

"You don't want to do that, sweetheart." Jacob's voice was low, warning. "The gossips will have a field day if you just up and leave."

He didn't give a damn about gossips, she thought, but unfortunately, at this point, those gossips were beginning to steal her peace. The question was, did she give into his warning, or do as she wanted, which was to stand up and leave?

Placing her hands in her lap once again she turned to look at Jacob. "You are becoming an irritant, Mr. Donovan."

Justice snorted in surprise. "She just figuring that out?"

Neither she nor Jacob glanced at him.

"Give me time." His smile was pure arrogance and far too much charm. "I intend to grow on you."

Not if she could help it. And she would help it. She didn't need him growing on her. She didn't need this man stealing parts of her she'd never recover. And that was exactly what he'd do.

Damn woman. She was as stubborn as the mountains and as damned pretty as a sunrise, Jacob thought as he pulled his truck into her driveway a few hours later, behind the little sedan she drove. She'd refused every suggestion Rhonda and Chet had come up with that she work with either Jacob or Justice during the festival. Each time she'd held firm that they contact Tara.

He'd be damned if he'd contact Tara about anything.

"Jacob, I didn't invite you over," she informed him as he reached the side entrance to the house just as she was getting ready to unlock it. "And I don't have time for you tonight."

Didn't have time for him?

"Sweetheart, you better make time." It was all he could do to keep from snarling like a bear with a thorn in its paw.

Because he could see the need in her. He could almost feel it in the air around her, vibrating against his skin, fueling his.

Taking the keys from her hand, he unlocked the door and pushed it open, stepping inside ahead of her, more from habit than any other reason.

Low lights glowed within the house, just as they had the first night, the pristine rooms reflecting a woman who either didn't consider this house a home or either didn't know what a home should be. He was aware of her coming in behind him, closing and locking the door before hanging her purse in the coat closet and slipping her shoes from her feet.

The dress she wore was softer, flowy, rather than the straight skirt and blouse she'd worn to the bar the week before. It was sleeveless, the neckline scalloped, the hem coming just above her knees.

Perfect to fuck her in.

As she turned, his arm went around her waist, pulling her to his chest, as he watched the emotions that flashed across her face in those moments. Vulnerability, need, and hunger and just a hint of fear.

"Are you scared of me, Sallie?" he asked, using his free hand to tuck a fallen strand of hair back from her face.

Disbelief flashed across her pale blue gaze.

"I'm not scared of you in the least, Jacob," she assured him, her hands splayed against his chest, neither pushing him away nor clinging to him. "You'd never hurt me physically, but what you can do is turn my life inside out more than you already have."

More than she'd turned his life inside out? It seemed to him they were standing on equal ground there.

"Should I leave then?" He let his fingers stroke over her cheek, down to her neck, where he curled his fingers around the side of the delicate column. "If I leave, I won't come back." He lowered his head, touched his lips to hers, holding her gaze. "Unless you ask me nicely."

He didn't bother giving her time to say no. She'd had plenty of time from the second he pulled her to him.

His lips touched hers, brushed over them and he watched her gaze darken before her lashes drifted lower. He did what he should have the first time, tested her kiss, explored her lips and the need rising inside her.

He tasted her, allowed her to taste him, encouraged her to deepen the kiss, and felt her come alive in his arms. He felt it the moment her natural reserve fell away and she let herself become lost in the pleasure rising between them. Her hands pushed to his shoulders, then to his head. Blunt nails scraped over his scalp, slender fingers clenching in his hair as she rose against him, pressing as close as possible to his chest.

She made him crazy for her, intent on it, determined as he had never been in his life to make certain this woman was his . . .

"Damn you, Sallie. Wanting you is killing me." His

voice was tormented, filled with lust as he lifted her, dragging her dress above her thighs to allow the denim-covered length of his cock to wedge between her thighs.

His lips covered hers again, hot, hard, his tongue sinking past them to twine with hers as he ground his cock against the soft pad between her thighs.

"You're destroying my control," he groaned as his teeth nipped at her jaw, his lips smoothing over the little sting as the sharp caresses moved to her neck.

Sallie trembled with pleasure, at the heated touches to her flesh, his lips on her neck. His hard body moved against her as his lips took hers once again, his kiss dominant, sending exciting, sizzling pleasure washing through her.

Bracing her back against the wall, he lifted her legs until they were at his hips, his cloth-covered cock driving against her pussy. His moan was dark, dangerous as it vibrated against her lips. Like a man desperate for touch. As desperate as the woman he held.

The sound spurred her need, her hunger. She'd spent so many years untouched, alone, both inside and out, and now, Jacob's touch was like a narcotic, an exciting, addicting liquor. And she needed more.

Jacob's lips swept from hers to her jaw, stroking over it, claiming her flesh. He sapped any thought of resistance, left only her hunger.

Turning her head to allow her lips to press to his neck as well, she let her lips and tongue taste the tough male flesh as he kissed, nipped, and licked at hers.

He was marking her flesh again, just as she was his. His hands were beneath her rear, holding her in place as his hips rotated, driving her insane.

"I won't make it to the damned bed," he groaned, his voice a hard rasp as he palmed the rounded flesh of her buttocks. "I doubt I can make it to the couch."

She didn't care. She didn't want him to wait. She needed him now. Once his flesh touched hers, her vows to resist, to remain alone, dissipated as though they were no more than dust.

As his lips moved over hers again, she felt him moving and seconds later, her back met the couch and at the same time Jacob reared back from her. Callused hands pushed the skirt of her dress to her hips then hooked in the band of her panties and pulled them down her legs and tossed them aside. In the next breath he had her thighs spread, and a cry of shocking pleasure tearing from her.

With lips and tongue, he sent flames rocking through her senses as he found the bare, slick folds of her pussy and the swollen, far too sensitive bud of her clit.

Her feet dug into the cushions of the couch as he held her thighs apart with broad, callused hands and worked his tongue over her flesh, throwing her into such a chaos of sensation that thought was impossible.

She hadn't known such pleasure except with him. She'd had only her memories of him, memories of the firm dominance and male hunger that spilled over her when he took her that long-ago weekend.

"Jacob . . ." Her fingers fisted in the cushions beneath her, hips arching to get closer, only to feel his hands sliding beneath her to clench in the swell of her buttocks.

He held her to his mouth, his tongue lashing at her flesh, circling her clit. He licked, sucked at it, as she fought to writhe beneath the torturous pleasure.

It was so good . . .

Her head tossed and her hands slid into the thick strands of his hair, fingers clenching as his tongue sank into the needy depths of her vagina. Moisture spilled to each thrust of his tongue as sensation, sharp and fiery, tightened through her body.

Sallie gasped for breath, a cry slipping past her lips as his lips shifted once again and his tongue raked over her clit. Each pass of his tongue over the swollen bit of flesh sent flares of jagged sensation tearing through her and pushing her closer to an edge that felt liked insanity.

"Jacob, please . . ." She gasped, whether for mercy or release, she wasn't certain.

There was no mercy in his diabolical lips and wicked tongue. Each lick, each draw of his mouth and heated kiss, pushed her higher, harder.

"So good . . . Oh, God, Jacob . . ." She moaned as his lips covered her clit, drawing it tighter into his mouth, sucking it with devastating results.

The explosion that tore through her was cataclysmic. Waves of pleasure washed over her, arching her closer to his mouth, her thighs straining as his broad hands held them apart. Ecstasy swept through her in resounding explosions that shook her to the depths of her senses.

She was still reeling, attempting to make some sort of sense of the chaotic pleasure when she felt him move over her, the thick head of his cock pressing inside her.

Tremors still raced over her. Her inner muscles were clenched tight and her clit vibrated with the excess of sensation when he began forging his way inside her.

"There, sweetheart." The graveled croon whispered at her ear as a cry tore past her lips. "That's it. Tighten that sweet pussy on me."

God, the pleasure.

Jacob was drowning in it.

Lowering his lips to where her neck and shoulder met, he couldn't help the need to grip the flesh there, nip at it, suck it.

Her head went back, a cry tearing from her lips.

Jacob felt her legs lift, her knees gripping his hips, hips churning as he thrust inside her, burying his cock full length in the hottest, tightest pussy he'd ever possessed.

Tight, slick flesh gripped the sensitive head and shaft, rippling over it, suckling at it like the sweetest lips. Pleasure swamped his mind, tore aside defenses and a lifetime of wariness and distrust.

Her hands gripped his shoulders tighter, nails digging into the flesh. Small tremors began to race through her, the muscles of her vagina clenched tighter, stroked and sucked at his dick until the effort it took to hold back his release was more than he knew he could hold on to.

"Jacob . . ." Her nails bit deeper as his thrusts increased, his cock plowing harder through the fist-tight grip she had on him. "Oh God, I needed . . ." A broken moan tore from her.

"What, baby?" Bracing his knees, he gripped her hip with one hand, her hair with the other as he dragged her head farther to the side to allow his lips to play, to claim the sweet flesh there. "What do you need, Sallie?" he whispered at her ear. "Tell me what you needed."

"You," she breathed, her knees tightening as he began thrusting harder, her answer ripping through him, fraying the hold he had on his own need to come. "I needed you."

Him.

The pleasure tightened around him, inside him, building to a point that he had to lift his head from her, clench his teeth, and it wasn't enough.

He felt her come. Fuck, he felt her inner flesh grip him tighter, suck at him with increasingly slick, hot contractions. His name was a cry on her lips, and he was lost.

Fuck. Lost inside her, spilling his seed with hard, fierce ejaculations, he fought whatever feeling those words pulled at inside him. Rapture raced through him, pure, white-hot pleasure he'd only found with this delicate, prickly little woman.

And he spilled inside her, without protection.

Holding her while the tremors of her climax rippled over her and his own release weakened him, Jacob lay against her, barely able to keep the majority of his weight from her delicate body.

Small whimpers left her throat as her teeth clenched at his chest, holding on to him with everything she had.

Had another woman ever held on to him so fiercely? He knew there hadn't been. He knew, in his entire sexual lifetime, no other woman had ever affected him to this point.

Just this woman.

This wasn't going to end well, Sallie thought later as Jacob held her against his chest, her head tucked beneath his chin. He'd carried her to her bed, undressed her and himself, and took her again, wringing another brutal orgasm from her before he was finished with her.

Now, in the dark stillness of the room, he was simply holding her, as though he somehow knew she needed to be held. And he couldn't possibly know that. She hadn't told anyone how desperately she ached to be held by him, to feel the security, the warmth she'd felt so long ago.

And she fully admitted she was crazy to allow it. When he didn't seem inclined to get up and rush from the house, she should have rushed him from it herself. Instead, here she lay, basking in his warmth, feeling it seep through her flesh, move inside her, arrowing to that frozen, icy core she often felt growing inside her.

Six years.

Six years ago, she'd spent one incredible weekend with a man that swept her off her feet and stole her heart. He'd disappeared when the weekend was over and from the moment she realized he wasn't returning, the hurt and lost dreams had begun freezing inside her.

And now here she was, in his arms again, and the frozen shards were slowly unthawing to reveal the ragged, pain-filled edges she hadn't known she was hiding from herself.

"You're thinking too hard." His lazy, satisfied drawl had her fighting a ragged, broken sob.

That sound, the gentle rasp of his voice, the warmth in it, was so reminiscent of the man he had been six years ago that she could feel her heart breaking anew.

"Maybe I'm wondering why you haven't rushed from the house as fast as possible." It wasn't a lie, exactly.

Somehow, lying to him wasn't something she found easy to do.

His hand stroked down her back then up to her shoulder once again.

"Too late to worry about it." He sighed with a thread of drowsiness. "I'd have stayed the last time I was here if I could have. Someone managed to break into the house while I was here and Gram was alone. That was the emergency at the ranch. I've spent the better part of this week trying to figure out who it was."

Sallie sat up, pulled the sheet around her breasts, and stared down at his shadowed face.

"She's okay?" she asked, concerned as a frown knitted her brow.

"She's fine. She fired Granddaddy's shotgun on him." He chuckled as his hand ran up her arm to pull her gently back to his chest. "A load of buckshot came at him as he went out the front window. She nicked him good, though. Unfortunately, I haven't figured out who it was yet."

"Is someone with her now?" She'd hate to think he left his grandmother alone.

Mary Ann Donovan was a tough, feisty old lady, but facing off a home intruder would be scary for anyone.

"Yeah, despite her objections." He gave another of those rough little chuckles. "She reloaded her rifle and placed it close to the bed too. I hope she doesn't shoot my foreman. John wouldn't like that much."

Sallie couldn't help but grin at the thought of the older lady shooting John Grange. He was rarely in the best of moods if his expression was anything to go by whenever she saw him. That might make him a bit ill-tempered.

"Why are you here, Jacob?" The question fell from her lips before she could stop it. "You're not exactly known for choosing lovers from Deer Haven. And you definitely didn't spend the night the few times you have."

He was silent for several long moments. Long enough that she wondered if he was ignoring the question.

"Maybe I'm lazy" he finally said quietly. "And it's damned comfortable here."

"Maybe . . ." she said. "But I don't think that's the case."

"How 'bout I promise to answer that question when I figure it out?" He sighed. "Then, we'll have a nice long discussion concerning it."

She almost grinned at the confusion in his voice. He might not recognize her, he may have even completely forgotten the one weekend he spent with her, but knowing he felt some of what she was going through was nice. Because she didn't understand herself either.

"Gram gave me orders to bring you to the ranch tomorrow," he said then, that bit of confusion still lingering in his voice. "If you're not busy."

His grandmother would probably hunt her down if she refused a summons, she thought, amused. Mary Ann Donovan was known for her determination.

"I wouldn't dare refuse," she told him with a light laugh. "She might come after me with that shotgun."

It couldn't hurt. His grandmother was a nice woman. They'd met several times at different functions she'd attended, and she had always been friendly. Nosy as hell, but friendly.

"Or she'd use it on me." He grunted. A second later she felt the yawn he tried to smother.

It would be okay, she promised herself again. He'd leave again soon and then she'd probably not see him again, other than chance meetings. Her past would stay a secret, and until she had to run again, life would go on.

The regrets would mount, she was certain, and when it was over this time, the pain would go deeper. But at least he was here, now, holding her, warming her.

For this moment in time, she felt safe.

"Come on, baby, lie down here and let me snuggle. You're damned soft and you've worn me out." The lazy amusement in his voice did nothing to quell her misgivings, but she lay down next to him and let him pull her into his embrace.

His warmth seeped into her, wrapped around her like nothing else had ever done. She just wanted to sleep in his arms one more time, she told herself. To sleep deep, secure, as she had during those long, cold nights in Switzerland.

Just one more time, and she'd be content.

And she knew it was a lie.

chapter six

Jacob knew it was a dream.

He always knew when it was a dream.

He stared down at Sallie and watched in agonized lust as his cock pumped in shallow thrusts past swollen, reddened lips.

Innocence filled her face . . . Sallie's face. A younger, far less cynical version. Her hair was darker, her face a bit fuller, her features not as defined, but it was definitely Sallie.

And she was loving his dick as he instructed her on how to take him deeper, how to allow the swollen head to fuck clear to her throat. He could feel the heat, the snug suction each time she swallowed on the wide crest.

Her expression mesmerized and filled with her sexual excitement, he watched as the generous length and girth of his shaft was slowly, agonizingly slowly, consumed.

He could feel the swallowing motions, the spasms of her throat on his cock as he took her and pulled back, pushed in again. And it was killing him, because he knew she'd never done this before. Knew she'd been a virgin for him.

Fuck, he wasn't going to be able to hold on to his control. His need to come was killing him, stealing his control and demanding he give her his release. He wanted to feel it shooting from him, filling her throat as she swallowed . . . and then she moaned . . .

Jacob awoke, sweat beaded on his forehead, his muscles tense as he fought back a groan. The fingers of one hand gripped the base, holding back his release as his jaw clenched with the effort not to come.

Beside him, Sallie was awake. He knew, by God, she was awake. He could feel the tension in her body, a heavy watchfulness as he turned his head and stared into her drowsy face.

"Jacob . . ." she whispered. She slowly sat up. "I could go . . ."

"Go where?" She wasn't leaving. He flipped the sheet back, revealing his erection, watching as her gaze shot to it and her tongue peaked out, swiping quickly over her lips. "You're needed right here, baby."

If lust wasn't pounding through his veins like a runaway train, he'd be able to decipher the strange combination of sensual hunger and wariness that swept across her face. But it was. The combination of the dream and the woman he'd been tempted by in those dreams for years, in the bed next to him, pushed any misgivings to the back of his mind.

He wanted her mouth. Wanted it consuming him,

driving him crazy with pleasure. Lifting his arm, he slid his hand into the back of her hair, urging her to him.

"Give me that sweet mouth, baby," he demanded, remembering every erotic second of a dream that felt far too real.

Reaching out, she touched his cheek, her hand caressing from his face, along his neck, moving slowly, sensually to the aching flesh rising between his thighs.

Her expression was somber, something almost saddened tinging her features and just as he was ready to pull back, to rescind the demand, she moved. Easing along his body until she knelt between his thighs. Just the way he wanted her. Just as she had been in his dreams.

Naked, her breasts swollen, nipples hard, she glanced up at him again, and goddamn, that look on her face. Just as it had been in his dreams.

"You know what I want," he growled, watching her lashes lower, a flush spread across her cheeks. "Give it to me, Sallie. All of it."

She'd teased him with it that first night, taking him only so far when he'd thought for certain she'd give him that ultimate pleasure.

This time, she'd give him what he needed.

Her head lowered, her tongue swiping over the throbbing crest before she went lower, licking, kissing, until she reached the taut sac of his balls. She played there, laving the tight flesh, sucking lightly at it as Jacob felt his breathing accelerate.

As she began her return journey, he opened his eyes and watched her, nearly shaking as she made her way to the lust-darkened crest once again.

"Fuck yeah," he groaned as she let her mouth cover

the sensitive head, her tongue licking, stroking as she sucked at him lightly.

She had to ease her way into it, some part of him urged caution when he wanted to rush her. Let her set the pace, take him at her comfort level. If he did, his reward would be the most erotic fucking blowjob outside his fantasies.

Her eyes drifted closed as she went lower, working his cock along her tongue, easing down marginally then slipping back, returning. Each time she went a little lower, pulled back, licked, and sucked as his balls tightened further.

He was going to blow. Just the thought of what he knew was coming . . .

"Fuck. Yes." She went lower, her tongue flattening as he felt her swallow when the wide crest met the back of her tongue. "Make me crazy, sweetheart."

She pulled back slowly, breathing through her nose, swallowing as she moved her mouth along his cock until once again, he was poised at the back of her tongue.

"God, yes," he growled. "Your sweet mouth . . . Fucking tight . . . hot."

She was killing him, shredding his control.

Jacob's thighs tightened, his jaw clenching with the effort to hold back a desperate groan.

"That's it . . ." His voice was graveled, rough. "Sweet baby . . . so damned good."

He could feel her easing closer, swallowing, taking him deeper as sweat ran along his temple. Ah God, it was killing him. It was his fantasy, part of the dreams that haunted him, step by step. Every sensation. Every stroke, every strike of pleasure that frayed his control.

Until the moment he felt her take him all the way.

Jacob stared down at her, feeling the incredible sensation of her throat tightening on him as she swallowed before she eased back, returned, holding him for brief seconds then releasing him again.

"Fuck, Sallie . . . God, I'm not going to last." He could barely talk, barely breathe.

She went down on him again, and this time, she took all of him. He felt the rippling, tightening pressure, the heat of her mouth, her tongue moving against him.

She eased back.

On the next slow penetration, her lips met the base of his dick, her throat tightened on him, and he lost it. Without warning, a shattered groan tore from his throat as he felt the swollen crest expand, felt her tighten, and his release erupted.

Violent, fierce, his come blasted down her throat. The pressure increased as she swallowed, struggled to hold in place as the ecstatic flashes of pure rapture tore through his mind. In that moment, fantasy and reality merged, the haunting vision of a younger Sallie, the present vision of her, and the two so striking he couldn't separate them.

As the final, hard eruption of his release jetted against the back of her throat he felt her easing back again, slowly, her tongue working over him as she swallowed, caressing the over sensitive crest with each beat of his heart.

He wasn't finished with her yet. Still hard, locked in a place where nothing mattered but this woman and returning to her the sheer ecstasy she'd given him.

"Ride me, baby," he demanded, reaching for her,

lifting her as she rose from between his thighs. "Come on, own me."

"Ride me, baby. Come on, own me . . ."

Sallie fought not to cry out as the words repeated the past. The last time he'd taken her in Switzerland, the way he'd pulled her up his body as the taste of him still lingered in her senses.

She fought to breathe, to separate the past from today, the man he had been from the man he was now. But she couldn't. They were the same. As he pulled her to him, lifting her until her thighs gripped his hips, he was still shockingly hard and so ready for her. And she was so slick, so wet, her body screaming out for his.

"Jacob . . ." she whispered his name as she fought herself, fought the certainty that he was stealing her heart in a way she'd never recover from.

The broad crest pushed past the bare folds between her thighs, drawing a gasp from her at the stroke of heated pleasure. Pressing against the narrow entrance to her sheath as her hands braced on his hard stomach, Sallie watched his face, his eyes, as he began impaling her.

She shook her head, gasping at the sensations tearing through her. The pleasure-pain of the penetration, her need for more, and the look on his face, so hard and dominant, weakened her. Her defenses were being torn to shreds. Her resistance against him was destroyed in those moments.

The pleasure was indescribable. With each inch forged inside her, she lost herself to him more. Just as she had before. She could feel it and the battle to hold back was lost as each inch of his broad shaft pushed inside her.

"Feel good, baby?" His hands gripped her hips as she rocked against him, taking more and more with each motion.

"Jacob," she breathed his name, her voice rough.

One hand moved from her hip to her breast, his fingers finding her nipple and creating another firestorm in her senses.

"Tell me." The demand was powerful, his voice grating with an excess of pleasure. "Come, baby, talk to me."

A helpless whimper escaped her lips.

"So good," she sobbed, tightening as his hips jerked, his cock burying deeper. "Oh God, Jacob, it's so good. So hard, so good."

She could barely think.

She cried out as she moved against him, felt him stretch her farther.

"Yes," she moaned. "Oh God, Jacob, please, more."

She needed him to fill her, to take her.

Instead, he was taking her by slow, measured increases despite her attempts to move on him, to take more of him.

"Please," she cried out, her nails raking his abs. "It hurts so good, Jacob. Make it hurt so good . . ."

Six years ago that plea had broken him. It broke him again.

Sallie was barely aware of her sharp, desperate cry as he thrust inside her, hard. Holding her hips, he pulled her lower, his head lifting to cover a nipple as he pushed harder, deeper, taking her, stretching tight, sensitive tissue and stroking over hypersensitive nerve endings.

She was awash in such fiery sensations that processing them was impossible. His mouth sucked at her nipple, his tongue lashing it as he began pounding inside her, hard, jackhammer thrusts that pushed her fast and hard into an orgasm that had her screaming out his name. Shudders tore through her, her nails dug into his shoulders, and she was certain she'd die before the shattering sensations could ease.

He didn't give them time to ease. With a growl, he turned, laying her back on the bed, still buried within her. He went inside her deeper, harder. He didn't let up despite the hard contractions of her sheath, her sobbing cries. And before the first orgasm could ease, she felt herself being pushed into another.

He was tireless, relentless.

His lips covered hers, his tongue pushing against hers, his kisses deep, voracious as he fucked her. Pumping inside her with powerful driving thrusts, he didn't let up, gave her no mercy. He gave her the most incredible rapture, driving her into another orgasm that threw her harder, higher as she sobbed out his name, her lips moving to his neck as he released them, and she bit.

The growling groan that rippled from him came as his thrusts increased into her desperate, clenching sheath, then drove deep. She felt his cock thicken as her release rocked her. A second later, the furious pulse of his semen shooting inside her extended the ecstasy, stealing her mind, her will.

Hard, wracking shudders tore through her body as she willingly gave herself to the madness. His lips were at her shoulder, her neck, and she knew he was marking her again. Claiming her in ways he hadn't six years ago. Claiming her in ways she knew she would never recover from.

What the fuck had happened?

Jacob fought to catch his breath as Sallie's legs eased slowly from his hips to the bed, her shudders of release beginning to settle as he continued to fight for breath, for a semblance of sanity.

In his entire sexual lifetime, he couldn't remember ever experiencing such a violent release. He felt as though he'd poured part of himself inside her. More than just his sperm. And for a second, one maddening second, he wished she weren't protected. He wanted to mark her in a way she'd never forget, never be able to fight.

He wanted to fill her, see her growing round with his child, and know beyond a shadow of a doubt she couldn't walk away from him.

He was losing his mind over her. He'd never lost his mind over a woman . . . except in his dreams.

Easing from her, Jacob rolled to his side and dragged her against him, his arms around her, his hands stroking her, gentling her as the last tremors washed through her. And he knew to the bottom of his soul that this felt far too familiar, it felt too much a part of him. Somehow, somewhere, he'd been here with her before.

chapter seven

Was there such a thing as simple coincidence?

Hours later, Jacob considered that question, though he knew the answer to it. In his life, with his past, there was no such thing. Especially not significant coincidences such as years of dreams, a familiarity with the subject of said dream, despite the fact that her features refused to come into focus. And now, those features could be seen, and the face was Sallie's.

As he drove her to the ranch later that afternoon, he could feel a warning curling in his gut, tightening it with a foreboding he knew better than to ignore.

Had he checked into her background yet?

He hadn't.

For some reason, he couldn't make himself do it. Couldn't make himself give Justice the order to do it. A part of him simply wasn't ready yet.

And still, he was bringing her to his ranch, his home, despite his misgivings where her past was concerned.

Despite his certainty that he needed to demand answers from her, needed to demand why he felt as though she belonged solely to him.

He didn't believe in past lives, so he couldn't use that as an excuse. And déjà vu was just the other side of the coin.

"You do know the betting with the ladies in that auxiliary group is going to go crazy once they learn you brought me to the ranch for lunch, don't you?" Her pale blue eyes watched him curiously as a grin curled at her lips.

The question wasn't enough of a distraction from his thoughts, but he'd take whatever he could get.

"Gram is part of that troublemaking little group of women." He shook his head at the thought of it. "Trust me, she's probably already pushed that little betting pool as high as it can go."

From the corner of his eye, he watched as she turned her head to stare out the passenger side window for a second before turning back to him, a smile teasing at her lips.

Damn, she was pretty. He knew she was unfailingly polite in public unless pushed, and once pushed, could slice a man wide open without uttering the first four letter word. He'd seen her in action at the supply store when one of the ranchers had decided to take his surly mood out on one of the young cashiers there.

Within minutes she'd been at the girl's side, icy cold, like a mother bear defending her cub. When the rancher left, he'd been forced to go to the next county to get his supplies for months. No one ever went after Sallie's employees after that.

He'd seen her carry purchases out for young mothers whose hands were full, and seen her laughing with the old men that flirted with her. She was well-liked, in some cases adored, and was slowly making herself a part of the community.

"You've never married, that makes all those mothers and grandmothers nervous," she informed him as she crossed her jean-clad legs and flicked him an amused glance. "They have to have hope you'll marry so their little girls will stop wishing for you and settle down with nice, unassuming young men they can control."

"Is that what it is?" He grunted, amused. "And here I just thought they enjoyed messing with my personal life."

"I have no doubt that's part of it too." She lifted her hand to brush the fringe of her bangs back and that motion seemed so fucking familiar he had to clench his teeth against the need to demand why. Why the hell did it feel like he knew her far better than he should?

"What about you?" He knew he was pushing it, but he was dying to know what the hell was driving him insane where she was concerned. "Gossip says you're divorced?"

Tension tightened through her instantly. He could feel it, even if he hadn't seen it in the stiffened line of her shoulders.

"Yes. Divorced," she agreed readily, her voice cooler now. "Young and dumb, you know?"

The nervous smile she shot him was followed by another brush of her fingers against her hair before she linked them together in her lap.

"Happens," he agreed, nodding as though he couldn't feel that edge of nerves and fear reaching out to him.

"Left him back in Oklahoma?" Was the bastard still a part of her life?

"When he left the house, I never saw him again." She shrugged. "I have no idea where he went or what he's doing."

She was stiff, staring straight ahead, though she was so obviously fighting to appear relaxed. Jacob forced himself to bite his tongue, to hold back his questions. If Sallie arrived at his home upset, or angry with him, then Gram would strip his hide.

He almost grimaced at the thought. His grandmother was scarier than any director or enemy he'd ever faced in his life. Not for a second would he consider bringing her wrath down on his head. He remembered the switch she'd used when he was a kid far too well.

"When it comes to exes, that's probably best," he stated, as though the subject were closed. "I can be a possessive man, you know."

Her head swung around, eyes narrowed suspiciously. "Why would you be possessive of me, Jacob? I wouldn't advise such a thing. It won't work out."

His let his brow lift mockingly as he slid her a quick look.

"We'll have to see about that," he murmured. "I might be able to convince you to like it."

She'd better learn to like it. He'd marked her, spilled himself inside her. As far as he was concerned, she already belonged to him, whether she liked it or not.

She had no doubt she wouldn't, Sallie told herself firmly as she pushed away the fear that Jacob was about to become nosy about her life. She couldn't afford his nosiness or his suspicion. When she'd met him six years before, he'd been using another name, a cover, which no doubt meant he'd been an agent of some sort. Considering they were in Switzerland at the time, she was guessing CIA, which meant she was going to have to be very careful if he kept his focus on her.

No, she was going to have to break this off quickly. She should have already realized he'd been an agent of some sort while he was in Switzerland. The moment she was introduced to him as Jacob Donovan, but no one called him Jake, she'd known something was wrong.

She'd thought for a while that perhaps he'd just lied to her about his name for some other reason. So she couldn't find him once he left, perhaps he was married at the time, but according to gossip, Jacob had never been married.

If he had been or even still was an agent, then she was in a hell of a lot of trouble.

She'd never imagined he'd want more than another one-night stand. She was already off-balance and uncertain, terrified that her past was going to return, and she'd have to run again. Terrified that she wouldn't run in time.

That was her greatest fear. Or even worse, Jacob would finally recognize her. How humiliating would that be? For him to know that she was so desperate for his touch that not only could she not resist him, but she couldn't resist him after he'd already walked away from her once.

And losing him again . . . After that morning, could she survive it? It had been like a flashback to that last morning in Switzerland, a near exact reenactment of how they'd taken each other again.

"Here we are." She was drawn from her thoughts at his quiet announcement and looked up from staring sightlessly at her entwined fingers.

The single-story ranch house sat peacefully in a wide, summer green valley, its back to the rising, forested land bordering it on one side. Stables, a barn, and corrals dotted the landscape some distance from the house. It was a lazy, peaceful summer day here. A small group of livestock grazed in a fenced pasture, while several horses stood placidly in a boarded corral.

It was a familiar sight to Sallie now. She'd visited enough of the ranches that Dillerman's supplied that she was familiar with the efficiency. Jacob's operation wasn't as large as, say, the Culpeppers', but the fact that it was successful showed in the neatly painted buildings, the care in the ranch yards, and the neat, careful landscaping around the house.

"It's beautiful," she said softly, her gaze roving over the flowering bushes and strategically placed trees for shade surrounding the house as well as the rest of the valley.

"Gram has strict standards." He shot her a grin, but she saw the pride in his expression as well.

His grandmother may well have strict standards, but so did Jacob evidently.

Following the asphalt drive to the garage attached to the house, he parked and cut the engine to the vehicle.

"Let me get your door," he told her as she reached for the latch. "Gram will lecture both of us otherwise."

Mrs. Donovan was actually known for her strict views

on what was or was not polite when it came to men and women. Those who knew her found it amusing, but if she was around, those men who knew her took notice.

So, Sallie stayed in place as Jacob jumped from the truck and made his way to the passenger side to open her door and help her from the cab. Placing his hand on her lower back, he walked next to her to the front door, where he then opened it and stepped back for her to enter. The subtle wink he shot her as she passed him sent a wave of warmth curling through her.

As though they shared a secret, an acknowledgment that he may be the polite gentleman now, but once he got her alone, that veil would drop, and he'd become the hungry, dominant lover she was becoming familiar with.

Entering the house, she put thoughts of Jacob the lover and the past behind her, and greeted Jacob's grandmother as the older woman moved to them.

Mary Ann Donovan was a small woman, delicately boned and full of energy. At seventy-three she still drove her own car, was rumored to slip out occasionally in Jacob's old Mustang, and if the gossip was right, kept all her friends in trouble with their children and grandchildren when they joined her in her sense of fun. Someone had even mentioned a near arrest when she and several others had helped another friend slip from the retirement home her children had placed her in.

She was entertaining, filled with warmth, and loved her grandson above all things, Sallie had heard.

"It's about time Jacob got off his butt and brought a lady friend to visit me," Mary Ann told her as Jacob stepped outside to talk to his foreman after a light lunch. "I was beginning to despair that he'd do something other than watching his cows."

The affection in her voice touched Sallie. Yes, rumors were correct, Mary Ann Donovan treasured her grandson. What would that feel like? she wondered. Grandparents or parents that so loved a child that their voices filled with it when talking about them?

"I think that's a qualification for ranchers," Sallie stated, hiding her grin as Mary Ann sat a cup of tea in front of her. "Watching their cows is high on their list of priorities I've heard."

Mary Ann gave a roll of her almost sapphire blue eyes. "His priority should be a wife and babies." She sighed longingly as she watched Sallie with just an edge of calculation. "I'm not getting any younger, you know."

Sallie sipped at her tea and watched Mary Ann patiently. It was obvious she'd already decided Sallie was going to provide those grandbabies.

At another time, in another life, Sallie thought sadly. How she would have loved to have that future with him.

"Have you mentioned this to Jacob?" Lowering her cup, Sallie tried to keep the conversation from focusing too heavily in her direction.

"Oh, just every day." A flash of her youth filled her face as she laughed back at Sallie. "Perhaps you should mention it, dear. The two of you seem rather close." Those bright eyes flicked to Sallie's neck.

Heat swept up her face. Sallie felt it with an edge of resignation. The marks didn't embarrass her, but the fact that this spry little woman knew how they got there wasn't comfortable.

"That wouldn't be a good idea, Mrs. Donovan," Sallie told her softly. "Jacob needs a wife that will make him happy. One that can stay, have those babies, and build a life with him. I'm not that woman."

Because monsters followed her. Because if she was found, she would have to run.

If she wasn't caught.

And God help her if she was caught.

Mary Ann sat back in her chair, her cup cradled between both hands as she lifted it to her lips, and Sallie could have sworn she saw the barest edge of a satisfied little smile just before she sipped at the tea.

Now she knew where Jacob had inherited that look. It could be downright dangerous to her and to Jacob, if she weren't careful.

Jacob reentered the house through the back door, just in time to hear his grandmother's suggestion and Sallie's answer. He'd spent some time while he was in the CIA in interrogation, so he knew nuances to tone and expression, and what his grandmother likely didn't catch, he did.

Sallie was scared, and it wasn't the fear of a woman facing an emotion or a man she was uncertain of. Sallie was frightened of something far more tangible.

"Well, Jacob can be a rather determined man," his grandmother said, not really a warning or statement. "Once he sets his mind to something, he doesn't fail. And I like you, Sallie," she said, surprising him and obviously Sallie as well. "You seem like a good girl. But you have a spirit. Standing up to Jacob when he's surly won't always be comfortable but I don't think you'd have trouble with it."

Only once had he failed, Jacob thought, stepping outside the house just as silently as he entered it. Identifying the young woman that drifted through his dreams for so many years, her face blurred until the day he met Sallie.

Hell. He hated the thought of nosing into her past without her knowledge of it. He'd put that behind him when he left the agency and swore he wouldn't let his suspicious nature mar any relationship he had. Over the years, he'd accepted that somehow, somewhere, he lost something or someone important to him. He'd been in too many blast areas and wounded far too often as he navigated the covert world he'd worked within.

Suspicion and coincidence were two different things, though. There were too many coincidences where Sallie was concerned, and far too many signs that there was more to her than a transplanted Oklahoma girl determined to live her life without the heartbreak most women suffered.

And now, the fear that flashed for the briefest second in her expression and shadowed her voice assured him there was more to her.

There were times he cursed the abilities he brought with him out of that damned agency. He'd been recruited straight out of boot camp at eighteen and worked exclusively with the CIA until twenty-five. That last mission had nearly killed him. While lying in that hospital, he'd known it was time to go home.

Walking quickly around the house to the front door, he stepped inside, ensuring his grandmother, as well as Sallie, were aware of his entrance. Both women looked toward him as he entered the house, his grandmother's expression was quieter than he expected, and Sallie's was that cool mask that showed nothing but polite interest. He hated it.

"Sorry it took so long." Striding the open living room to the dining room, he kissed his grandmother's cheek before giving Sallie a slow, easy grin. "Come for a walk with me. I'll even introduce you to my favorite horse."

There was a marginal warming in her gaze and that shadow of fear dissipated.

Taking her hand Jacob led her from the house for a walk to the stables. The soft breeze drifting through the valley softened the summer's heat. There was still a stiffness in her body, a wariness that hadn't eased away.

Pointing out the two barns he explained the different uses for them as he led her to the stables. He didn't have a favorite horse, really, but he was damned if he hadn't been desperate to get the fear out of her eyes. He did have his best horse. The chestnut stallion was temperamental as a two-year-old when carrying a rider, but gentle as a lapdog with the saddle off.

"He's beautiful," Sallie said softly as the horse leaned his head over the stall door for attention.

"Ornery as hell." He chuckled as he leaned against the wall next to her as the horse nickered softly. "Put a saddle on his back and he becomes Satan's child."

Damn he wanted to kiss her. Wanted to taste her kiss while that gentle curve of enjoyment was in place on her lips.

Sallie glanced back at him with a smile. "He's here to look pretty, not carry your heavy butt around."

His brow arched. "You look pretty, he looks like a horse."

A soft blush stole up her cheeks as another smile tugged at her lips.

"He's pretty too," she assured him, easing her hand from where she'd been gently stroking the stallion's face. "And he knows it."

Turning to him, she lifted her head and her pretty, pale blue eyes still soft with pleasure. She was irresistible. And Jacob was a hungry man. Cupping her cheek, he lowered his head, watching the need that filled her expression.

Slowly, keeping his gaze on hers and watching her eyes darken, her lashes lower, he let his lips brush against hers in a kiss filled with promise.

Sallie knew she was in over her head, had known it since the night she'd allowed him to take her home from that bar. As Jacob eased her closer, his arms going around her, his lips parting hers to make way for the slow glide of his tongue, she felt another part of her heart melt and open for him. Her lips parted, took his kiss, met his tongue with her own, and a part of her began weeping with the loss she could feel coming closer.

"Hey, boss, you got a . . . oops . . ." Inquiry turned to amusement as Sallie jerked back in surprise, heat rushing up her face at the knowledge that they'd been caught in the moment. "Uh, sorry, boss."

A rueful grin pulled at his lips and he stepped back from her, turning his attention to the ranch hand.

"What can I help you with, Kenny?" he asked, the lazy amusement and simmering lust in his voice showing on his expression as well.

"We got a problem with the computer in the office;

you might need to look at. I have everything shut down for now, though, if you'd like to look at it later."

Jacob didn't stiffen, there were no signs of tension, but Sallie could feel it nonetheless.

"I need to get back to the house anyway," she told him easily. "It sounds like it could be a problem."

A rancher depended on his computer system just as much as any other business.

"I'll look at it after I take Miss Hamblen home," he stated, but Sallie could sense the question in the statement.

"Sounds good, Mr. Donovan." The older man nodded then gave Sallie an apologetic smile. "Good to see you, Miss Hamblen."

"You as well, Kenny," she said. "Tell Missy I said hello."

Kenny's wife was one of the store's regular customers, often coming in to make purchases for the ranch and for Kenny. No doubt Kenny would also tell his wife about what he'd interrupted.

"Will do." With a brief nod, the ranch hand turned and left the barn, once again leaving them alone.

"You could hang out with Gram," Jacob suggested, his voice low, the brush of his lips against her ear gentle. "I wouldn't have to leave after taking you home then. I could spend the night."

There was definitely no question in his tone now. It was a sexy, far too tempting demand. One she had to refuse.

Shaking her head, Sallie stepped back slowly. "Lily's staying the night. I promised I'd help her with one of the online business classes she's taking."

The class wouldn't take more than an hour or two, Sallie knew, but she also knew Lily was desperate to get away from her parent's home for a while. Between Shay and her parents, she was being driven to distraction over her refusal to return to the more traditional college experience. Right now, that was the last thing the younger woman needed.

"She needs to get her butt back to college." Jacob sighed, a hard look crossing his face. "Or actually give her parents a good reason for not doing so."

Sallie merely shrugged. Anything she said could only make the situation worse. Lily had confided in her at a time when she had been weak. Sallie wouldn't betray that confidence. Even inadvertently.

"Seems to me it should be her decision." She moved past him and headed for the barn's entrance.

He didn't say anything, which could mean everything or nothing where Jacob was concerned.

Returning to the house first, Jacob informed his grandmother of their departure.

"Come back soon, dear." The quick hug the older woman gave her surprised Sallie, at first. Mrs. Donovan wasn't known for hugging anyone and everyone, she was actually known for being more distant than most. "Visit anytime."

That wasn't an option for her, and Sallie knew it. She'd already made friends, made herself a part of the lives around her, and she'd sworn she wouldn't do that. She'd promised herself she wouldn't care enough about the people around her so much that leaving would break her heart.

And what had she done, she asked herself as Jacob

drove from the ranch. She'd gotten close to Lily and Shay, to her assistant, Tara, and even the often-interfering women on the Ladies Auxiliary. Instead of renting, she'd bought a house, because she'd loved it once she saw it and instead of a one-night stand, she seemed to have acquired a lover. At least temporarily. She was under no illusions that he'd stay.

"Sweet Kyra." The words whispered through her memories. "A man would be a fool to let you go."

And yet, he had let her go. He'd left her bed and never returned. She'd extended her stay in Switzerland as long as possible, using every excuse she could think of, and it had been in vain.

She'd been eighteen, a virgin, and she'd thought herself so very smart and sophisticated. She'd been warding off advances since she was fifteen, heard every lie a man could tell, or so she'd thought. She hadn't expected a man who didn't whisper promises, but instead danced with her in a rose garden, helped her slip into the kitchen for cookies, and then shared them with her after pouring both of them a glass of milk.

Dressed in her ball gown, all but giggling, she'd carried the plate of cookies while he held the milk and they slipped back out again to enjoy the treat as snow drifted around them. He'd placed his evening jacket over her bare shoulders, warmed her against his side. Then dared her to a game of cards after the party.

And she'd invited him to her room, tempted him with the offer of a new deck of cards, and met the hunger in his gaze with her own.

That night, she'd given him more than just her body, her innocence. Not love, she assured herself. She hadn't known him long enough to give him her heart fully. But still, something she'd never been able to recover again. No touch rivaled his. No kiss was as sensual or held the same power over her own arousal. He'd lived in her memories like a ghost determined to haunt her.

He would always haunt her. That realization was a sobering one and not entirely pleasant.

Glancing over at him as he drove, she saw the thoughtful expression on his tanned face. He drove with one hand, the other arm rested casually against the window at his side. Sunglasses covered his face now, the late afternoon sun shining bright and hard through the truck's window.

He didn't seem to be in the mood to talk, but that was okay too.

Pulling her own glasses free of her purse, Sallie put them on and sat back in the seat, watching the scenery go by.

"Don't start coming up with excuses to kick me out of your bed as soon as I drop you off," he suddenly spoke some minutes later. "You do, and I'm telling you, Sallie, the next time I get you under me, I'll make damned sure you don't come up with excuses again."

He glanced at her, determination and sheer arrogance filling his face.

"Threats?" she asked, arching a brow. "Those don't work on me, Jacob."

He wouldn't hurt her, she knew that much, but there were rumors, hints that perhaps she hadn't experienced Jacob at his most sensual either. No details, nothing ominous, but Tara had once laughed that one of his few lovers from the area swore no man had ever ridden her as hard, as powerfully or dominantly, as Jacob had. When asked what she meant, she'd told Tara that Jacob did things to that no other man ever had.

"I'd never threaten you, darlin'," he promised with a slow, far too knowing grin. "Not in the bedroom and not with anything rough. At least"—he paused, his grin deepening—"not unless you asked nicely."

She had to fight not to lose her breath, not to blush or stammer. The man was too confident already.

"Holding out on me, cowboy?" she murmured. "And here I was certain I'd already seen all the tricks you had to offer."

She wasn't the brightest person when it came to this man, she thought once the words left her lips. But the thought of him being rougher . . . of experiencing the implied acts Tara had related from his former lover, tempted her, aroused her.

"Ah, sweetheart." Sensual, wicked, the curve of his lips had butterflies attacking her stomach in ways a grown woman should never experience. "That's a dare, you know? That ain't nice."

His tone assured her that he might be rather pleased by that.

"It's been a long time since I was accused of being nice," she assured him, enjoying the teasing despite the knowledge that it would only hurt more when he walked away. Or when she had to run.

"It's been a long time since I've been dared," he countered, laughing over at her. "You're a bad girl, Sallie. I might have to spank you."

"You might have to try." The challenge was given, and she understood it hadn't been missed.

The thought of a sensual spanking, only previously read about, had her entire body clenching and lust spiking her blood. Each time Jacob had taken her, she'd sensed more, sensed hungers he wasn't allowing himself to let free. Should he decide to loosen the reins on his hungers, could she meet them or be overwhelmed by them?

"Teasing me when you know I can't stay and meet that little challenge tonight might get you spanked sooner than you imagine," he warned. "And that cute little ass could be in trouble if I get started petting on it, Sallie."

She lifted her shoulder negligently, as though the threat didn't bother her but the smile that teased her lips was nearly impossible to control. "Promises, promises."

She wanted all of him, just once. All his hunger, his wild lust, everything she could feel he kept contained when he was in her bed. All the things he'd given her in Switzerland.

She wanted more than she should.

Far more than her heart could bear.

God, what was she going to do now? And how the hell was she going to let him go when everything inside her was demanding she fight for more?

chapter eight

Jacob could swear he was still sweating when he pulled into the small parking area behind his ranch foreman's office at the main stable. Sallie had him so damned sexually riled before he arrived at her home that he'd had to force himself to leave her house after walking her in.

That woman made him crazy for her and he couldn't figure out why. There was something about her, almost familiar. Almost as though he'd found something he hadn't known was lost.

No, that wasn't exactly right. He'd known she was lost, he just hadn't known from where, or her identity. But since Sallie's arrival the hazy image of a woman in his dreams was no longer so hazy. She now carried Sallie's face. A younger, less wary Sallie whose eyes stared at him with shining dreams and innocence. And he was damned if that made sense to him. Because he knew for a fact they hadn't met.

Normally, he had an exact memory, photographic in

many ways. There were only a few instances in his life that his memory of the time was less than perfect, and only once that a complete block of time was gone. That one time, though, he'd had a partner, and if there'd been a woman Jacob had been involved with, his partner would have said something.

Hell, when he'd first come to consciousness after the explosion that nearly killed him, he'd even asked John what he'd lost, memory wise. Nothing but the mission, John had assured him, the heavy disgust at the loss of information filling his voice. If there had been anything more, the other man would have told him. It would have had to have been a part of the report John had turned in after he'd been debriefed. Yet nothing had been there.

A week was absent from that Switzerland operation. The only point in his time when more than a few hours had gone missing.

Rubbing at the side of his jaw, he fought to make sense of it as he drove into the ranch yard. The dreams, the woman, the slowly forming knowledge that somehow, somewhere, he'd forgotten something. And that was only a single moment in time, a matter of days, when that could have happened.

Parking, Jacob moved from the truck, determined to quickly take care of whatever problem the computer was having and get back to Sallie. He wanted answers. And he wanted them now.

Neither John Grange, nor Kenny, was in sight, but Justice Culpepper's Harley was parked at the corner of the building and the owner was leaning back comfortably in the manager's leather desk chair, the computer open before him.

"Makin' yourself at home, Justice?" Jacob asked as he strode into the office, his brow lifted mockingly.

"Took you long enough to get back." Justice grunted, his gray eyes glancing from the computer screen. "I was about to send a search party out looking for you." A grin touched his lips then. "Except, I pretty much knew where you were."

"Hmm," Jacob murmured, still watching the other man. "I'm going to assume you lied to Kenny about the computer, or somehow convinced him to lie to me." He glanced at the laptop then back to Justice.

A broad shoulder lifted in reply as a cool smile shaped the other man's lips. "I lied to him. I figured it would be rather hard to convince him to lie to you."

Rather hard would probably be an understatement. Kenny was easygoing, friendly, but, like Grange, he and Jacob had saved each other's asses one time too many in the past to consider such betrayals.

"I'll assume you had a reason?" He'd better have a damned good reason.

Justice grimaced at the question. "You know what a paranoid bastard I am, Jacob. We made a deal two years ago when we learned how our county was being used by those bastards to traffic innocent kids and terrorists. You were nearly killed and our trust in neighbors went to hell in a hand basket. I'm not willing to let that happen again."

Yeah, it had. Learning men they dealt with daily were as evil as any enemy they'd ever faced hadn't been easy.

The knowledge had nearly cost Jacob his life. It had cost the Culpeppers their peace.

"What does that have to do with anything now?" Jacob asked. "And why couldn't it wait until morning when I returned from Sallie's?"

A heavy breath expelled from Justice's chest at the question. "Because Rancor just called from Oklahoma on the physical background check I reinitiated on your very pretty Ms. Hamblen," he stated heavily as anger snapped into Jacob's mind. "I don't know who she is, my friend, but Sallie Hamblen she is not. Sallie Hamblen's living a nice, comfortable little life in Europe with her husband while someone else is using her past, her Social Security number, and her identity. And I think I'd like to know why."

The somber heaviness in the other man's expression attested to the fact that he didn't like what he'd found any more than Jacob liked hearing it.

"You're certain?" Jacob wanted to be sure, dead fucking sure, because once he confronted Sallie, there would be no taking it back. And hell yes, he'd damn sure be confronting her over it.

Doubting Justice wasn't an option. They'd been friends for too long and the pact they'd made two years before was too strong. But even more, he'd never known Justice to outright lie. He and his brothers had been raised in hell and honed by monsters. The men those experiences had molded the Culpeppers into had no give, little mercy, and a certain code they lived by. One they wouldn't break, for any reason.

"Rancor doesn't make mistakes when it comes to this and you know it," Justice reminded him as he leaned back in the manager's chair. "He's still chasing some leads down, but we're damned sure she's not Sallie Hamblen. We're just not certain who she is yet. But he'll figure it out before he gets back."

Hell, he'd known this was coming. He should have checked her background himself, should have ignored that little voice in the back of his mind that for once wanted to learn who his lover was, rather than check into her as though she were a criminal.

"You went through our contacts in the government?" Jacob asked as he turned his back on his friend and stepped to the window looking out onto the main pastures.

Vibrant summer green filled the view, interspersed with the white board fences. Calm, peaceful, just what he'd sworn his life was going to be two years ago. No more chasing adrenaline, dodging bullets, or watching blood fly.

"She's not CIA, FBI, or any other government agency and she's not in WITSEC. Sallie Hamblen is nothing to no one within the government. Not an agent, a former agent, or in any sort of investigative or protective detail. She's nada there. I checked myself," Justice assured him. "I even stole her wineglass from the restaurant once she left after the meeting with Rhonda and Chet. No hit. Period."

No hit. With the contacts and databases at their disposal, there would have been a hit if she was listed with any law enforcement or government agency.

"Private," he muttered, crossing his arms over his chest to keep from hitting something.

"And a damned lot of money covering her trail," the

other man bit out, a thread of anger filling his voice. "I like her, Jacob. She seems like a fine woman, but hell, a lot of enemies seem like fine people, don't they?"

People like the mayor and several deputies that had been involved in the mess they'd found two years before.

"Fuck," he breathed out, glaring into the peaceful summer setting outside the office. "What made you re-initiate the background check?"

He turned to face Justice once more, wishing there were some damned way to deny the fact that Sallie was lying to all of them.

"She's watched you for three years whenever you were around." His friend sighed. "No dates with anyone else, no hints, rumors, or gossip about a lover, male or female, until you. It just sat wrong with me, Jacob. I can't help it. Only a woman in love, or a woman with an agenda, is that focused. And hell if I believe in love enough to let it go."

The statement had Jacob's neck tightening, his gut rioting. Yeah, there was something off there, and he'd known it. Something that just didn't add up and he hadn't wanted to face it, or admit it to himself. Sometimes, in the dead of night, when crazy-assed dreams brought him awake, Sallie was his first thought and the image haunting those dreams.

How long had it been since he'd allowed himself to trust a woman far enough to want more than a night or two in her bed? And he sure as hell didn't trust women as distant and secretive as Sallie seemed to be. But with her, damn, if he hadn't been so busy in the past three years, he would have already had her in his bed.

"Tara says she's the same way with everyone at the store," Justice continued. "They don't know shit about her, even now, three years later. No family has visited, she doesn't go out of town to visit family and they damned sure don't contact her there. The real Sallie Hamblen has no immediate family, but there's cousins, etc. According to the cousins, they haven't seen her in over ten years, since she went to Europe to live with a distant cousin after her parents died. So, I didn't really think about it during the initial check. But too many things started bothering me, I guess."

Yeah, that was Justice, and the rest of his brothers as well. Come to think of it, Jacob was a paranoid, suspicious person himself, yet, he'd ignored all the signs that something wasn't adding up with Sallie.

"She's running scared," Jacob muttered then. "She keeps everyone at arm's length, doesn't make close friends, doesn't date. Her home holds very few pictures or mementos, and she stays at home rather than socializing."

"She also has a strict policy that none of her pictures hit social media, no matter what. She told Tara she hates social media and doesn't like being a part of it." He shrugged. "Some folks are like that but, like us, they usually have a reason for it."

Because anything that went viral could possibly come with a hell of a lot of danger, Jacob thought. They evaded pictures and Justice even had someone hired to ensure any pictures of himself, his family, or Jacob ended up either gone or out of focus both on accounts as well as the devices of whoever posted them. Though, most people knew they were rather camera shy and respected their privacy. Deer Haven wasn't a large metropolis, and most people he associated or socialized with, they'd known for years.

"How soon before Rancor is finished chasing down his leads on her identity?" he asked, wondering if waiting before he confronted Sallie should be an option.

Justice shrugged with a shake of his head. "Not sure. He's waiting to see if I want him to fly to Europe. I wanted to talk to you first."

Waiting wouldn't be an option.

Jacob nodded slowly. "I'll let you know. I think I'll have a talk with our little imposter first, see what she has to say about it."

The brooding look on Justice's face was tinged with regret. "I sure hate this, Jacob." He sighed before rising to his feet. "I like her. Hell, I like her a lot. But even more, I know you do."

Like her?

Fuck no, it went a hell of a lot deeper than merely like, and Jacob knew it, just as Justice suspected it.

"I need Pride to set up a watch on her." And he hated that like hell. "Three men on eight-hour shifts whether I'm there or not."

Justice nodded again. "He should be heading there now from where he was waiting at the café in town. I called when the cameras showed you heading from the main road to the house." He flicked his fingers toward the security monitors above the desk. "I wasn't sure when you'd arrive, so I waited."

Because Jacob would have known the house was being watched and he'd have damned sure checked it out the second his instincts warned him something or someone was focused on Sallie.

Son of a bitch.

It would have been nice not to fight a battle with her that involved more than her own stubborn nature. Not that he was going to let that stop him. At least, not yet. Something inside him had already marked her as his, and he was damned if he was ready to let her go yet.

"I know you have sources I don't," Justice stated when Jacob remained silent. "Maybe you should check with them, see what you can learn."

Sources. Yeah, he had sources, but using them wasn't something he liked doing. At this point, he was beginning to wonder if he had a choice. Learning who she was, the danger she was in, was too important. He couldn't imagine her being a threat, everything inside him recoiled at the thought of it.

"You have the information Rancor tracked?" he asked Justice then.

Nodding, the other man closed whatever he was looking at then pulled the flash drive and extended it to him.

"What are you going to do?" Justice asked, rising to his feet, his expression concerned.

Jacob's brow arched. "Find out who she is and why she's pretending to be someone else." And by God, he wanted to know why she was lying to him and who she was running from.

Night had fallen before Lily declared she was finished studying. Sallie had all the curtains firmly closed, the lights on the end tables next to the couch providing the only light in the room, and a glass of wine as she fought against the nerves that had haunted her the past few nights.

It happened occasionally, the nervous tension, the urge to pack and run, to make certain she wasn't being followed. It hadn't happened in the past year or so, at least, not until she'd allowed Jacob back into her bed.

He was like an addiction, she told herself, taking another sip of the wine. One she couldn't seem to get out of her system.

"I'm tired of studying. We should go out and have fun." Lily leaned back against the couch, giving Sallie a self-effacing smile as she closed her laptop and set the device aside.

With her black hair in a ponytail and a mischievous smile, Lily looked like a teenager rather than the twenty-three-year-old woman Sallie knew her to be. Lily was sharp, for all her innocent looks, and she'd already experienced enough to know that the world was rarely a nice place to be.

"I just want to sit here, relax, and enjoy my wine." Sallie waved the suggestion away as she curled her legs to her side and sipped at her wine. "I think I've had enough excitement for a while."

The grin that edged at Lily's lips had Sallie's eyes rolling.

"Cousin Jacob filling your life with madness and mayhem?" She laughed. "And here I thought he was boring for a single man. Especially one who had all the women chasing after him."

It was a good thing she didn't have wine in her mouth,

it would have gone all over the couch. Boring was the last thing she'd call Jacob.

Unfortunately.

"He can be time-consuming. A bit high-maintenance for certain," Sallie drawled, wondering for a second if Jacob had managed to figure out his computer problems. He hadn't called as he said he would and he hadn't returned. For some reason she'd expected him to come back when he finished with the computer.

"I've never heard a woman say that." Leaning forward, Lily watched her intently, a look Sallie wasn't exactly comfortable with. "He really likes you, Sallie. Jacob's not had a woman that he's focused on like this, ever. Sometimes, he's almost seemed kind of lost, I guess. Or waiting . . ."

"Stop, Lily." Sallie couldn't let her friend finish. She couldn't bear to hope when she knew nothing could come of it. "This isn't anything serious. Don't read anything into it."

It was the same advice she gave herself countless times a day. She couldn't let herself hope. Hoping meant she had far too much to lose if she was found again.

She was going to have to call investigators soon. This was going to have to end. She couldn't keep living like this, never knowing, unable to truly live.

"Because you're scared," Lily softly accused, her gaze compassionate.

"Because nothing can come of it." Sallie shook her head definitively, despite her regret. "You and I both know that."

And not because she was scared, but because Jacob

had already walked away from her once, and she couldn't trust him to stay this time, couldn't trust that she meant anything more to him than a few nights of fun and games in her bed.

"He took you to see Gram," Lily pointed out. "He wouldn't have done that if he didn't care about you, Sallie. You two have danced around each other for three years. You think others haven't noticed it?"

"I haven't danced around anyone." She scoffed. "I've always been very polite."

Lily snorted at the claim. "Too polite. And he always watches you. Especially the few times you've come to the bar with us. He always shows up, always watches you."

Sallie stared back at her for a long moment. Lily worried, she knew. And she'd always believed Jacob could protect Sallie and Sallie had always known she could never ask.

Gripping her wineglass in both hands, Lily looked down at the dark liquid for long moments. When her head lifted, there was something determined in her gaze. "Jacob is a bad ass," she warned Sallie then. "If he knew . . ."

"Stop!" Fear shot through her, tightening her chest and roiling through her stomach as panic threatened to edge into her mind. "You promised me, Lily . . ."

"I'm not going to say anything," the other girl exclaimed. "But Sallie, Jacob and the Culpeppers could help you. I swear it."

And as much as she wanted someone to help her, the thought of Jacob knowing who she was, possibly remembering, knowing he'd already walked away from her once, was more than she could bear.

What would he think? Would she see disgust in his eyes, or a complete lack of knowledge? To know he'd forgotten her entirely would destroy a part of her that she didn't know would ever recover.

"No, Lily," she repeated, careful to keep her voice firm, to keep Lily from arguing further. "No one . . ."

The house went black. Every light blinked off and didn't come back on. Fear rushed inside Sallie. This was no normal outage. This was her worst nightmare. Jumping for Lily as she went to rise to her feet, Sallie jerked her friend to the floor no more than a breath before the sound of glass exploding through the house and a door splintering could be heard.

There was a heartbeat of time that regret, grief, and sheer terror vied for supremacy inside her. But even as those emotions whipped through her senses, Sallie was moving, desperate to escape, to get Lily away from the danger.

"Run." Sallie gasped, pushing Lily toward the back guest room. "Out the back window. Now."

She moved to follow Lily, had every intention of escaping with her friend, and she would have, but as she cleared the couch, heavy fingers tangled in her hair, pulling her back. The pain shot through her scalp to the back of her neck, dragging a cry from her lips as the shock of it shattered her senses.

Her hands went back, nails digging into the wrists as fingers twisted cruelly into her hair. Her heels scraped across the carpet, fighting for traction as she cried out, desperate to ease the pressure on her skull.

Fuck, he was going to pull her hair out. Every strand. From the roots.

"Where is he, bitch?" The vicious snarl behind her had terror racing through her.

She knew that voice. She'd heard it once before, years ago. It was this voice that sent her running, sent her fighting for her life through the night.

Gasping, crying out at the pain as she was jerked to her feet, Sallie fought the tears and a distant part of her prayed Lily had made it out of the house.

She should have left months ago, she acknowledged as a forearm wrapped around her throat, threatening to strangle her. When the panic attacks had first begun, she should have known it was time to leave.

"I warned you, you can't hide." The hiss at her ear was followed by the tightening of his arm around her neck, blocking much needed air and the ability to think. "He can't hide. Now where the fuck is he?"

Sallie clawed at the arm around her neck, shuddering, attempting to kick back at the legs she knew must be behind her. Legs she couldn't find. There had to be legs back there, right?

"Where is he?" The snarl again, filled with rage, as the arm tightened further around her neck, stealing her air, threatening to steal consciousness.

chapter nine

"Right here."

Jacob's answer came through a dark stillness, a silence that had been smothering. The forearm around her neck released with the sound of an ominous crack and Sallie's sudden freedom.

She felt the weight that had pinned her slumping to the floor, lifeless. She knew it was lifeless. Jacob had just killed a man because of her.

As a broken sob escaped her lips, she stood trembling, shuddering in place, knowing who was behind her, knowing any measure of mercy Jacob might have held for her, would no longer exist. He had been forced to take a life, there was no way he could ever look at her the same, or touch her with any gentleness.

She felt the tear that eased from the corner of one eye, felt the loss searing her, tearing at the deepest part of her heart. Bitter knowledge swept through her as she fought the sobs trying to break free, as well as the panic building inside her.

"Clear." His voice was cold, like ice, sharp and clipped as he spoke behind her. "Get Lily to the ranch."

It took her a second to realize he wasn't talking to her, and she didn't question who it was.

Thank God Lily was okay, safe. At least her friend had gotten away.

Sallie wanted to move. She needed to move, but fear, and something that went far deeper than regret, held her rooted to the floor as she felt Jacob staring at her, waiting. Like the specter of death, he stood towering over her, a dead man at his feet, and death in his voice.

"Let's go!" Jacob's demand was accompanied by a firm grip on her arm as he all but dragged her away from the fallen body to the back door. "Pride's waiting till we leave to take care of this fucking mess."

Beneath the ice was a burning rage. She could hear it, feel it. He was furious, and who could blame him? She'd endangered his cousin and forced him to kill.

Sallie stumbled as they neared the door, shaking her head desperately.

"No," she whispered, barely able to speak, her voice shaking to the point that she could barely understand her own words. "No, I have to leave. I have to go . . ."

And of course, Jacob didn't argue. Before Sallie realized his intent, he simply wrapped his arm around her waist and picked her up off her feet. Within seconds they were out the door, and he was all but tossing her into the pickup that braked at the back door a second before one of his men jumped from the driver's seat, leaving the door open.

"Grange and a couple of our men are holding perimeter around the house," the other man informed Jacob as Sallie was lifted into the cab. "We'll take care of this and meet you back at the ranch."

With a sharp nod Jacob slid behind the wheel, slammed the door closed, and reversed from the car port.

"Buckle your seat belt," he ordered, pulling out onto the road and increasing speed. "Now!"

Buckle her seat belt? She reached for the strap, missed it, and tried again. Catching it in fingers that felt numb and disassociated from her mind, she tried to pull it around her but once again, felt it slip away.

As she reached for the belt a third time, Jacob's arm reach across her, causing her to flinch as he jerked the seat belt around her and clipped it without so much as a word.

"I'm sorry," she whispered, wishing her voice would steady, to stop the hateful trembling.

She'd thought she'd defeated that once horrendous trait. When under pressure, when frightened, there had been a time when her voice trembled so horribly she couldn't make herself understood. Her stepfather had always grimaced with distaste when it happened and her mother's gaze had always been filled with such disappointment.

Jacob didn't speak, didn't make so much as a murmur of acknowledgement at the apology. Risking a glance at him, Sallie swallowed with more than a little trepidation. His expression looked carved from stone. No anger, no concern, nothing. Just completely impassive ice.

It was terrifying.

Gripping her hands in her lap she stared down at her

fingers rather than the imposing profile, shadowed by the night and the dim glow to the dashboard lights.

He was furious, she could feel the anger rolling off him in waves, pouring toward her, and surrounding her. And she deserved it. Because she'd been so desperate for just a little time with him, she'd caused his cousin to possibly be hurt, or worse. And everyone knew Jacob was terribly protective of his female cousins.

She'd known what she'd found with him wouldn't last, but she hadn't expected it to end with his hatred.

For six years the memory of his touch had been her secret lover on long, lonely nights. She'd compared every man against him and none had measured up. She'd held those memories to her heart, warmed herself with them even as she assured herself she hadn't loved him.

And she'd known better.

She'd often told herself and others, she'd never been in love, but it wasn't true. She'd loved. For one impossible moment in time, she'd loved a man who had walked away from her with surprising ease and never returned.

It was breaking her inside, tearing her apart, piece by piece, and she couldn't stop the pain from resonating through every part of her. It tore at every defense she'd ever built between herself and anything or anyone else who could hurt her. But she hadn't had any defenses against Jacob, had she?

All she'd had was this unreasonable need for one man. A man who must surely hate her now.

Jacob could still feel the overwhelming terror that threatened to flood him when he stepped into the darkened house to see Sallie in the killing grip of the bastard behind her. Small, fragile, her neck arched back as she struggled to breathe, and still, she'd fought to get free. Clawing at the bastard's arms, trying to kick back at him, terror filling her expression and the small, strangled cries she'd managed to make despite the pressure on her neck.

It had been all he could do to stay silent long enough to slip up on the bastard and eliminate the threat. The fact that Sallie had stayed on her feet, despite the shudders racking her body, still had the power to amaze him. And now, she was apologizing to him, and he knew if he made the mistake of speaking to her before he pushed back the utter rage tearing at him, then he'd never make it safely to the ranch before completely losing control.

Releasing that anger against her was unacceptable, but damn her, if she had just trusted him. All she'd had to do was tell him she was in danger; he would have protected her. No one would have touched her; he would have made sure of it.

"We have your grandmother safe, Lily's en route, and the trash is being disposed of," Justice spoke through the secured communication device Jacob had tucked in his ear. "Grange has an ID on the bastard too. Sallie's assailant was Jorg Deverson. He's linked to the Swiss-based militant group, Forefront, that you were investigating when that explosion nearly took you out about six years ago."

Forefront had been small but heavily financed. Its main goal had been the destabilization of political and economic partnerships between Switzerland and other major nations. Notably, America and Europe. Rumor was they'd disbanded when their leader had been killed as well.

Jacob frowned at the information. He didn't remember the week before that explosion or the members he'd identified in that warehouse before the world went to hell.

"Looks like he came prepared, according to Grange," Justice continued. "Silenced weapon at his back and a small pack equipped with all the tools needed to torture helpless women. Bastard even had several devices he must have meant to rape her with."

His hands clenched, fingers nearly numbing at the grip he had on the leather-covered steering wheel.

Yeah, that sounded like the information that did exist on the group.

They had been responsible for the torture and murder of another young woman in Switzerland just before Jacob had nearly died investigating them. A translator working for Germany had been found, tortured to death, just days before a German politician had been assassinated. Jacob had been given the task of identifying the group members and taking out whoever had given that order. And to this day, he still wasn't certain if he'd managed to complete the mission because the memories of that last week had never returned.

"I'll be waiting at your ranch for you," Justice finished his report. "You have a team in front of you and one following, if you need them."

Personally, he would have ditched the help and gone hunting himself, if he didn't have Sallie's safety to consider. But there was Sallie. And there were questions he was determined to find the answers to. Who was she?

Why did he know her, yet not remember her? And why the fuck couldn't he get answers where she was concerned?

With those final words from the other man, Jacob reached up and deactivated the small communications device before returning his hand to the wheel. He didn't look at Sallie, though he could feel her eyes on him, feel the fear and uncertainty he glimpsed on her face.

"Lily's fine," he stated, forcibly controlling his voice and his need to jerk her to his side. "She's with Pride. They're ahead of us, heading for the ranch. Once I talk to her, she'll be sent to the Culpeppers' to join Gram until I have this figured out."

"There's nothing to figure out." She was all but wheezing, desperation and an edge of panic filling her voice now. "I need my car . . . my purse . . . I'll leave . . ."

She would leave? Well, wasn't that just incredibly thoughtful of her. He'd be damned if she was going anywhere without him.

"Over my dead body." Jacob had to force the words past his lips as he shot her a hard glance. "I'll be damned if you're going anywhere. How many fucking times have you run, Sallie? How long has this shit been going on?"

He had a stranglehold on the steering wheel as he fought to keep from stopping the vehicle and demanding answers now, demanding she explain why he couldn't let her go, and why she wanted to go when she was in so much danger.

"It may well be over your dead body." The pain in her voice lashed at him, made his chest ache in a way it had only ached after the dreams that haunted him. "I had no idea they were this close, Jacob." Her voice broke and he heard the ragged breath she took before continuing. "I wouldn't have stayed if I'd known. I wouldn't have seen you in danger or risked Lily."

She wasn't crying, but he could hear the need in her voice, and in her words, he heard something more.

What the hell made her think he needed protection? She was crazy, he decided. Why did she think he wasn't strong enough to protect her? Son of a bitch, what kind of man was she used to that she had remained alone, believing it was in her place to protect everyone from whatever danger followed her?

Until he'd all but forced himself into her life, she'd been alone. She'd arrived in Deer Haven alone and she'd remained alone but for a few friends. She'd would have been scared, always looking over her shoulder. She was still scared, he realized. She pushed anyone who tried to get close to her away, distanced herself, in case she was found.

"You actually think I need you to protect me?" He couldn't help the snarl in his voice. "Goddammit, Sallie, you should have told me you were in danger. You should have let me help you."

Let him help her?

Sallie could only shake her head. No one could help her; she'd learned that the first time she'd run. A neighbor had heard her screams and he'd nearly paid with his life. She'd never forget the blood that soaked his shirt, or her terror after her attacker had run.

She'd been lucky . . . too lucky, she knew. Whoever she was running from didn't want to kill her yet. Unfortunately, she had no idea what they did want from her.

"This is the third attack, Jacob," she whispered. "If they were going to kill me, I'd be dead. I don't know who he wanted, or what he was trying to accomplish. But he's never cared if he hurt anyone who's tried to get in his way whenever he catches up with me. All I can do is run and try to hide again."

"Who's he looking for?" he snapped. "I heard him demand where 'he' was? Who?"

"I don't know." The cry was torn from her. "I've never known. I'm divorced, I didn't live a dangerous life, my ex-husband didn't stay in contact. I'm a nobody. Whoever's been chasing me has to be crazed."

A nobody. And she actually believed that? He could hear the certainty in her voice, in the pain and confusion that filled it.

"Crazed?" he snapped as he made the turn to the ranch. "Baby, the man who attacked you is linked to a Swiss militant group with delusions of becoming a major terrorist presence. A fucking assassin. So you wanna tell me why a fucking terrorist has followed you from wherever the hell you came from and just what he fucking wants from you?"

Sallie flinched, the uncontrolled response part shock, part terror.

The deepened pitch of Jacob's voice was filled with danger, suspicion, and knowledge. He knew her background listed her as being from Oklahoma. Everyone knew that. It was her standard answer since her stepfather had drilled it into her on the drive there three years before.

He was suspicious of her, and a terrorist had targeted her. A Swiss terrorist. She'd been to Switzerland once in her life, and she'd met Jacob, as well as her ex-husband, there.

Where is he?

It was the same demand that had been made each time she'd been attacked.

The first time had been only hours after her ex-husband had served annulment papers on her and left. The husband that hadn't been able to touch her in all the time she'd known him. To this day neither she nor her stepfather knew where he'd disappeared to.

"You better find some place to hide, baby," John warned her as he paused at the front door after giving her the annulment decree, staring at her somberly. "At this point, that bastard has screwed both of us."

Who the bastard in question was, she'd never been certain.

Swallowing past the fear in her throat, Sallie watched as Jacob pulled the truck into the opened garage door, the panel sliding closed again as he parked.

"Inside." The controlled anger in Jacob's tone was nerve-racking.

Sliding from the truck as he strode to her door, she glanced at his closed, brooding expression and wanted to rage at fate and whoever the hell had managed to get her into this mess.

John had to be the culprit. From the moment he'd showed up on her doorstep after she'd returned from Switzerland, her life had been crazy.

Stepping ahead of him, Sallie entered the house through the garage entrance into the kitchen, rubbing at the ever-present aching chill in her arms. She wished she could go back to the days before when Jacob had held her, when his touch had warmed her. When she'd felt surrounded by his need for her rather than his anger.

"I need to leave, Jacob. I can't stay here." She turned to face him, regret and aching weariness filling her.

She'd fit in in Deer Haven, been accepted by those she called friends. She had loved her little house and the life she had been building for herself. She'd ached to see where the hunger she and Jacob shared would have gone. Leaving was going to break not just her heart, but her soul.

"Not happening." He stomped through the kitchen and into the open living-dining area to the wood bar on the other side of the room. "What you're going to do is help me figure out why the hell someone equipped to torture you to death attacked you in your home. And we're going to do it tonight." He poured himself a drink then turned back to her, his gaze hard, flat as he took a healthy swallow of the drink.

Equipped to torture her? Her attacker had knocked her around when he found her, broken her arm the last time, terrified her. But he'd always been interrupted as well. Had he decided to stop playing with her after losing track of her for three years?

"Jacob, my stepfather, and his investigators have been trying to figure this out since it began." She wanted to sob at the impossibility of it. "If he can't do it, then there's no way you can."

The hard, mocking laugh that left his throat scraped over her nerves and deepened the trepidation already growing inside her.

"We'll get to why you believe that," he assured her,

his smile sarcastic. "But just let me tell you who you're dealing with, sweetheart. The CIA has connections no one else can hope to touch. And that's what I am. Trust me, I'll figure it out, and whoever the hell it is, they'll pay, the same way that bastard in your house paid. With their fucking life for daring to believe they can target you in my fucking territory. So, let's start with who the hell you really are, why don't we, and go from there."

Sallie could feel herself paling, the color leeching from her face at the confirmation that he knew she wasn't Sallie Hamblen. She felt herself freeze inside, fear gathering into a lump of ice in her belly.

Oh God, she couldn't do this. She couldn't stare into his face and tell him who she was, and see a complete lack of recognition. And that was what she'd see. She hadn't meant enough to him at the time that he'd even remember her, or else he'd have recognized her, or at least asked her if they'd met.

Her looks had changed, but the eighteen-year-old she'd been was still present in them. If he was an agent for the CIA, then he should have recognized her anyway. Wouldn't he?

"I want to leave . . ."

"No." His lips curled back from his teeth in such a primal snarl that she found herself almost hypnotized by the sheer alpha intensity in the look.

God, she was depraved, because that look made her instantly wet, her nipples hard, and her body sensitizing, readying for his touch.

What the hell was wrong with her?

The glass thumped to the bar and Sallie watched his

gaze narrow, watched the dangerous stillness that came over him a breath before he began stalking toward her.

She couldn't move. She stared at him, watching the intense sexuality that shadowed his face now. It pushed back the anger, but the impression of danger hadn't been eliminated.

"Jacob, please . . ." she breathed out, her voice a thread of sound as his hands gripped her hips, pulling her against his hard, obviously aroused body.

"Please what, baby?" he growled, his head bending until the sound whispered over the sensitive shell of her ear. "I don't care one bit to please you. But I won't let you go."

Before she could argue, before she could protest, one hand locked in the hair at the back of her head, her head pulled back and his lips taking hers in a kiss so primal and filled with hunger, she became lost in it.

It was a grave mistake, she knew. A part of her was terribly aware of the power she'd just given this man over her. To allow him to know how his sexual dominance affected her was something she may well regret later. Or not.

Oh God. The pleasure.

Her lips parted beneath the hunger in his kiss as the chill that had filled her eased away. There was nothing cold, nothing else that could touch her when Jacob held her. The heat of his hunger and his arousal wrapped around her, filled her, heated her.

Wrapping her arms around his neck, Sallie burrowed her fingers into his hair, clenching the thick strands as she lifted closer to him. Nothing mattered but this kiss, this man, and this single moment in time.

Perhaps, this last memory to hold close before she was forced to run again, to release the only warmth in her life.

As her lips parted beneath his, a moan slipped from her throat at the lash of his tongue against hers. It was a possession, a kiss that owned. And Sallie was helpless against it.

The hand at her hip moved, caressed, pushed beneath the silky sleep top she wore to frame the swollen, aching curve of her breast. Her nipples throbbed for his touch and the folds between her thighs grew slicker, wetter than ever.

She needed him. Desperation began building inside her, the need for more, for the hunger and the pure dominance she sensed inside him overtaking her. She wanted all of him. Everything she'd felt he was holding back on her, hiding from her. He was always so careful with her, touched her with such gentleness when she could sense he wanted more. When she wanted more.

She trembled at the thought, tugged at the hold he had on her hair and moaned at the dark, sensual pleasure that raced through her as he held her in position.

His kiss deepened, his hold tightening on her as she felt herself suddenly lifted, turned, and a second later Jacob sat her on the counter separating the kitchen from the dining area. Still controlling the kiss, devouring her lips, he pushed her legs apart and slid effortlessly between them.

Sallie couldn't halt the breathless moan that escaped her. Separated by denim and silk, the hard, thick length of his cock rubbed against her, pressing firmly into the aching mound of her pussy. Her clit throbbed

with the pressure, the swollen bud demanding relief. Gripping his hips with her knees she tried to get
closer, to still the ever-growing hunger raging through
her body now.

"Jacob . . ." she gasped, delirious with pleasure as he
released her lips, his kisses moving along her jaw, interspersed with the heated nips of his teeth.

And oh God, she loved those little bites as they moved
lower. Angling her neck to the side, her hands falling to
his shoulders, she dug her nails into the material of his
shirt and arched closer. Still gripping her hair, he tugged
again to pull her head to the side, and again, she fought
it, almost crying out at the sensual pain that lashed at
her senses.

"Damn you," he snarled against her neck, his hold
tightening as he increased the pressure. "You don't know
what you're asking for."

But she wanted it. With each touch, Sallie shud-
dered at the increased pressure, desperate cries falling
from her lips. Tightening her thighs around his, she dug
her nails deeper into the material of his shirt, her neck
arching for another of those sharp, heated kisses that
never failed to mark her flesh.

"Jacob, I'm still here, buddy . . ." Mocking, amused,
Justice spoke behind her as Jacob seemed to snarl
against her neck. "And I think Lily blushed before she
ran back to your office."

Sallie laid her head against Jacob's shoulder, eyes
closed, and not for the first time, wished she could make
Justice Culpepper just disappear.

chapter ten

Of course, Justice had no intentions of disappearing.

As Jacob lifted her from the counter, Sallie caught a glimpse of Jacob's friend standing on the other side of the living room, just watching them curiously. Lily was nowhere in sight. But that didn't surprise her. Lily would be too wary after what had happened at the house. And like Sallie, she wouldn't be looking forward to Jacob's questions. And even less, whatever Justice had to say. Lily had a volatile relationship with that particular rancher.

How Justice Culpepper and Jacob had become such friends, she couldn't imagine. Justice was a pure ass from what Sallie had seen, and it seemed many shared her opinion, even if they did get along with him. Jacob, by contrast, was well liked and there were few people who had a problem with him. Of course, Jacob wasn't as social as Justice, nor as prone to fight. The

Culpeppers were known far and wide for their ability to fight as well as to party.

"Justice, I might end up killing you," Jacob growled as Sallie stepped away, her head lowered, her expression hidden from him.

"Yeah, so you and everyone else keep threatening." Justice grunted, resigned. "I thought you'd like to know Pride has everything taken care of in town and he's on his way back. He found Deverson's hotel room too, right in town, and there's signs he wasn't alone."

Jacob saw the subtle flinch Sallie couldn't fully hide at the other man's words.

"He left two of our men to see if they could track the partner. We should have an update soon," Justice concluded. "It would help if we knew why a Swiss terrorist cell has targeted one little Dillerman's manager, though."

Jacob watched Sallie shake her head before taking a deep breath and moving to stand next to the dining table, one slender hand gripping the back of a chair for support.

"Sallie, stop running," Jacob told her, trying to sound reasonable. "Those bastards are going to kill you. Is that what you want?"

It wasn't what she wanted. It couldn't be, he tried to convince himself. There was far too much fire, too much fight inside her.

"I met my ex-husband in Switzerland six years ago," she stated, pushing one hand through her hair, the desperation in her gaze causing tension to build through him. "When I returned home, he followed with my step-father several months later and we married before the year was out." She swallowed tightly before drawing in a ragged breath. "I've been running since the night he gave me annulment papers and walked out of the house a year later."

Years. Jacob fought to hold back his anger. She'd been running for years. She'd been alone when she came here three years ago, so she'd been alone when she began running, he had no doubt. Delicate, fragile, she'd had no one to lean on, no one to protect her during that time.

"Who is he?" It wasn't a gentle demand and Jacob knew it. Knew it, but could do nothing to soften it.

He watched her tongue flick against her lips nervously.

"He was my stepfather's aide. John Dillon. But he couldn't be behind this . . ."

Jacob could hear her talking, he could even assimilate the reasons why she believed her ex-husband wasn't behind an assassin's attack. But he knew something he didn't believe she was aware of.

Jacob knew John Dillon.

Or at least the man who had used the identity John Dillon while in Switzerland, working as Ambassador Rance Dougal's aide. But at that time there had been no information that the ambassador or his wife had children with them.

"Ambassador Dougal didn't have any children with him at the time he was there," he bit out, but as he stared at her, memories slowly began to form. "Who the fuck are you?"

Pain. Anger. Disillusionment. Jacob watched the emotions flicker across her face before she breathed in raggedly.

"My name is Kyra Sallie Dougal. I'm Rance Dougal's adopted daughter. While I was in Switzerland, I was there as Kyra Bannon and introduced as part of his staff . . ."

Kyra Bannon. Young, so very pretty he'd found her irresistible. He remembered that when he hadn't before.

And in that second, memories raced over him.

". . . an intern, Jake . . ." Rance introduced the pretty young woman jovially. "Kyra Bannon . . . Dance with Jake, honey, it's a party . . ."

Eyes filled with dreams, a laugh as sweet and smooth as honey and filled with warmth.

A virgin until he touched her . . .

His, until the world had blown up around him.

"If this goes bad, tell Kyra I was coming back to her . . ." Jake told his partner, the man posing as an ambassador's aide.

"I'll tell her," John promised. "Watch your six, buddy. I don't like the feel of this . . ."

Minutes later the world exploded around him. It was weeks later before Jacob had come out of the coma he'd been left in. And his partner had been there. Unfortunately, Jacob's memories of the mission hadn't been present.

"What did I forget?" Jacob remembered asking. "I feel like I've lost a part of myself."

"Months' worth of busting our asses to identify these bastards," John had cursed. "Hell, buddy, this is bullshit."

Not once in those weeks had his partner mentioned the woman Jacob had forgotten, or even hinted at the fact that she existed. Someone so important her memory had haunted nearly every night of his dreams yet he hadn't known why, hadn't known who she was. Until now.

Until she found him.

Until this moment he'd forgotten the woman he'd meant to hold as long as humanly possible. A woman he'd wanted to know, that he'd meant to return to. Instead, the son of a bitch that had remembered her lied to Jacob, to Sallie, then for some unfathomable reason, married Jacob's woman.

The bastard was a dead man.

"Jacob . . . ?" Justice began to pull back only at the quick look Jacob shot him.

The thing about having friends you once worked with in covert ops? They knew your history, your business, and they never forgot a fucking detail. And that was Justice.

Jacob couldn't, wouldn't address this in front of the other man. He clearly remembered the sense of pride Sallie had displayed as a young woman and now he understood the anger mixed with the hunger she'd felt for him when they met once again, three years before.

He hadn't returned for her as he'd promised her and he hadn't remembered her when he came face to face with her again.

No wonder she'd reacted as she had when they were introduced just after she moved to Deer Haven. Joy, hope, and just as quickly, despair and anger had raced through her expression.

It had confused him at the time, the memory of those

flashing emotions, there then just as quickly gone. Replaced with that damned polite look she gave everyone else, as well as him, every time she saw him after that.

And now he knew why that pissed him off every time he saw her, and why the dreams had intensified in the past few years, that shadowed image slowly becoming Sallie's. Because once he'd seen her again, known she was close, letting her go was impossible. That part of himself that he'd given her in Switzerland, refused to release her.

"Justice, get Lily to your place with Gram," Jacob ordered. "You get info in later, call me immediately."

A quick nod and Justice strode back to the study. A minute later Lily hurried into the room, dressed in jeans, a T-shirt, and sneakers she kept in his spare room. Sallie walked straight to Lily and gave her a quick hug.

The two women were close friends, something Jacob had used since Sallie had come into town, to ensure no other man poached on what he'd already claimed as his woman. Lily had kept him updated with what Sallie was doing, if any men were approaching her and how Sallie handled it. Until Jacob, she'd handled it the same each time, with complete indifference.

"I'm sorry, Lily," Sallie whispered, her voice torn with regret. "I'm so sorry . . ."

Painful and filled with sorrow, her tone was heavy with the guilt she carried for any danger Lily had faced. Sallie's heart, as Gram had told him a year ago, was far too soft, and her compassion and guilt complex too well defined.

"Don't be," Lily berated her gently. "Jacob will fix it, I promise."

The confidence in her voice was almost humbling. He'd fought to protect his little cousins for as long as they'd been born, knowing the faith they had in him made that sometimes frustrating job worth it.

Now, if Sallie would just trust him to fix whatever she was running from. His cousins would end up making him crazy if there was anything left of him after Sallie drove him insane.

Pulling back, Lily shot Jacob a warning look. "You know I hate that biker wannabe you're sending me off with."

She and Justice had never had a friendly moment between them that he knew of.

"Be nice, fruitcake," Justice drawled behind her. "Remember who controls access to my pool."

"Like I'd so much as dip a toe in that orgy hole," she stated disdainfully as they left the house. "Pervert."

The door closed on her accusation and blocked Justice's reply. Jacob was certain there would have been an equally sharp comment.

"Those two act like they hate each other." Jacob shook his head at their relationship before breathing out roughly and turning back to Sallie. "You'll stay here. But I bet you guessed that one."

Sallie glanced at the floor a moment before meeting Jacob's gaze squarely.

"You know John, don't you? I saw Justice's face. He recognized John's name." She'd seen it, the warning Jacob had shot the other man when he nearly said something about it.

"Sallie . . ." His expression was closed, implacable. And she hated it. There was no regret, no sense that it even bothered him that he'd forgotten her when she'd never been able to forget him.

"Forget it." She sliced her hand through the air almost furiously. "Of course, you knew him. You remember him. You remember Rance as well, don't you? You just forgot the stupid little fool you spent the weekend screwing, right?"

Sallie felt her heart breaking. Right there, staring back at the lack of emotion in his face, her heart shattered. And it shouldn't have. She knew better . . . Still, she had to keep her lip from trembling, tears from filling her eyes because the pain was like daggers digging into her heart and twisting in vicious, gouging stabs.

"I need to contact Rance," she forced herself to push the words past her lips. "He'll send someone . . ."

"No!" The snap in his voice, the instant denial made no sense to her.

"Yes, Jacob." She had some pride left, she assured herself. "I should have never stayed long enough for this to happen. One of his investigators will come for me and I'll disappear. And you can just forget me once again." It was all she could do not to sob as she spoke, not to completely break apart.

She should have left. But Jacob had been there, and she'd been unable to resist praying for just a little more time.

"You're not leaving. You're not running again," he said it as though it were his choice to make. As though it were suddenly his business.

"I don't have a choice . . ."

The smile that almost curled his lips had her taking a step back even as her body blazed with heat.

"Run then," he growled, covering the distance between them far quicker than she could move to evade him. "See how far you get before I drag your ass right back here."

She stared back at him in complete shock.

"Why?" The throttled cry tore from her throat, jagged and confused. "Why does it matter? It didn't matter to you six years ago, so why let it now?"

She couldn't escape his hold or the warmth of his larger body as he pulled her to him. One hand held the back of her head, dragging it back to stare into her gaze.

"Who do you think that bastard was looking for tonight?" Anger throbbed in his voice. "They may want John first, but as soon as they find him, want me to tell you what they're going to do?"

Nose to nose, fury burning in his eyes, he glared down at her.

Sallie shook her head. Or tried to.

"They'll send their assassins right back here." The snarl in his voice matched the one on his face. "Because it's not that fucker you married that Forefront's after. It's his partner. They're after me. And I'd just as soon stop them here."

John Dillon's partner.

"No . . ." John's partner? "You said you were CIA?"

"And John was my partner in Switzerland." He released her slowly then stepped back, raking his fingers through his hair. When he turned back to her, a mocking smile curled his lips. "The same partner who assured me that all I forgot in an explosion that nearly killed me, was the information in my head. He never mentioned the woman he knew was waiting for me."

She could barely process that information, process his declaration that he'd been hurt.

"John was CIA?" she whispered, barely able to push the question past her lips because she couldn't deal with the information that he'd been hurt, nearly killed.

"John is still CIA as far as I know," he informed her, pushing the fingers of one hand through his hair.

Regret, rage, and frustration flashed across his face then and when his gaze returned to her, she could have sworn she saw a dark, enraged sorrow.

"We were investigating a new militant group that had moved into Switzerland. They were kidnapping lower level employees attached to foreign political figures, torturing, and killing them. We spent months identifying the group behind the deaths and were attempting to identify senior members when I was caught in an ambush." Jacob shook his head and turned his back on her, pacing to what appeared to be a newly installed window before turning back to her. "I forgot everything from that week, for years, then slowly, details began coming back, but nothing we hadn't already known. Except you . . ."

Except her. He hadn't remembered her. He didn't remember her.

"And John knew we'd been together?" The sense of betrayal she felt went far deeper than she expected, and she knew it shouldn't. John's betrayal of her had begun well before they'd married and continued through the time they'd spent together. She'd already known he'd somehow used her, that she'd been a means to an end.

She just wasn't certain what the end game had been for him. But how had he ever imagined she knew anything about a militant group?

"John knew," he said sharply. "John knew every second of that operation and where I spent my time. He was my backup."

John had known about her weekend with Jacob, and no doubt he'd known what they'd spent those three days doing.

Jacob watched the painful realizations flicker across Sallie's expression and knew the sense of betrayal she was likely feeling. She'd thought she was married to John, that she'd meant something to him.

Rage festered inside him, clawing at his guts with jagged talons at the thought. The son of a bitch had married Jacob's woman. Dared to touch her. Hid the memory of her from him. He'd break every fucking bone in his body for it when he got his hands on him. And there was no doubt Jacob would catch up with him first. For all their brutality, Forefront hadn't managed to build itself to the power it dreamed of being, nor had it enlisted killers sharp enough to hunt well-trained, experienced agents. That was why they were hunting Sallie. They intended to interrogate her, torture her, believing she had to know her ex-husband's location.

They'd come to the ranch searching for her, meaning to interrogate his grandmother, and when that hadn't worked out for them, they'd found Sallie. They'd been tracking her for years, searching for John, knowing John would lead them to the man that had fouled their ambush and killed some of their top generals during that explosion.

"John knew," she whispered, mockery curling at her lips despite the pain that filled her expression. "Explains a lot." The broken sound that escaped her may have meant to be a laugh, but it came out as more of a sob.

This wasn't a situation she should have ever had to face. It was his fault she was in danger. His fault she was running.

"Come on, I'll show you to your room. I need to talk to my men and you need to rest."

"Like hell." Before Sallie could stop herself, she grabbed his arm, surprised when he came to a stop. "You think I'm just going to bed like a good little girl? Really, Jacob? If you knew me, you'd know better."

"Get some rest, baby," he suggested, staring down at her, hunger sizzling in his gaze. "Because I promise, I'm going to see just how bad you are later. Now, come on . . ."

He strode away from her as though he believed she'd obey his autocratic little demand. She had no intention of obeying anyone at this point. The lies and betrayals were growing around her and it was pissing her off. She'd been attacked, hunted, used and she was damned sick of it. She wasn't going to be ordered like some pet by a man who hadn't even cared to remember her.

Crossing her arms over her breasts she stayed in place, and simply stared at his retreating back until he stopped halfway up the hallway. He turned back to her slowly, his gaze narrowing on her, his expression dark, so damned sexy. She felt her nipples peaking again, the flesh between her thighs sensitizing and growing moist at that look.

He was powerful, dominant. A man unlike any she

had ever known in her life, before or after him. He'd ruined her for another man. He'd taken her to the very depths of her soul, and there was no getting past him or the memories of his touch.

"Sallie." Dark, deep, his voice whispered of sin and sex and had moisture spilling from her vagina. "If I get my hands on you, I'm not going to be the man you've taken in the past weeks. Trust me, I haven't given you the full brunt of the lover I can be because I didn't want to scare you. But after this morning, that's going to change. If you're ready for that, fine. If not, move your ass now and give me time to get a handle on myself before I fucking touch you."

Of course, she'd known he was holding back. She remembered the lover he'd been in Switzerland and the pleasure he'd gained in teaching her things she hadn't known her body was capable of.

She remembered her complete inability to tell him no. And she knew if he touched her as he had that weekend, she'd be putty in his hands. There would be no saving herself then.

Jacob watched as her arms fell slowly to her sides and she began walking toward him. And she should have hurried, because as she moved, her fragile body so damned sexy, so alluring, his dick was like steel beneath his jeans.

He was going to rip those clothes off her. The soft, gray silk floated around her body like a dream, hinting at the soft curves, firm breasts, thighs that tempted a man beyond his ability to control his hunger.

Hazy, barely there, the memory of her on her knees, watching her take him in her mouth and the incredible pleasure of knowing she belonged to him, drifted through his mind as it had that morning in his dreams. She'd learned to take him as he liked, learned to trust him, to love him as no woman ever had.

How the hell had he forgotten her?

The brightest spot in his life and he'd allowed that memory to be taken from his mind. To be stolen from him along with the memory of that god be damned investigation.

"I don't like orders," she muttered, nearing him. "Nor do I like threats."

She loved the right kind of orders, he remembered as half-formed memories drifted through his head. Remembered how slick and wet she'd get for him, how she'd scream in pleasure when he took her to that edge of reason before allowing her to come around him.

And she'd refused to tell him who she was when she'd come to Deer Haven. Three additional years he'd lost with her. Years she could have spent in his bed, in his life, and she'd kept her mouth shut. She'd refused both of them that time.

"And I don't like being kept in the dark," he all but snarled, turning on his heel once again and leading the way to his bedroom. "Get some rest. I'll be a few hours. And come morning, I'm sure we'll have plenty of other matters to argue over."

Not that he intended to argue them with her. Come morning, he intended to revisit the nights he'd lost, and a hunger he'd never had for any other woman.

Now, he clearly understood why he'd restrained his cravings, his needs. Why he'd pulled back and refused to visit the darker passions he'd known before that explosion. Because that man belonged to only one woman. This woman. And he'd be damned if he'd restrain them any longer.

Stepping back, he allowed her to go around him and into the bedroom. The big bed was turned back invitingly, waiting for them. Here, in his room, she'd be safe, warm. Once the door closed and she locked it from the other side, no one but Jacob would be able to open it from the hallway.

"Lock the door once it closes, no one else can get to you then. Shower, watch television, sleep, whatever you choose, but don't leave this room," he told her, once again allowing his gaze to drift over the seductive allure of her silk-covered body. "Get some rest. Once I know what the hell is going on, we'll talk."

Her lips thinned, those oddly colored pale blue eyes shooting darts at him despite the hard points of her nipples straining beneath the top of the lounging set.

They'd talk, he assured himself. He'd let her know what he learned, then they'd revisit those lost nights and searing heat that flared between them every time he touched her. And he'd make damned sure no matter what happened, she'd know to never, ever walk away again until he returned, no matter his condition.

"I'll be back later." He quickly closed the door, then waited.

Seconds later he could hear the lock engaging, and knew she was safe until his return. And that was all that mattered.

Sallie was safe.

chapter eleven

Jacob had every intention of revisiting some of the memories that had slowly reemerged through the night. Heated, so-fucking-sexy memories that his cock tortured him with his need for her. By the time he made it back to the house, tiredness was weighing on him, so rather than joining her in his bed, he made do with the guest room. Just till daylight, he assured himself.

Unfortunately, he was awakened just after daylight by the abrupt ringing of the cell phone he'd left lying on the table next to the bed. Slapping one hand to the offending instrument, he lifted it from the bed and glared at the muted glow of the caller ID.

"What?" he answered as he flipped the cover open and brought the device to his ear.

"I'm heading there," Justice snapped into the line. "Rancor managed to dig some information up and we'll need your woman in on this."

His woman. That was exactly what she was, his.

"We'll be waiting in the kitchen with coffee," Jacob assured him. "See you when you get here."

Rising, still dressed in everything but his boots, Jacob pulled them on, left the guest room, and headed for his room, where Sallie slept. Where he should have just crawled into that big bed with her last night and loved her until neither of them could do anything but collapse in exhaustion.

He was still kicking his ass for that oversight when he reached his bedroom door, and it pushed open.

Sallie still wore the silky lounging set from the night before but one of his shirts was worn over it. The white cotton fell to her thighs and hung loosely on her much smaller frame.

Lust hit him with such a surge of hunger it shocked him.

"I need clothes." She stepped around him quickly after glancing at his face. "Lily mentioned she and Shay didn't have extra clothes here."

She didn't need clothes, she needed to take her ass right back in that bedroom and let him go crazy on her. But goddamned, that would take hours. He didn't have hours.

"I'll have Pride take Shay to the house to pack a bag for you." Damn it, not touching her was killing him and he knew better than to touch her right now. He didn't want Justice walking in and seeing how sensual his Sallie could be.

"My purse, phone, and tablet as well," she demanded with a frown. "I need to be able to talk to Tara about the store."

"Make a list." He nodded sharply, noticing the way

her fingers clenched nervously in the material of the overly large shirt she wore. "I'll be out in a few minutes if you want to make coffee."

After a cold shower. If that even helped. Images of the three days they spent in her hotel room were slamming into his head, drawing his balls tight, and tearing at his determination to wait before he took her.

Memories previously forgotten were drifting through his mind, coalescing at points, making him nearly rabid to take her, to once again experience what he knew had been the most erotic weekend of his life.

Sallie edged away from him, eyes widening marginally as he fought to keep from jerking her to him.

"Maybe breakfast," she muttered, turning as she spoke and hurrying down the hallway toward the kitchen.

Blowing out a hard breath Jacob gave his head a curt shake and stepped into the bedroom, looking around. Other than the soft spice of her scent there were few signs she'd slept there. The bed was made perfectly, pillows fluffed. Everything as neat and tidy as it had been when he'd left the day before.

There were no signs of anger, fear, or volatile emotions. No pillows thrown, nothing to indicate she'd lost control of herself. Not once.

Jaw clenched, tension raging through him, Jacob glared at the room, the bed and swore that when he found out the identity of the person or persons behind this—they'd die. And they'd die hard.

Justice arrived just as Sallie was cleaning the last of the breakfast dishes from the sink. She'd been nervous since Jacob had informed her of the rancher's call. Whatever he'd learned the night before couldn't have been good if it required a visit rather than a simple phone call.

Didn't the elder Culpepper ever sleep, she thought in disgust as he poured himself coffee and snagged several of the large biscuits and sausage she'd left on a plate on the stove. If it weren't for the fact she'd actually seen him eat, she'd swear he was a robot.

"Rancor called right after I got home last night," Justice stated as Sallie put another pot of coffee on.

Turning, she watched as he and Jacob seemed to face off from standing positions on each side of the dining table. He turned to her curiously after making that statement. "Did you know you and John Dillon weren't legally married?"

A curious sense of relief rolled through her, as well as a healthy measure of suspicion.

"There's a registered marriage license," she pointed out. "It was a rather large wedding too. I'd say over two hundred and fifty guests."

Justice gave a slow nod. "According to what Rancor learned, John Dillon isn't his real name but the woman he married eight years ago, he married under his legal name."

Sallie could feel Jacob watching her closely. What was he looking for? Betrayal, hurt? That wasn't likely.

"Did you know?" she asked him. His dark, implacable expression gave a warning.

His jaw flexed dangerously. "I knew."

Well, surprise, surprise. Why had she even bothered to ask?

"Thanks for the heads up." She turned back to the coffee maker and poured herself another cup of the dark brew. She had a feeling caffeine was the last thing she needed. Her nerves were already raw.

So many secrets, she thought, so many lies. She had to fight back the rage, fight back the need to throw the coffee, cup and all, and watch it shatter.

The way her life felt shattered.

"Yeah. Evidently, Rancor's source wouldn't budge on his real name," Justice continued as she turned back to them.

"John Kenton Mayler," Jacob state quietly. "I'm surprised you were able to learn as much as you did. John and I were extremely deep cover."

"Does he know your identity as well?" Justice frowned back at him thoughtfully as Sallie wondered if John's wife had any idea how much of a bastard her husband truly was.

"No. It was information he volunteered while I was in recovery. I wasn't in nearly such a sharing mood." The fact that he hadn't trusted his partner was clear. But hell, he hadn't even trusted his lover, had he?

"What about Rance?" Sallie asked then. "Did he know who and what John actually was?"

How far had her stepfather betrayed her?

"He knew about the operation," Jacob stated, his hands settling on the back of the chair, his expression stoic. "I don't know if he was aware that we were the agents. But I contacted his aide last night. He's supposed to call sometime later tonight."

Sallie had no idea what Jacob was thinking, or feeling. Neither his tone nor his expression betrayed much emotion. But she could feel the tension radiating from him, feel his anger building.

God, what had happened to her life? How had she managed to endanger so many people?

"I didn't tell anyone about you." Sallie fought to keep her voice from shaking. Her entire life was out of control and she had no idea how to fix it. "This isn't because of you, Jacob."

"Maybe you should have." Hard, cool, his tone caused her own anger to flare back to life.

"Perhaps you're right," she agreed, her smile tight and hard. "It would have been far better had everyone believed as I did, that I was no more than a weekend fling you had no trouble walking away from."

She slapped her coffee cup to the counter rather than throwing it, and inhaled deeply, fighting to control the hurt building inside her chest. Pushing her fingers through her hair she tried to remind herself it wasn't his fault; she should have known to leave the second she realized he was there.

"John never hinted he knew Jacob?" Justice asked, his voice lacking any mockery for a change.

He would have had to actually talk to her about anything first, she thought, realizing just how little she and her ex-husband had communicated.

"When he gave me the annulment papers, he said I better find someplace to hide, because someone had screwed both of us." She turned back to Jacob once again and watched the muscle at the side of his face flex dangerously. "I don't know who he was talking about and he didn't stick around to explain it."

"If John had needed me for information, all he had to do was contact Langley and I'd have been notified," he said, frowning at the information. "Besides, he knew I didn't foul that operation. The men I was at that warehouse to identify were warned at the last minute. They were just unlucky enough that the explosives went off before some of their leading members could get out. Who set the explosives or why, we had no way of knowing."

Justice's phone chose that moment to ring. Turning from them, he answered quickly, pacing to the other side of the room as he spoke in a low tone.

"You should let me leave, Jacob," she tried again, though she doubted it would work now any more than it had the night before. "I think John managed to get himself in trouble after the two of you parted ways and his enemies believe I'd be leverage. This isn't about you."

How could it be, no one had known about him?

He stared at her for long seconds, his predatory gaze gleaming with anger.

"Stop wasting your breath, sweetheart," he growled, his arms going across his powerful chest. "If I have to tie your ass to my bed to make sure you stay right here, then that's exactly what I'll do."

And as exciting as that would be, Sallie thought, it wasn't going to solve anything. Running might not save her life, but it could save him, his friends. His family.

"Pride's coming up on the turnoff to the ranch." Justice walked back to the table. "Said he has some clothes for Sallie if we want to walk out and collect them." The look he gave Jacob was a warning. The fact that Justice wanted to talk to Pride without her presence was evident.

"If you'll bring my stuff in, I'll shower," she told Jacob as she shot Justice a knowing look. "You boys can have your little visit alone."

Far be it for her to intrude, she thought mockingly.

She was too damned sharp, Jacob thought, his gaze meeting Sallie's squarely. She carried her anger well, but it was there, and it was building. And being cut out of the loop wasn't helping that anger either.

Whatever Pride was bringing in other than Sallie's clothes, Justice wasn't certain about letting her know until he had a chance to discuss it. And though Jacob wasn't certain how he felt about that, he knew Justice. Justice wouldn't make that call if he didn't feel it was needed.

"Get her things," he ordered Justice then turned back to Sallie. "I won't keep anything from you. I promise."

Her lips quirked with subtle mockery.

"Sure you will." Her disbelief wasn't in the least subtle. "But at least try to stay away from explosions this time, hmm?" An arch of her brow and she turned back to the sink, singularly ignoring both of them.

The message was silent but all the more powerful for the fact that she said nothing more.

Damned pure, stubborn will, Jacob thought. Sallie had a surfeit of grace and a steel backbone that he was only now realizing existed within her. He hadn't seen her cry, she hadn't exploded or gone into hysterics.

No, she'd just turned her back on both him and Justice and picked up her cup of coffee.

When she turned back, cup in hand, a slender brow arched quizzically. "I think that's Pride's truck I hear coming up the drive." She nodded toward to the door. "I'd really like that shower, if you don't mind."

Jacob couldn't help the amused quirk of his lips. Damn, by the time he got his hands on her, he was going to be so hungry for her, he'd probably end up coming in his jeans before he ever got around to spanking that delectable little ass.

For now, he'd let her get her jibes in, he thought as he left the house. She was angry, and she had a right to be, just as she had a right to be hurt. And he had a right to protect her, ensure her safety, and hear those broken little screams of pleasure she made.

A right to once again be the man he'd been until he'd lost the memory of her. His subconscious hadn't forgotten her, nor had that part of him allowed him to be the lover he'd been with Sallie, after her.

He was fine with that. She was back. And now, by God, she'd get all of him.

chapter twelve

Sallie had showered and dressed and was pacing the open living-dining area with her tablet in hand and the Bluetooth phone receiver at her ear as her assistant brought her up to date with the store. Dillerman's was the leading farm supply station for three other counties and Sallie knew the place never ran smoothly.

If she didn't make it back to her own home and back to work within a few days, she'd have a mess on her hands.

"Justice has a killer order in, so does Jacob and three other smaller ranches we picked up in the past weeks. We're running low on feed of every variety and seriously, Sallie, you're going to have to do something with your supply manager. Davison refuses to order supplies in enough quantity to cover the store if there are problems. If we're completely out of feed and have to wait for supplies to come in when the Culpepper or

Donovan orders come in, trust me, Grange and Keller are going to come down on our heads, not Davison's."

She'd talked to Davison several times about the feed and regular ranching supplies, but he still wasn't listening.

She made a note to check the supply numbers and order herself if needed before Tara moved on to floor sales.

She still wondered why she bothered to make the store a success. Dillerman was a total asshole with seven stores in three states and rarely bothered to pay attention to them unless they were losing money. He'd given Sallie the job without references.

For some reason Rance Dougal had decided he needed to keep her alive after the first attempt on her life. And she had to admit, he'd gone out of his way to try to hide her each time she'd been found. Credible identities and the paperwork needed to go with them were always provided, job opportunities as well as cash to survive.

She'd bought the house in Deer Haven out of a small inheritance left to her by her paternal grandparents and placed the rest in a safe deposit box in a bank nearly a hundred miles away, just in case she didn't have time to contact her stepfather when and if she had to run.

She'd learned over the years to protect her own six, as John had once called it. *"Always protect yourself, Sallie,"* he'd warned her. *"People will fail you and not even mean to. It's your six, so watch it yourself."*

Frowning as she listened to Tara complete her report, Sallie realized John had given her quite a bit of advice during their year together. Advice she'd used in the past years since he'd left.

Had he known once he left, she'd become a target?

"I think that's everything, Sallie," Tara finally called an end to the list of complaints, problems, and general concerns. "I'll get a summary of everything together and email it to you."

"Thanks, Tara," she answered as the front door opened.

"Oh, I almost forgot," Tara said hurriedly. "Some guy has called here for you twice. Name was Rance. He wants you to call him ASAP. It sounded really important."

All too aware of the fact that Jacob now stood behind her at some point, Sallie inhaled slowly before answering. "Okay, I made a note of it," she said easily. "Send me the summary and I'll go over it in case I forgot anything."

Disconnecting the call, she tried to push aside her unease at the information that her stepfather was searching for her. He never made an effort to contact her. Once he'd deposited her somewhere, he rarely concerned himself with her unless she called after running again. So why was he attempting to contact her now?

"You should have waited to contact the store." Jacob stepped around her, his frown disapproving as he stalked to the coffee pot.

"I didn't tell her where I was," she assured him, the demanding tone irritating her already sensitive nerves.

She watched as he strode to the coffee and poured a cup. His shoulders were stiff and tense, and she wasn't certain if it was anger or a sense of danger she could feel rolling off him in waves.

Whichever it was, he wasn't happy.

"You wouldn't have to tell them where you were if they have the right equipment and managed to tap into your office phone. Which they likely have." He turned back to her as he raised the cup and sipped at the steaming liquid.

Sallie felt her heart nearly stop in fear. Her hands shook so bad she nearly dropped her tablet and she felt terror racing through her.

"Jacob . . ." she whispered, her voice trembling. "I didn't think . . ."

She should have thought. She should have known better, or at least made certain it was okay to make the call.

He gave a little shrug of his shoulders. "Don't worry, the connection here is encrypted enough to cover you. I'm a paranoid son of a bitch when it comes to protecting what I consider mine."

It was enough to cover her?

After scaring the shit out of her, it was enough to cover her?

"You bastard!" Tearing the Bluetooth mic and receiver from her ear, she threw it to the table before placing her tablet beside it and turned to face him furiously. "What was the point in scaring me to death? Is that how you get your jollies? You scared the life out of me."

He sipped at the coffee again, then without breaking her gaze, placed the cup back on the counter and crossed his arms over his chest. His expression was dark, too sexy, and tinged with a shadow of anger. Yeah, he was mad, and he had a right to be, she thought. She'd rather mucked his life up a bit, but that was no reason to terrify her any further.

"To make a point." Arrogance settled on his expression so naturally it was easy to tell it was a part of him. "The encryption on my Wi-Fi connection is good, but nothing's perfect, so watch what you say when online or using the cell. It would be easy to guess where you are, at this point, but hard to get to you if you'll cooperate."

If she would cooperate.

Now he was talking to her as though she were a child.

"You don't have to do this," she reminded him desperately. "I offered to call Rance. He'll make arrangements . . ."

"Yeah, that's worked out for you in the past, hasn't it?" He grunted, crossing his arms over his chest as mockery gleamed in his brown eyes. "This makes the third time you've been found. And this time, they were serious about it, baby."

She stared back at him, the truth of that statement racing through her mind and once again filling her with a sense of uncertainty and helplessness.

"Thank you for that reminder, Jacob," she stated, frustration eating at her. "It doesn't change the fact that you're not responsible for my safety. I never wanted to put you in danger."

"No, you wanted to save your ass all by yourself." His voice raised just enough that she no longer had to suspect he was angry. "Have you ever asked anyone for help, Sallie? Or did you just decide you were going to die without a fight?"

"Without a fight?" she asked painfully. "I've been

running for over four years, Jacob. I've fought the only way I know how."

She wasn't some super-secret spy or tough-assed agent with an alphabet agency to back her and she had no idea why her life had gone to hell. And she had no idea what he wanted from her.

"You've run. That's not fighting. And Dougal let you run rather than using his connections to help you," he snarled, dropping his arms from his chest and moving to her before she could evade him. "And what did you do when you came here? When you saw me? Did you ask for my help?"

Sallie lifted her chin, surprise and disbelief coursing through her. "Ask you for your help?" she repeated softly. "A man who forgot my very existence. Why, Jacob, would I have asked you for anything?"

"Because you did remember." Hard hands gripped her shoulders, holding her in place when she would have jerked from him. "And you should have known I would have never forgotten this willingly."

This.

One arm went around her, pulling her to him, lifting her into the hard length of his body. A powerful hand cupped her jaw, lifted her face, and his lips commanded hers. It wasn't a simple kiss. Nothing like it had been in the past weeks. It went beyond a kiss. It was ownership, and oh God, in this, she wanted to be owned.

By him.

He parted her lips forcefully, his tongue forging past them, rasping against hers and creating arcs of exquisite pleasure. His kiss electrified her. It pleasured her.

His lips slanted over hers, moving against her. There was nothing teasing in the possession, nothing gentle. It was demanding, and he took what he wanted, gave what she had been longing for, without apologies.

Sallie's arms wrapped around his neck, her fingers burrowing into his hair, clenching in it, desperate to hold him closer. She wanted the heat and security, the power and the promise of him, to wrap around her. To own her.

He'd filled her fantasies for six long years. His face had been the one she searched for among crowds. It was his kiss, the memory of his touch that had sustained her.

Now, that kiss burned through her, over her. It was harder, more dominant than it had ever been, even six years before. He kissed her as though he were as starved for her as she was for him. As though he had missed her touch as well.

God, she loved his kiss. The way his tongue stroked over her lips, licked at her, held her mesmerized with pleasure and the promise of more to come.

Now, Sallie strained to get closer, to absorb every sensation, the hand at her hip pushed beneath her top, caressed over the bare, sensitive flesh of her waist to the curve of her breast. Tingles of electrified pleasure raced through her, swelling her breasts, tightening her nipples further.

She ached. She needed, even more than she had that first night at the bar. Her senses scattered as that hand moved between her breasts, flicked open the catch of her bra and released the material.

"Goddamn, yes," he groaned, pulling back enough

to nip at her lips as he rubbed against the sensitive tip with his thumb.

Her nipples throbbed at the touch, the need for more surging through her with such power it clenched her womb and sent moisture spilling to her sex. She could feel her clit, swelling, aching for touch, for the extremity of pleasure she knew only he could give her.

Pulling back, he stared down at her for long moments, his gaze heated, lashes lowered as Sallie fought to drag in air. Then, she felt her T-shirt lifting, clearing her midriff.

"Lift your arms." The graveled sound of his voice sent sensation racing down her spine.

Lifting them, she stared up at him, excitement thundering in her blood as he pulled the shirt from her and tossed it only God knew where. As she lowered her arms, he pushed the straps of her lacy bra over her shoulders and did away with that as well.

"Jacob," she whispered, not so certain of this now.

She thought he'd take her to the bedroom, somewhere that no one would come in on them.

A grin tugged at his lips, his hands falling to the snap of her jeans.

"Let's get you out of these, baby," he murmured, voice rough, his gaze hungry. "Let me see that pretty body."

Sallie lost her breath. She felt as off-balance as she had the first time he'd taken her. She couldn't slow her breathing, or the rise and fall of her breasts as he watched. Her nipples were hard, and far too sensitive as he stared down at them, his expression tighter now, his own breathing rough.

"The bedroom . . ." Her breath caught on the words as pleasure lashed at her senses.

"The bedroom later. This now . . ." he whispered, his head bending, his lips covering the hardened peak of her breast and sucking it inside the heat of his mouth.

His tongue licked, his mouth sucking at her. The pleasure rose inside Sallie like a wave, gathering, crashing against her, only to gather again and rush through her with such need she was crying out at it. With each surge of sensation, the need inside her only grew.

Raising his head, Jacob gripped her hips and lifted her and Sallie found herself on the counter once again, staring back at him in dazed excitement as he gripped the waist of her jeans.

"Lift." The order was a growl of hunger.

Bracing her hands on the counter, Sallie lifted her hips, gasping as he jerked her jeans and panties down in one quick move. Ridding her of the denim, he stared down at her, a dark flush on his face, his breathing uneven.

"Lay back, baby," he made the demand as his hands gripped her hips and he pulled her rear closer to the edge.

Lying back, Sallie stared up at him as he gripped her legs just behind the knees, pushing them back until her feet rested at the edge of the marble.

She was fully, blatantly exposed to him now, her thighs spread farther apart by his broad hands.

"Absolutely perfect," he murmured, his hands lifting from her to grip the material of his shirt and pull it over his head, revealing the tanned expanse of his chest.

The flesh stretched over powerful muscle and rippled

with tension beneath a light mat of dark golden hair that arrowed to his abs and disappeared beneath the band of his jeans.

Jeans he was slowly loosening. First the wide belt, then the snap and zipper, the material parting to allow him to draw the thick shaft of his cock free. The wide, bloated crest was dark with lust and sheened with pre-cum.

"This is why you should have told me you were in danger, Sallie," he growled. "Because no pleasure has ever been this fucking good." His expression tightened as he notched the wide crest between the slick folds of her pussy.

Pressing her thighs farther apart, he pushed his hands beneath her rear, lifted her, and with a groan that was more a growl, sent his tongue tunneling hard and fast inside the slick, aching depths of her sex.

He wasn't giving her the slow gentleness she'd known since he'd come to her bed in Deer Haven. He wasn't holding back this time, wasn't refusing to give her every part of his hunger. No, she had it all now, just as she had in Switzerland and it was destroying her senses.

Too much . . .

Sallie cried out at the fiery pleasure that tore through her, the feel of Jacob's tongue taking her, pushing inside her . . .

Oh God, licking at her inner flesh, devouring her, destroying her.

She was sure she would have screamed, if she found enough breath to do so. She was fighting to breathe, to hold on, to anything, as the pleasure began to erupt inside her again.

He was consuming her. Not just her flesh, but her senses. With his lips and tongue, he owned her, possessed her in ways she had no idea she could be possessed until she exploded to the hungry thrusts and licks of his tongue.

Dazed, perspiration slickening her flesh, she was only barely aware of him straightening, moving between her thighs until the dark, mushroomed crest of his cock notched between the slick folds between her thighs.

"Jacob . . ." She stared up at him, heart racing, fighting to breathe as his gaze dropped to where he was preparing to take her.

A second later, a whimper left her lips, the feel of his shaft, iron hot and steel hard, pressing against the entrance to her body, stole her breath.

Could she take more? Could her senses survive another wave of the brutal pleasure?

"I dreamed of you, ached for you." He groaned, his expression savage with lust. "I've woken, my dick spilling into my own hand as I dreamt I was spilling into your sweet flesh."

Sallie fought to breathe, panting, mewling whimpers of extreme pleasure falling from her lips as she felt her inner flesh giving way to the brutally slow impalement. And she watched him. The savage, dark lust in his expression, the glitter of hungry need in his narrowed gaze.

"Jacob . . . please . . ." She tried to protest the excruciatingly slow penetration.

It was killing her, parting her flesh in a way that made her aware of every erotic pinch of sensation. He hadn't taken her like this in the past weeks. Not like this. Not with the brutal hunger and sheer intensity he was displaying now.

This was the lover he'd been during that incredible, erotic weekend in Switzerland. The lover determined to own every part of her. Heart and soul.

"Ah, baby, it's so fucking good." His tone was grating as he held her thighs apart, his gaze locked on the impalement of her body. "So fucking hot." A grimace pulled at his expression and he pushed deeper, his shaft working deeper inside her. "God. Damn. Sallie, baby . . ." The harsh, graveled tone was followed by a short, sharp thrust that had her lifting closer with a shattered cry.

She'd never imagined so much pleasure before Jacob. Never known it could lay waste to her control in such a way.

Her head thrashed against the counter as sensation raced through her body, from nerve ending to nerve ending, like wicked bolts of inner lightning she had no hope of escaping.

"That's it, sweetheart," he crooned as her hips moved, fighting to push him deeper, harder inside her. "Take me. Work that sweet pussy on me just like that. Ah God, Sallie . . ."

A hard, driving thrust buried him those final inches inside her. He filled her, overfilled her, the sensations dragging a breathless scream from her as her hands tightened on his arms, feeling the muscles bunch and flex beneath her palms.

"Sweet heaven, Sallie," he groaned as he came over her, his lips moving to her neck, stroking the sensitive flesh as his hips bunched, his muscles tightening as he pulled back, dragging the flared head of his cock over tender, nerve-rich tissue. "So fucking sweet and tight . . . Fucking you is better than a dream . . ."

Heat surged through her, lashed at her. The erotic words sinking inside her senses and pushing her higher as more of her juices spilled to lubricate his way. Her inner muscles clenched around the retreat, hips arching to hold him inside her.

"Jacob, please . . ." she whimpered, she begged. "Oh God, please. It's not enough. Not enough . . ."

His groan sounded torn from his throat, ragged and in the next second he pushed inside her harder, faster, burying several inches. He didn't stop. Each fierce impalement took him deeper, possessed her senses, as well as the emotions she'd kept locked inside her for so many years.

His touch, his lips at her neck, hungry kisses, stinging little nips that she knew would mark her skin later, and she didn't care. She loved carrying his marks, loved knowing he lost himself to the pleasure just as much as she did.

Her nails bit into his scalp, moved to his shoulders, and she fought to memorize every second of the incredible pleasure he was giving her. She wanted each moment branded into her brain, as vivid as it was now, to take out and remind herself that if only for a brief time, once all this was over, Jacob held her.

She was lost in the almost painful ecstasy surging through her. Agony and ecstasy, a mix of pleasure and pain so extreme she had no idea how to process it.

As he thrust into her, pushing her deeper into the sensations amassing inside her, she fought just to hold on to enough of herself to survive with just a piece of her heart intact. The pleasure was that extreme, that intense. She wanted it to last forever. To never lose it.

To never lose him.

Holding tight to him, she lifted her lashes and stared up at him, caught immediately by the savage hunger in his gaze. His eyes held her, locked her to him. Her breathing became harder, tighter, and she swore she felt a part of her open to him as her orgasm caught her so unaware that she had no time to prepare herself for it.

Ecstasy slammed inside her. Her eyes widened, a whimper passing her lips as Jacob's eyes narrowed and his thrusts increased, pushing her over that final edge and sending her flying.

The explosions of pleasure were cataclysmic, rapturous. Destructive. They tore through her mind, through her heart, and she feared they just might have laid waste to defenses she might have maintained against him, before this moment.

With a final, desperate thrust Jacob buried inside her a final time, his harsh groan vibrating around her. His hips pushed against her in several minute, hard jerks as she felt his shaft throb, pulse, his release pulling a hard grimace to his face before his eyes drifted closed.

Sallie collapsed beneath him, a final shudder working through her body before she felt the last of her strength ease from her limbs.

And she wondered if she could ever survive once she recovered and if there was any way she could ever be the same again?

chapter thirteen

Jacob gave Sallie enough time to catch her breath before easing his cock from the fist-tight grip her pussy had on him. He wasn't nearly satisfied yet, but hell, he didn't think he'd ever have enough of her. She was fiery, explosive in his arms, and kept him on his toes. That sharp little mind of hers took in too much, and pieced things together far too fast.

Adjusting his jeans and zipping them, he helped her from the counter and watched somberly as she rushed to find her clothes and dress. She didn't say anything, but he glimpsed the shaking of her fingers and her desperate attempt to control her breathing.

Yeah, he'd taken her like an animal, and he knew it. But she did that to him. It was the reason he'd rushed from her bed before, desperate to keep his control around him long enough to keep from scaring her off.

Breathing out heavily, he dressed as well, knowing now wasn't the time to rush her to his bedroom for seconds and further destroy both their senses. The information Justice had brought him earlier needed dealing with and as the other man had warned him, that information could threaten more than Sallie's life. It could threaten any hold he had on her at the moment. She was too determined to run again, to try to hide, no matter the danger. And he was just as determined to keep it from happening. She'd run too long, too hard, it was time to stop.

The past six years had built a wariness in her, an anger he couldn't even blame her for. She had believed he'd simply walked away from the fragile trust and innocence she'd given him that weekend in Switzerland. She'd returned to the States, married, and watched another man walk out of her life with no explanations. Then her life had been filled with nothing but the fight for survival while some bastard played with her. And they had been playing with her.

She had no reason to trust him now, no reason to stay with him once this was over and he couldn't even blame her if she did intend to walk away from him.

Once they were both dressed, he stood at the end of the counter and watched as she brushed her hair back from her face, her pretty pale blue eyes watching him uncertainly.

She looked so delicate, so damned fragile standing there that the rage he'd fought since she'd been attacked reared its ugly head once again.

Six years ago, he'd marked her as his and then again, the night he'd left the bar with her. During the years without her, Jacob had known he'd lost something important at some time, something that had changed him, left him lost, searching. That search had ended when Sallie had come to Deer Haven, and by God, he wasn't going to let anyone take her from him again.

And he damned sure wasn't letting her run again.

"John was supposed to find you and let you know I was coming back for you if anything happened," he told her when she started to turn away from him.

She froze for a moment then turned back to him slowly, gripping her hands together in front of her. She was tense, defensive, and in her eyes, he could see the vulnerable emotions she tried so hard to keep concealed from the world.

Jacob felt his chest tighten at the flash of pain she tried to hide. It was there, shadowing her face and darkening the blue of her eyes. She'd lived with the loss of what they'd found together, and she'd dealt with it. He didn't think he'd have dealt with it nearly so well.

"It doesn't matter, Jacob." She gave her head a hard shake before looking around the room as though searching for an escape. "It was a long time ago."

"It does matter. Because he knew about you. When I woke in the hospital he was there. When we realized I'd lost that entire week, I knew I'd forgotten more than mission information. I asked him what I'd lost." His fingers ached to clench into fists, and he ached to hit something when she stared back at him, her expression vulnerable and filled with uncertainty. "He never mentioned you."

It didn't change the fact that he'd lost those memories of her until she'd turned up in Deer Haven and confronted him with the truth. He'd forgotten her, when he knew to the bottom of his soul that she'd haunted him every day of the past six years.

"I waited," she said, clearing her throat, looking down at her hands for long moments. "I was supposed to leave the next day, but I waited for nearly a week."

She shrugged as though it hadn't mattered, as though she hadn't been hurt.

"I asked some of Rance's staff if they knew Jake Rossiter." Her head lifted, pride sparking in her gaze. "No one even knew you. Rance claimed he'd introduced so many people that night that he wasn't certain." She swallowed tightly, one hand lifting briefly, almost help-lessly before she dropped it once again. "Sometimes, I wondered if you were a figment of my imagination."

Jacob rubbed his hands over his face, frustration and anger tearing at him. They should have had time to learn about one another after she came to Deer Haven. Should have had a chance to figure this out before she found herself in danger once again.

She'd been betrayed, lied to, and he was going to have to jeopardize everything she may still feel for him now by revealing the information he had. When he got his hands on John Dillon and Rance Dougal, they might not survive the meeting.

"When Rance introduced me to John, about a week before I met you, I could tell he was trying to play matchmaker," she said, causing Jacob to still and watch her closely. "John called several times in that week after you left, but even he claimed not to know Jake Rossiter."

Jake Rossiter had been his cover name. The name, the

background, all of it, just as much a lie as those told to her by Rance and John.

"Did either of them ask you about me once you returned to the States?" he asked her, because he knew both men, and they had damned sure known him.

Sallie shook her head. "No. And I didn't mention you to them or anyone else again."

She turned away from him then, stared around the living room for long seconds, her shoulders tense. Jacob doubted she knew it but he could see her expression through the dim reflection of the window across from her, and the naked pain on her face had him vowing to kill both men.

"I've spent so many years running, trying to figure out why," she said, her voice almost too soft to hear. "I don't even know what living is anymore."

She wrapped her arms over her breasts, holding on to herself as though she'd never known what it was to hold on to anyone else.

Jacob couldn't bear the sight of her, standing alone as though she were lost.

Moving to her he pulled her into his arms, ignoring the stiffness in her back as it met his chest.

"The running is over, Sallie," he snarled, his lips at her ear, his arms crossed over hers. "It's done here and now. Remember that. By God, accept it. You're not running again."

He let her go when she jerked away from him, watching her turn back to him, anger sparking in her face. He preferred the anger to that bleak, heartfelt pain.

"I should have left the moment I realized who you were." The tears she refused to cry thickened her voice.

"I should have never stayed, Jacob. I should have never let you become involved in this."

His lips thinned in irritation for a moment. If she was going to keep on, he was going to paddle her bottom for believing she had to defend everyone else.

"I'm getting a little tired of your lack in confidence in me, sugar. Keep it up and I'm going to give you something to do with that pretty mouth besides doubting me."

Her eyes narrowed on him, the pale blue color sparking with anger.

"I don't doubt your arrogance in the least," she snapped. "Or your stubbornness."

She was a fine one to talk about someone else's stubbornness. She had to be the most stubborn woman he'd damned well ever met.

"At least there's something you don't doubt." He snorted, not even bothering to hide the fact that her statement amused him. "Keep doubting the rest of me and I'm going to spank that pretty ass of yours."

Her face flushed, anger and arousal an intriguing mix in her delicate features. Damn, he could do her all over again. His dick was just as hard now as it had been before he'd fucked her.

"But if I remember correctly," he continued, a fragment of a memory revealing itself. "You liked being spanked."

Glaring at him, she crossed her arms over her breasts as though she thought she could hide the appearance of those tight little nipples from him.

"You're an ass, Jacob."

"And you'd rather run than face the past," he accused

her. "And before you bother to deny it, sweetheart, think about this. You could have come to me at any time and told me who you were. You opted not to."

Her eyes widened, lips parting briefly as though in disbelief.

"I was supposed to know you'd forgotten the time you spent with me because of some damned explosion? Or that you were some super-secret spy for the CIA? For all I knew, for all I know, I'm just one woman among many." She sneered back at him. "Get over yourself, why don't you? You're not God's gift to all women and you're damned sure not Superman."

He grinned back her, making certain to inject just the right amount of mockery in the amusement. "Neither is your ex-husband or the bastards stalking you. They're not even smart enough to find who they're looking for when he's right under their nose."

That one amazed him. And oh yes, he knew exactly who they were looking for. Once Justice and Rancor knew where to look, who to question, all kinds of interesting information had made itself known.

"And you're so certain whoever's been attacking me is after you?" She gave the cutest little roll of her eyes. "Really? We were together for three days, six years ago. What would make anyone think I was more to you than a weekend fuck?"

If she wasn't careful, she was going to get fucked again. The sound of that word passing lips that looked so damned innocent was making even his balls hard.

"I know, because Justice and his brothers have more contacts in certain circles than any one family needs. But since they're on my side, I tend to be thankful for it." He shrugged. "What he discovered was that somehow, the group I was investigating learned I'd spent the weekend with you. Once they regrouped after the explosion, they tracked you back to the States and put you on the run, hoping you'd lead them to me."

She pushed her fingers through her hair in frustration, disbelief filling her expression.

"After all these years?" Her arms went across her breasts once again as she watched him skeptically.

"Some men don't know when to give up, darlin'." He grinned again and leaned his hip into the counter, wishing to hell he could have fixed this for her when she first showed up.

"This sounds a little far-fetched, you have to admit." She frowned back at him, but he could see the beginnings of suspicion in the intensity of her gaze.

He nodded as though he understood her doubt.

"You'd think," he agreed. "Tell you what. Pride caught a glimpse of John in town this morning. He and Justice and three of my men are out tracking him now. When they catch up with him, they'll bring him here and we'll ask him what he knows about it."

Jacob intended to rearrange the man's face real good for him. If John was lucky, Jacob might let him live. No promises, though. It was actually kind of doubtful.

Sallie took a step backward, staring back at him in disbelief. She didn't pale or appear guilty. She looked shocked as she rubbed at her arms as though chilled.

"That doesn't make sense." She shook her head, her arms dropping slowly, only to cross again as though trying to keep warm. "I haven't seen or heard from him once since the night he delivered the annulment papers. Why would he be here?"

Why was John here? Why had Rance arranged for Sallie to hide here, in his hometown, right beneath his nose?

Jacob didn't believe in coincidence, not to that degree. Coincidence was a winning lottery ticket when someone didn't have gas money. Sallie being here, that wasn't coincidence, it was by design. And Jacob wanted to know exactly what Rance Dougal thought he was doing when he neglected to inform him that she was here and in trouble.

"I'm going to bet it's for the same reason your attacker was in town. Hoping you'll lead him to me," he guessed. "Too many things tie this to me, baby. And it just pisses me the fuck off that you've been terrorized this way. I'll be sure to let John know how I feel about it once we find him. And Rance Dougal has his own questions to answer, because he damned sure knew Jake Rossiter, and he knew I was an agent."

Sallie had a very bad feeling Jacob would do something a hell of a lot worse than just question John. She could see it in the hard, predatory glitter in his fierce gaze. Just what she needed, another person to weigh on her conscience, though she had a feeling John just might receive a harsher sentence from Jacob than those who had tried to help her had received from her attacker.

"Don't use me as an excuse for violence," she demanded, wondering exactly how she was supposed to handle this one. "What the hell has gotten into you?

Everyone who talks about you says you're not possessive." She ticked the points off on her fingers. "You're not violent, you're easy to get along with." Bracing her hands on her hips she stared back at him suspiciously. "People don't know you well, do they?"

In an instant his expression hardened, turned savage as his gaze went cold.

"People who know me, know better than to fuck with me, or to fuck with what's mine." He moved before she could evade him, one hand locking in the strands of hair at the back of her head, the other gripping her jaw, holding her in place. "And like it or not, baby, you're mine."

Sallie felt her lips part in surprise a second before he delivered a hard, possessive kiss. His tongue pushed past her lips, stamping his ownership on her senses, on a part of her heart she'd been certain she'd managed to hold back from him.

As she stood beneath his kiss, her hands fisted in the material of his shirt and felt the dominance, the sheer power of the man holding her, and memories of the three days he'd spent in her hotel room six years ago swept over her. This was the kiss he'd given her before he'd left her that last day, promising to return. It was this kiss, this sense of belonging to him that she'd never been able to escape.

To have him state that ownership, to take it so blatantly was a shock, a certainty that somehow, someway, she'd entirely lost control of this situation.

His head lifted, his thumb raking over her swollen lips as Sallie fought to right herself, to make sense of the sudden cessation of pleasure, of a claiming she'd never recovered from in the past six years.

"Remember that, Sallie." He stepped back from her, his voice darker, graveled. "Because I promise you, anyone else that even entertains the idea of hurting you will pay for it."

He released her just as suddenly as he'd restrained her and stomped to the front door, leaving the house entirely.

Sallie stood in place, watching as the door closed behind with a snap and knew she'd just lost precious ground if she had any hope of enforcing her own wishes in this little relationship developing between them.

Ground she'd better regain fast.

This was crazy. She glanced around the room she stood in, swallowed tightly, and tried to figure out what she should do. She'd considered contacting Rance when Pride had first returned her phone and tablet to her, but something had warned her to wait.

It was still warning her.

If her mother were still alive, perhaps that call would have already been made, though Sallie wasn't certain of it.

And it wasn't as though it had done her any good to run, she reminded herself. Three identities and relocations in nearly five years, and still, she'd been found.

But if it was all some elaborate plot to draw Jacob out, why hadn't they just clued her in during one of the attacks? What was the point in terrorizing her and keeping her on the run this way?

And Rance, what the hell was he doing calling her office? He'd never called to check up on her before. She'd always had to contact him and wait for him to come to wherever she'd managed to run to once she'd been found.

He'd lied to her about knowing who Jake Rossiter was. That thought was sudden knowledge she couldn't forget. John had lied to her, and if he had, then she had no doubt Rance had as well.

But why?

Lifting her hand, she nibbled at her thumbnail as she walked to the front door, opened it, and stepped out onto the wide front porch.

The sun beat down, bright and filled with heat. The lush green pastures and neat barns and stables were given only a cursory glance as Sallie stepped to the cushioned outdoor sofa that sat against the house. Curling in the corner, partially hidden by one of the wide support beams, she tried to make sense of her stepfather's motives, as well as those of her ex-husband's.

If Rance and John knew Jacob, then they knew he'd lost that weekend they'd spent together, so why not just tell her? Better yet, why not contact Jacob and tell him?

Why had they lied to her?

God, she wanted to call him, to demand the answers she needed, but that little foreboding she felt at the thought wouldn't leave her alone. And it wasn't the first time she'd felt it. Each time she'd had to run again and contacted him, she'd had to fight that edge of panic and make herself call.

Movement from the corner of her eye had her looking up from where she'd been staring sightlessly at the verdant green of the lawn just beyond the porch. Jacob stood at the top of the steps, watching her silently.

For a second, indecision raced through her before she made up her mind and breathed out heavily. "Rance never calls to check up on me, you know," she told him quietly. "But Tara said he's been calling, demanding I check in with him. He shouldn't be aware anything happened."

Jacob frowned at the information. "Did you call him?"

She shook her head. "No. In the past, I've only called him once I've had to run again. I didn't have to run this time."

His expression took on that dangerous, predatory look once again. "I'll take care of it," he promised, the sound of his voice as dangerous as the look on his face. "I'll take care of him and John both."

Sallie nodded at the statement. Both John and Rance had lied to her, had hidden the fact that they knew Jacob. He could take care of that. She had other things to take care of.

"I need my car," she told him firmly, rising to her feet. "I have to be at work tomorrow, and that's not up for debate." She could see the denial in his face. "You want to catch the bastard, do whatever you have to do, but it's destroyed enough of my life. If I'm going to stay in Deer Haven, then I'm not going to lose any more than I already have."

"Neither will I." He bent to her, nearly nose to nose with her. "You want to go into work, fine. But you won't be going alone."

"Stop trying to intimidate me, Jacob." She pushed

against his chest, rising to her feet, and staring back at him, certain she should be wary of the look on his face.

Part predatory, sexually intent, and demanding.

"I'm not trying to do anything, baby," he assured her, his tone way too autocratic to suit her. "I'm simply stating fact. You won't be alone."

What was it with men like Jacob—men that many called alpha males—that made them think their word was law and every woman in their vicinity was to obey their every wish and whim? She'd never obeyed well. It had been her stepfather's biggest complaint, that she didn't obey his idea of how she should dress, talk, or act. She didn't make the right friends, refused to attend the proper parties, and acted as though she had no civility at all.

Even her mother had been incredibly critical of her inability to adapt, as she called it. But then, Megan Dougal had been very adaptable. The perfect ambassador's wife, the ultimate hostess. Always perfectly dressed and in complete control of herself and her surroundings. Her mother attended the proper parties, made the proper friends, and ensured she behaved in a dignified, class-conscious manner.

To see them together, no one would have known Megan Dougal and Kyra Bannon were mother and daughter.

"Don't make the mistake of believing I'm easy to control, Jacob," she warned him. "This situation has me terrified, but as much as I want to hide in a dark room and pretend I don't exist for a while, I've never allowed myself to be that person. If I'm going to stay rather than run, then until I have no other choice, I won't find that dark room."

"I'd never allow you to be placed in a dark room, sweet Sallie," he murmured. "Unless it was a bedroom and I was there with you."

Her eyes narrowed, irritation vying with arousal.

Damn him, he shouldn't be able to make her want him like this. He'd just taken her in the kitchen and her body was more than willing to have him do it again.

"You're about to piss me off, Jacob," she warned him. "And you really don't want to do that."

A dark, mocking brow lifted as if Jacob was curious. "Could be I really don't care if do. I think I could handle your anger."

"Don't make that mistake, Jacob," she snapped, staring back at him, the admittedly short fuse to her anger began to burn. "Just because you can arouse me, never believe you'll control me. I won't be dictated to and I damned sure won't be controlled. Now, I have to be at the store before eight in the morning. I'd appreciate my car, or a ride. Don't make me call someone to come pick me up."

Turning on her heel she stalked to the door, then turned back to him.

"And I'd like to be present during your call to Rance, if you don't mind," she asked him, careful to keep her tone brisk and cool. "Now if you'll excuse me, I have things to do."

chapter fourteen

It didn't surprise Sallie in the least that Rance canceled the scheduled phone call with Jacob that evening. His aide was properly apologetic, but Mr. Dougal had been called away on another business matter.

Sallie rolled her eyes at the excuse. It was the aide's standard excuse for Rance's missed appointments. The aide, Ray Masser, didn't have much imagination when it came to lying for Rance, and Rance simply didn't care.

"Does he know who you are?" she asked Jacob when he disconnected the call and placed the phone on the desk.

Jacob leaned back on the desk and crossed his arms over his broad chest as he frowned at the question.

"He knew Jake Rossiter, though I doubt he knows my true identity or has the contacts to get it," he said, his tone brooding. "His security clearance wasn't anywhere near high enough for that information."

"I don't think he knew John was with the CIA either."

That one still had the power to bother her. Rance talked about his references once and seemed unduly impressed by the fact that John had worked with several other ambassadors and had a variety of overseas contacts that he felt would help with other political concerns he had at the time.

"Rance played with the idea of going into politics with the ultimate goal of running for president. A plan that never materialized beyond the discussion stage."

Her stepfather was intelligent, and entirely calculating enough for politics, but Sallie had always felt it was her mother pushing that agenda rather than Rance. With her mother's death, Rance had dropped the idea and worked at building his consulting business.

"You said John showed up just after your return to the States," Jacob reminded her. "What was his reason?"

Sallie glanced down at where her hands rested in her lap for a moment. She was uncomfortable talking about John with Jacob. There was too much pain involved in it.

"According to him, he was there to apply for the position of aide that Rance had available." She glanced up at him, caught by the steady focus in his gaze, as though he could see inside her for the answers he was searching for. "Rance seemed ecstatic that he was interested."

Rance and her mother had discussed it for days. John Dillon was known for both his overseas and stateside contacts according to his references. When Rance had checked said references, he'd been far more impressed with him than anyone else he'd been considering at the time.

"I bet he was," Jacob muttered, scowling at the information. "John's cover was already in place when the operation in Switzerland began. At that time, he was working as an attaché to the state department assigned to the embassy. His contacts and knowledge of politics were extensive."

Sallie nodded at that. "Mother and Rance were quite impressed."

"And you? Were you impressed?"

Sallie started back at him silently for long moments before she gave a light shrug. "I married him."

Jacob's expression hardened in an instant, his gaze narrowing on her.

"Did I mention I actually spent several years working with some of the agency's most experienced interrogators?" His tone was harder than his expression. "You don't have the training to lie to me, baby, don't pretend you do."

Sallie inhaled slowly, deeply. "I don't recall lying to you, Jacob," she told him coolly. "You asked if he impressed me. I merely answered you."

He straightened from the half-sitting position against the front of his desk, his arms dropping to his sides as he regarded for long, silent moments.

"Why did you marry him, Sallie?" he asked her then. "Were you in love with him?"

Was she in love with him? She wanted to laugh at the question.

No, she hadn't loved him. She'd been too hurt, too angry that Jacob hadn't returned for her as he'd promised. She'd been humiliated, confused.

"You don't have the right to ask either of those

questions." She didn't even bother to hide the fact that she didn't appreciate the inquisition.

There was no way to answer him without revealing far too much of herself and how she'd felt about Jacob. Unfortunately, time hadn't erased those emotions and the past month had only strengthened them.

She'd been a fool for him then and evidently, she was still a fool for him.

In the deepest part of her heart Sallie ached for what might have been had he not been in that explosion and hurt so bad he'd forgotten her. If he had returned as he'd promised, at least there would have been closure.

"I have every right to ask those questions," he snapped. "I didn't walk away from you, Sallie. You know that now."

Sallie swallowed tightly at the regret she heard in his voice. She wanted to beg him to tell her how he felt all those years ago. But she liked to think she did still have some pride left. Whatever he'd felt had been wiped away with his memories, and it hadn't had the time to lie in wait inside him, to shadow every possible relationship until he realized only one person could relieve that ache for touch, for warmth.

What was wrong with her? She knew women who claimed to love one man while they slept with several others. They would cry and swear their heart belonged to another while taking a succession of men into their beds and making do with the fantasy that they were with the man they loved.

Maybe her imagination just wasn't good enough to allow herself to do that.

"Why I married him or how I felt about him doesn't

have anything to do with the situation I'm in now," she informed him.

"It does if I have to kill the bastard," he snarled. "Because if I find out he was a part of this, I will kill him, Sallie. No matter how much you fucking cry, he'll be dead."

Sallie pushed to her feet from the couch she'd been sitting on, anger surging to the surface to meet his.

"Do what you have to do, Jacob," she told him furiously. "I've lost five years of my life because of someone's determination to either find you, or him. But for your own sake, be certain of the reason you're killing him. I'd hate for you to learn you've killed an innocent man." She jabbed a finger in his direction as she fought to control her anger. "Whoever the bastard that attacked me is looking for, he deserves killing. But remember, I was married to John for a year. If it was you he wanted, he could have asked me about you at any time."

"He knew you had no idea what my real name was, or the fact that I was an agent," he pointed out. The dark, furious tone should have had her retreating rather than facing him, but her own anger was impossible to push back. "He would have kept pushing, until either you or Rance broke and contacted me or found me. Rance brought you here, Sallie. Why did he do that?"

Her lips thinned at the accusation in his tone. "Because Myron Dillerman owed him one hell of a favor and believed Rance needed to get his dead wife's daughter out of his life, that's why." Her voice rose despite her attempt to calm down. "And it was no more than the truth. Mother made Rance swear he'd continue to protect me before her death, and he keeps his promises whether he likes it or not."

And she'd accepted his help because she had no idea how to protect herself from the unknown assailant that seemed to find her, no matter where she ran.

"Coincidence?" The mockery in his voice was evident. "You believe you ended up in my hometown, right under my nose, because of coincidence?"

"No one knew who you were." She felt as though she were arguing with the wall. No doubt the wall would pay more attention to what she said. "How could you be a target when no one knew?"

"How could I have not been the target, because, baby, there's no way in hell coincidence stretches that far." He snorted derisively. "Somehow, Rance had to have learned who I was, and where I was. There's no other explanation."

"Then why not just send that bastard after you rather than me?" she argued. "Why use me to begin with?"

He stared at her for long moments, eyes narrowed, his expression far too calculating.

"I'll be sure to ask him," he drawled, a cold smile tugging at his lips. "If I don't hear from him by tomorrow afternoon, then I'll make damned sure he hears from me in a way he won't care much for. But I'll be damned if I'll sit on my ass and give some son of a bitch another chance at you."

Another chance at her?

"It's not me they want." She breathed out heavily and pushed her fingers through her hair in frustration. "Each time I was found the question was the same. 'Where is he?' Whether that was you or John, is anyone's guess. But Rance isn't involved or he would have just sent me to you. Being forced to keep his promise to Mother can't sit well with him after all these years, I imagine."

He'd done it though, and Sallie had always been grateful that he had. Without him, she would have no doubt been dead by now.

"He raised you," Jacob stated as though that should mean something. "He was the same as your father." ·

She lifted a brow and almost laughed. "Where do you get that?"

The look he gave her was almost questioning. "You were five when they married, Sallie. No more than a baby. That's a lot of years to help raise a kid and not care something for her."

She shook her head, almost amused. "I had a nanny until I was seven then I was sent away to boarding school. When I came home on vacations, the staff watched after me. Mother and Rance were usually somewhere out of the country. Switzerland was the first time I'd joined them at one of his postings." She gave him a mocking glance. "And even then, I was introduced as part of his staff, rather than Megan Dougal's daughter." She shrugged as he stared at her silently, his expression slowly turning implacable. "Since Rance is clearly avoiding your phone call, I believe I'll get more coffee."

She turned to leave the room.

"Your mother didn't even raise you?" Jacob's question caught her as she reached the door.

Sallie turned back to him, pondering the question.

"No. Sister Rebecca, the headmistress of the school

I was sent to, took care of that for her. Before her, Nonny made certain I had all the attention I could have wanted. Don't feel sorry for me, Jacob." She smiled back at him. "Nonny and Sister Rebecca were wonderful caregivers. I wasn't abused or neglected. No one dared to try to bully me, they were terrified to even try. Sister Rebecca could be quite imposing when she needed to be. I was loved. More so than I would have been if my mother had actually attempted to raise me herself. Now, about that coffee?"

He gave a short, sharp nod that she took as assent. Turning back, Sallie left the office and moved through the quiet house to the kitchen.

She'd seen the somber intensity in Jacob's look and knew he felt sorry for the child she'd once been. Sallie considered herself fortunate. Other than holidays and breaks, she'd had friends, laughter, and people who cared for her during those years. It was only when she came back to the Dougal household that she'd felt out of place and alone.

"My child would never be sent away," Jacob spoke behind her as she reached the coffee pot, his voice quiet but tempered with steel.

"If I ever have a chance to have children, then mine won't be either," she told him, focusing on her task rather than looking at him. "A child should be loved by his or her parents. Though, I was lucky. Mother and Rance could have actually kept me with them. I would have had a terribly lonely life if they had."

She'd seen enough of their lifestyle and their friends at the odd times they'd been in the country and she'd actually spent time with them, that she knew it wasn't a life that would have suited her. She'd been groped, leered at, and propositioned by the so-called social elite since she was fifteen years old, saw the children that had been raised by their friends, and thanked God daily that she'd escaped that life.

"Do you want children?"

Sallie stilled at the question, wishing in some small part that he wanted her to have his children.

"I do." She stared at the counter, blinking back emotions that threatened to swamp her. "I want a house filled with children. But I also want a man as committed to them as I'll be. One as committed to me as I'll be to him."

Dragging in a heavy breath she went about pouring the water into the pot and measuring the coffee grounds in.

"You didn't mention love," he pointed out. "Shouldn't you love him rather than simply be committed?"

She loved him, though. How was she supposed to ever have those children without him, because she couldn't stand the thought of another man's touch now?

Once the coffee started running into the pot, she turned back to him, her gaze meeting his squarely. "I'd never consider a child without it, Jacob. I wouldn't hurt myself or a baby like that. Children need two parents, not just one. But even more, they need parents who love each other. Parents that give them an example of what love and commitment truly are. I didn't have that and though my life was fairly easy, I knew I lacked it."

He moved to her slowly, almost as though he were stalking her, holding her gaze, staring into her as though he could read every secret she had.

"I spill myself inside you each time I take you," he said, his voice low, rough. "No protection is one hundred percent effective, Sallie. What if you were carrying my child? Do you think I'd let you or that baby go?"

"If that happens, then I'll do what's best for the baby, Jacob." It was all she could do. "That doesn't mean you'll have a hold over me. I won't marry you for the sake of a child. But I would work with you to make certain that child had the best possible life." She shook her head. "But I doubt it will happen now. If I recall, there was once or twice that you forgot to use a condom in Switzerland."

"Oh, I didn't forget." The curve of his lips wasn't one of amusement but of regret touched with need. "I did it deliberately, Sallie. And if I could ensure your protection didn't work this time, then trust me, sweetheart, that's exactly what I'd do."

Shock held her still, silent as Jacob turned on his heel and stalked to the front door, opened it, and left the house, the door closing hard and loud behind him.

She could feel her heart racing, blood thundering through her veins and she didn't know why.

What was that look on his face? The hard, chiseled features had looked carved from stone into an expression that assured her he meant exactly what he said, and he had his own reasons for it. Reasons that he was certain of.

She let out her breath, realizing she'd been holding it, and felt a rush of light-headedness as her hand moved slowly to her stomach, where she let it rest for long moments. The thought of carrying his child could make her weak with need, just as it had six years ago and she knew it was just as insane now as it had been.

He hadn't loved her. He didn't love her. It wouldn't matter how much she loved him, or how much he'd love their child if there were one, it would mean just that much more heartache for her. And that was the one thing she didn't need.

Why had he said that, though? What would make him wish her protection would fail?

chapter fifteen

He should have kept his damned mouth shut.

Jacob stalked from the house to the barn, self-disgust warring with the possessiveness he felt for Sallie.

Memories of the three days and nights they'd spent in Switzerland and the emotions he'd left that hotel room feeling were as sharp and clear now as they had been at the time. He hadn't wanted to leave her, but John had gotten information about the meeting being planned and the American scheduled to join the militant group. They'd had to move fast, and he hadn't had time to tell her that he wanted to keep her in his life. That he didn't want to lose her.

He'd already made the decision to leave the agency, to return to the ranch, and he'd wanted to invite her to his home.

Fuck, what had happened in that warehouse with that explosion and why the hell hadn't John told him about the young woman he'd left waiting for him? He'd kill the other man for that alone.

Strangely, memories of Sallie were crystal clear now, but the four days before and the morning of the explosion were still missing. At times, he was certain they were just a second away, then they'd dissipate like smoke in the wind.

He'd read the debriefings, discussed it with John while he was recovering after the explosion, but still, nothing clicked those memories into place. The doctors hadn't believed the memories would ever return while Jacob had known there was more missing than just operational information.

He wanted this over with and he wanted a full background on Sallie's life. Rance Dougal and his wife had thrown her away as though she didn't matter. They'd pushed a baby into a boarding school and left her there for others to care for.

The fact that she was the kind, compassionate woman he knew her to be was shocking to him.

For three fucking years he'd watched her, waited for her to mess up if the image she presented wasn't the woman she was. Rather than messing up, she'd only endeared herself further to those who knew her. As Justice had said, even he had liked her. Hell, his grandmother had mentioned her several times and asked why he couldn't get a sweet girl like Miss Hamblen.

And still, he'd waited, drawn to her, fascinated by her, and already claimed by her. Son of a bitch. He could paddle her ass for not saying anything to him. Instead, she had retreated, kept that cool mask in place, and acted as though she had no interest.

Until that night at the bar. When she'd looked at him, he'd seen the hunger in her, the aching need, and he knew she hadn't looked at anyone else like that as long as she'd been in Deer Haven. If she had, the bastard she looked at would have done the same thing he had. Marked her. Claimed her in return in a way she couldn't hide or deny. She belonged to him and John had known it. He had known it and he had dared to touch her, marry her.

Stopping on the other side of the barn, away from the view of the house, he pushed his fingers through his hair and gripped the back of his neck as he stared down at the ground. The other man had endangered her because he'd been a stupid-fuck and hadn't informed Jacob that he'd forgotten the woman he'd left waiting in the hotel for him.

She'd been running for nearly five years, scared, with no friends to help her, no family except a stepfather who had done no more than dump her somewhere with a new identity and no protection.

Had her marriage to John resulted in a child, as much as Jacob hated what the bastard had done, he would have never turned his back on Sallie's child. He would have made that child his own, treated him or her as his own. That was what a man did, his father had always told him. And Tyler Donovan had been a man of his beliefs. He'd taken a scraggly little eight-year-old with more chips on his shoulder than a kid should have. He'd adopted that child, raised that child, and called him his own far and wide.

Jacob hadn't been born a Donovan, but that hadn't mattered to his father, nor had it mattered to Gram.

The sound of a pickup pulling into the front drive had him pushing back thoughts of John and his own past. Blowing out a hard breath he made his way back to the front of the barn just as Justice, Pride, and Rancor were stepping from Justice's truck. The three men could have been an imposing sight if Jacob wasn't well aware of each man's strengths and weaknesses. They'd grown up together, though Jacob had followed his father's footsteps into the agency at a young age, the Culpeppers had each gone their own way before returning to the ranch.

Justice had stayed to help his father before taking over the Culpepper ranch and various businesses. Pride had joined the military before being discharged after he'd busted his knee, while Rancor had gone the college route before joining the FBI for several years.

Together, the three were a formidable group and not for the first time, Jacob was damned glad they were on his side.

"Gram's getting antsy." Justice stepped to the back of the truck and braced his arms over the side of the bed, watching Jacob in amusement. "She said to tell you to get this foolishness done with so you can get to the business of making those great-grandbabies she's waiting on."

All three men chuckled at the message, amusement filling their hardened faces.

"Yeah, and sometime before Lily carries out her threat to kill Justice in his sleep," Rancor drawled, a smile flashing across his darkly tanned face. "She threw a frying pan at him this morning."

Hell, Lily and Gram hadn't been there twenty-four

hours yet and already Lily was throwing things at him and Gram was antsy.

"I don't know, it's all pretty amusing if you ask me." Pride leaned against the passenger side of the truck, arms across his chest as he grinned over at Rancor. "Tell me we've been bored, and I'll call you a liar."

"Son of a bitch, they haven't even been there a full day yet." Jacob glared at all three of them.

"And what a fun, less than full day it's been." Pride was obviously enjoying it more than the other three.

"It was my head she threw that pan at," Justice groused.

"And my shoulder she hit." Rancor was fighting a grin. "I think Gram wanted her to throw the pot instead. I'm sure glad Lily ignored her." He rubbed at his shoulder as though the skillet had actually hurt.

Jacob wiped his hand down the side of his face and stared at the three men, wondering if they'd ever actually grown out of their teenage years. There were days he wouldn't swear to it.

"I thought if we put our heads together and put Rancor on the computer maybe we could figure some things out. I'd like to get this done, Jacob. None of them are safe until we do."

Jacob's eyes narrowed on him. "What happened?"

"Shay went to her apartment this morning to get some clothes before returning to her parents, and the place was trashed." Rancor was deadly serious now. "Completely trashed. I went and checked it out, and someone went through it with a hell of a temper tantrum."

"Anyone see anything?" Jacob questioned them.

"Nada," Pride answered. "And all I saw on the security cameras was some dumbass in a dark jacket, Stetson pulled low over his face. It could have been anyone. I have the file on a flash drive for you, though. Maybe, if it's your old partner, you'll recognize something about him."

He glanced up at the house. It would be dark in an hour or so, and damned if he hadn't had other plans.

He sighed. "Come on up to the house. Dougal's aide called and canceled the phone meeting we'd set up. Son of a bitch claimed Dougal was called away on other business."

"Yeah, all those oil wells probably need his direct attention." Pride snorted. "I feel for the bastard. Really I do."

Jacob just shook his head and led the way to the house.

It wasn't exactly what he'd intended to do for the night, but the other plans could wait a little while. Sallie was still there, and she'd be in his bed, safe. When he was finished, she'd be there, exactly where she should have been for the past six years. He'd content himself with that.

For now.

chapter sixteen

It was well after midnight before Jacob and the three brothers called it a night and the Culpeppers headed back to their ranch. Stepping into the house and setting the security, Jacob ran his fingers through his hair in frustration. There were still no answers, and other than memories of Sallie, he hadn't remembered anything further about the operation in Switzerland.

Forefront had been fairly new but vicious when it came to getting the information they needed. Torture was a favorite sport to them, especially when it came to women. And the women targeted had all been tied to or working for diplomats assigned to Switzerland from various other countries.

If Jacob had ever learned what their ultimate goal had been, then it hadn't been in the information he'd given his partner or the CIA before the warehouse explosion. And he hadn't remembered a damned thing once he'd awakened after the explosion.

"I have some inquiries out to several contacts in Interpol and Scotland Yard," Rancor had revealed as they went over the current information gathered. "They were looking into the group as well after the German chancellor and England's prime minister lost a young female staff member while in Switzerland that year. Belgium, France, Italy, and South Africa also lost female staff members during an international meeting earlier that year."

There had been a total of six young females tortured, raped, and murdered in the course of a year and it was only by a stroke of luck that the CIA had uncovered talk that a new militant group was behind the murders. Jacob and John had never learned why. All they'd managed to uncover was that Forefront, comprised of former Swiss military and law enforcement, were determined to change the course Switzerland had taken in intervening between nuclear nations in conflict.

The role of mediator wasn't where Forefront believed the nation should be concentrating and they believed they could change that course. How the murders of low-level female staff among those countries factored into that didn't make sense.

None of the women possessed a security clearance from their government that could actually net any information they could find useful. The women were more or less interns.

Jacob couldn't shake the feeling that he was missing something, or that he'd forgotten something vitally important to protecting Sallie. It was a nagging itch at the back of his neck, a tightening in his gut that refused to ease. What was he overlooking? What was the fog in his brain hiding?

He was missing a full week. According to John's debriefing, Jacob had been gathering information on potential members of Forefront while John hung back to gather intel on anyone following or showing interest in Jacob's movements. Whatever information he'd gathered that week, he'd obviously not shared.

According to John's report, a call had come in during the early hours of that last morning to a number Jacob had given to those he talked to when looking for information, providing the location of a suspected Forefront meeting. Jacob had told John he trusted the contact, and they'd decided to check it out before calling out the team assigned as backup.

Sipping at a glass of whisky, Jacob prowled the house, frowning, a long memory separating and forming in his mind.

"What the fuck are you doing?" John hissed when Jacob arrived at the location where John was waiting for him. "That woman's a threat and you fucking know it. You're going to blow this op."

"The only thing she threatens is my self-control." Jacob snorted.

"Get your head out of your dick, Jacob." Disbelief filled John's expression. "She's working you. She must be a hell of a fuck . . ."

Before Jacob could stop himself, he threw John against the brick wall they were using as shelter.

"That's my woman, fucker," he snarled. "Watch your goddamned mouth before I shut it for you. Permanently . . ."

The memory drifted away, but he could still feel the rage, the fury that burned inside him. She hadn't known anything about why he was there, and she hadn't asked a single damned question or questioned his reason for being with the embassy. She'd used the name Kyra then, her real name, Kyra Bannon, and in a matter of days she'd stolen his heart.

She'd told him who she was that first morning as she lay in his arms. A haunting loneliness had filled her voice, and despite the disgust he'd felt, he'd given John that information. And once Jacob had lost those memories and been sent back to the ranch, John had made his way to Rance Dougal's employ within months, and within the year, he'd married Sallie and moved into her bed.

He nearly threw the whisky glass he'd emptied before he managed to stop himself. The thought of John faking a marriage to the young, innocent Sallie ripped at his guts. She'd given Jacob her virginity, let him tap into her emerging sexuality, then John had betrayed both of them, married her, slept with her.

Pushing forward he rested his elbows on his knees and ran his hands down his face.

He wanted to kill the son of a bitch in that moment. He'd touched the woman Jacob had claimed as his own, and John had known it. He'd planned it. Jacob knew the man John was, a calculating son of a bitch who didn't care about anything but the mission he'd been given.

Sallie wouldn't have meant anything to him, but even now, John would use whatever advantage his relationship with Sallie might have gained him. And no matter how Sallie didn't seem to care about the man she thought she was married to, the fact that she'd been married to him gave John an incredible advantage.

Jacob would be damned if he'd allow that advantage to make a difference. Sallie belonged to him. She was back in his life now, in his bed, he'd be damned if he'd let that bastard hurt her or risk the hold he was securing on her heart. It wasn't going to happen.

She belonged to him.

Once again that single thought had his cock iron hard, filling his jeans and pushing at the material in an attempt for freedom. Not that he'd had much relief from the hard-on tormenting him since the day he'd glimpsed her in town, three years ago. Even then, some part of his brain had pushed him to remember even as he'd felt that overwhelming sense of ownership.

Mine.

She was in in his bed waiting for him. Sweet. Hot. Silken. God, every time he took her Jacob lost himself in her. Nothing mattered but tasting her, taking her, imprinting himself so deep and hard inside her that she'd never be free of him. Not ever.

Rising to his feet, his shaft so swollen and hard that walking only made the ache worse, he stalked down the hall to his bedroom. The scent of her was in his head, the taste of her teasing his senses. He couldn't get enough of her. He didn't want the taste of her, the feel of her to ever slip away. He intended to make certain he never lost her again. Not from his mind or from his heart.

He paused at the door, the strip of light showing beneath it, indicating she was still awake, and for a moment he wondered if he should go to the guest room. He could jack off and get a handle on the hunger raging through him.

Yet still, his fingers gripped the doorknob and turned it. He pushed the door open and stepped inside, immediately finding Sallie where she sat in the bed, her tablet opened and resting on her lap as she made notes in a notebook beside her.

Her head lifted, her expression a bit surprised, innocent. A moment's vulnerability flashed across her face, darkened her light blue eyes, and only fed the hunger tearing through him.

The blankets were folded to the bottom of the bed as she sat propped against the pillows. She wore one of those little shorty and tank sets. The scoop neck tank wasn't tight, but it emphasized the firm, rounded curves of her breasts and did nothing to hide the suddenly hard peaks of her nipples.

Holding her gaze, Jacob closed the door, sliding the lock in place.

"Jacob?" He could see the feminine need as her face flushed a pretty pink and her breathing escalated, pushing her breasts tighter against the material of her top.

He didn't speak. He couldn't yet. Lust was rising inside him like some creature that had taken possession of him.

He stepped to the chair that sat against the wall from the bottom of the bed and began working his boots from his feet.

Drawing in a deep breath, Sallie closed out the file on her tablet then placed it and the notebook on the small table beside the bed, still watching him uncertainly.

Dropping his boots and socks to the floor, Jacob rose to his feet once again and pulled his shirt over his head, tossing it carelessly to the chair behind him. Stripping his jeans from his body, he continued to watch her, his fingers gripping the base of his cock, hoping to relieve the pressure straining the engorged shaft.

Sallie lost her breath.

The sight of the thick, heavy length of his shaft, the engorged head dark and leaking pre-cum had her juices spilling and dampening her panties as he moved around the bed to her. Her breathing accelerated; her body sensitized.

He fisted the heavy length as he moved to her, his tight abs flexing, his powerful body appearing stronger, harder.

She could barely breathe as he came to her, her heart pounding in her chest when he came to his knees by the bed. Gripping her hips he turned her, pulling her legs to the floor and gripping the waist of the thin pajama shorts she wore.

Sallie gasped in surprised as he pulled them, along with her panties, over her hips and down her legs, tossing them aside. The tank came next. Lifting her arms with one hand he gripped the top and whipped it over her head. She didn't pay attention to where it dropped.

"Jacob," she gasped as his hands cupped her breasts, his thumbs rasping against her sensitive nipples.

"I love these pretty tits." His voice was hard, dark, his gaze focused on them as hunger creased his face. "And those sweet, hard little nipples."

Holding her breath, Sallie watched as he leaned closer, his head lowering to take the tip of her breast into his mouth. Pleasure seared her nerve endings, racing from her nipple to her clit before exploding in her stomach in a riot of pleasure. Pinpoints of heat screamed through her body, exploding along her nerve endings in a rush of mind-numbing sensation.

"Jacob, yes," she gasped, agonizing need clenching her sheath as liquid heat spilled between her thighs.

As he sucked, one hand plumped the neglected breast, his thumb stroking, rubbing the hardened tip. Sallie's hands gripped his shoulders, fighting to hold on to him, to hold on to anything to keep her senses intact.

He sucked firmly, his teeth raked over it, his tongue flicked like a playful demon intent on sensitizing the swollen tip even further, making her desperate. Her thighs tightened on the outside of his, the engorged crest of his cock brushed against her clitoris, making the ache, the need to orgasm imperative.

"Jacob, please. I need . . ." She needed him now.

His palm pushed between her thighs, found the saturated folds, and parted them, stroking with a whisper touch. A second later, his fingers pierced her, two sliding deep in a shocking thrust that sent flames licking through her channel. Sallie fell back on the bed as Jacob released her nipple, her hips writhing, riding the thrust of his fingers as ecstasy rose in a hard, overwhelming wave.

Just as she was certain she'd fly, the fiery strokes were gone.

"Don't stop." Her demand was a gasp of agonizing need now. "Please, Jacob . . ." Her wail ended in a gasp as he gripped the cheeks of her ass, lifted her, and brought the slick, lush flesh between her thighs to his mouth.

Jacob tasted the sweetness, the fresh, summer heat of Sallie's pussy and nearly spilled his seed. With her thighs spread wide, her legs resting over his arms, he held on to her, his senses completely immersed in what was rapidly becoming his favorite treat.

Only here, right here, with her cries echoing in his head, his tongue buried in the sweetest nectar he'd ever known, had he known true pleasure.

She was addicting, every taste of her, every cry, every caress he could give her, she took willingly, eagerly.

She gave herself to him completely.

As Jacob's lips and tongue stripped her of inhibitions and pushed her closer to the edge of rapture, Sallie felt the last defenses against him disintegrate. She'd known she was his. Completely. Totally.

From the first moment his gaze touched hers all those years ago, she'd known she belonged to this man. The years apart had never changed that. And now there was no hiding from it.

Sallie arched to the wicked hunger he ate her with. His tongue thrust inside her channel, licked, and tongued her until her orgasm exploded through her with a forced that stole her breath and resistance she could have had against him.

Shaking, shuddering in his grip, her release rained to his lips and tongue as she swore each of her senses flew outside her body and met his somewhere in a realm where nothing existed but the two of them.

"We're not finished, darlin'. Not by a long shot," he growled, the dark, husky sound of his voice stroking her senses. "Just lie there for me, sweet and warm. Look at me now, Sallie. Let me see your pretty eyes as I fuck the sweetest pussy I've ever known."

Sallie struggled to open her eyes, staring back at him,

her gaze locked with his as she felt the slow, stretching penetration of his shaft invading her.

She couldn't breathe. The steady, fiery invasion was more than she could bear. The pleasure was too much . . . Exquisite. Fierce.

He surged deep, hard inside her, filling her with a shocking wave of sensation that rode both pleasure and pain. Ecstasy blazed through her, brilliant and hot as her body jerked tight.

Jacob clenched his teeth, fighting the release boiling through his shaft as Sallie's sheath gripped his cock tighter than a fist, ripping, sucking at his shaft with ever increasing waves of pure rapture. Impossible to resist, destroying his control. A groan tore from his throat as his release gripped him, destroyed him.

His seed shot from him, heavy, hot streams erupting from his cock as he thrust inside the heated grip she had on him. It was more pleasure than he'd ever known in his life. Every sense he possessed was immersed in her, owned by her.

She was his. His heart, his soul. In that moment he knew, he belonged to her as well.

Completely.

He was hers.

Sallie lay still, silent, more than an hour later, exhausted, her body still resonating with the extremity of the orgasms he'd torn from her. He'd been relentless. Tireless. Riding her through each release and extending the ecstasy until she was certain it wasn't possible to ever be the same.

She watched now as he came out of the bathroom carrying a towel and washcloths and somehow her heart softened further as he carefully cleaned their combined releases from her thighs and the bare folds of her sex. His expression was quiet, brooding and when he returned to the bathroom, she forced back a sigh heavy with uncertainty.

He didn't speak when he returned to the bed, pulled her into his arms, then covered both of them with the blankets that had somehow been pushed to the bottom of the bed. Silence stretched between them, filled with unspoken words and emotions, with her uncertainty and whatever he was silently contemplating.

"I should have said something when I first came to Deer Haven and realized you were here," she said softly, feeling his arms tighten around her as she lay against his chest. "I didn't know about the explosion. I just thought . . ." She swallowed tightly. "I thought you'd forgotten me."

And the pain from that thought had been more debilitating than she'd ever believed it could be. Even the events that happened after she returned to the States, as crippling as they had been, hadn't hurt as bad as the thought that he'd forgotten her.

"You stayed in my dreams, my fantasies." His hand stroked down her back, his palm warm and callused, creating a delicious friction. "The night I was in introduced to you in Deer Haven, all I could think was how beautiful you were and how much you reminded me of the dreams that haunted me." He kissed her forehead, the slope of her cheek. "And the dreams came almost nightly. Until the day you told me what I'd forgotten, and then, memories of you began returning until I could account for every second we were together."

As she had always remembered those seconds. Remembered them and replayed them so often she thought she'd cease to exist without him.

"I wasn't going to leave Switzerland without convincing you to come here, to the ranch, when I returned. I knew that mission had to be finished first, though. I couldn't leave the agency until I finished it." Regret filled his hushed tone and sliced at her heart. "But I wasn't willing to let you go, baby. I was so determined to keep you that even after I forgot everything, you still haunted me."

"I loved you," she whispered. "I told myself I didn't, for so long. But I knew better. Every part of me knew better."

But still, she'd married.

Jacob couldn't say the words, hell, he had no right to say them. He had no right to think it. He'd forgotten her. He'd almost married himself, but the dreams of Sallie had become so damned prevalent there were times he'd been jerked into those fantasies, even when he was awake.

He'd lost more sleep during that year than at any time in his life. And he'd wondered if he was going insane.

"You love me now too," he told her, knowing it, feeling it each time he took her, each time he looked into her eyes. In every touch she gave him. "I love you, Sallie. And that's something I should have told you in Switzerland. There's nothing I'll ever regret more than I regret leaving that hotel room without telling you I loved you."

She lay against him silently, and though he wanted to press her to commit to far more than her love for him, for now, he let it go.

They had a battle to win, her future was at stake, and he was damned if he was going to allow anyone or anything else to take her away from him. If she couldn't forgive him for the past, then he understood that. He'd live with it if he had to. But he'd damned sure try to convince her otherwise.

Rather than pushing, he simply held her until they both drifted off to sleep, her head against his shoulder, her warmth chasing away the cold he'd felt for too damned long.

Holding her to him was a battle he'd continue when they woke, and when the cold light of day forced them to face the problems standing between them. Problems he wouldn't allow to stand there much longer.

chapter seventeen

He loved her.

Sallie held that knowledge close to her heart throughout the night and the next morning as she dressed for work. Jeans and blouses were about the extent of the clothing that had been packed for her, along with socks and sneakers. Ranch clothes, as Shay and Lily called them, but thankfully, it wasn't unusual for her to occasionally wear jeans to the office.

It was unusual to have to argue through her first cup of coffee, though.

"This is a bad idea, Sallie," Jacob stated as she took that first sip of coffee. "Your attacker, Deverson, wasn't working alone. There're signs he had a partner. Which means you're still in danger."

She could see the worry in his expression, in his raptor brown eyes. Striations of gold and hazel mixed with brown, creating a predatory, savage gaze that never failed to turn her on and make her breathless. In this case, the thought of the danger that could be waiting for her gave her a momentary pause.

"I've never been attacked outside my home." She shrugged, though the memories of it weren't in the least comfortable. "I doubt there will be any danger going to work. I'm in more danger away from it, I'd think."

His lips thinned, his gaze narrowing on her until his eyes glittered behind the heavy barrier of his lashes. He looked predatory. Dangerous. And so damned piratical her panties were wet.

Damn him.

"I'm going to work, Jacob." She watched him as she lifted the cup to her lips and sipped at the hot liquid.

She could feel his mind working, the calculation and brooding intensity were off the charts. He was certain he could get his way.

"I could tie you to my bed." His voice was low, dark, and dangerous. "And I could make you like it."

She nearly lost her breath because she knew she'd probably love it.

"And tomorrow I wouldn't warn you before I left. And if tomorrow didn't work, then the day after." She placed the cup on the counter, braced her hands on the edge behind her and watched him carefully. "I've been running for five years. Three of those years I've spent too frightened of myself and whatever I was running from to reach out to you. Don't make me run from you as well, Jacob."

The silent snarl that pulled at his lips was both sexy and amusing.

"First sign of trouble and we get your ass back here."

He pointed an imperious finger at her sharply. "You understand me?"

She nodded slowly. "Yes, Jacob, at the first sign of trouble."

She wouldn't take that from him. She didn't want him in danger. She wanted the danger over and she wanted the life she'd built here, the friends she'd made. The man she loved.

"Let's get it the hell over with then," he growled. "But tonight, you definitely get that spanking."

It may not be a good idea to tell him she was looking forward to it.

Or perhaps she should rethink that, she pondered as they drove into Deer Haven nearly an hour later. Jacob had given in, but he hadn't done so gracefully. His expression was still brooding and his lips thin with irritation. Or perhaps anger. He hadn't spoken much on the drive in.

"I still don't like it." The rasp of his voice was dark, resonating with predatory danger.

As he pulled into the back of the building, Sallie looked around carefully, a chill racing up her arms.

"Give me a few hours, Jacob," she said, her voice low. "There are some matters Tara can't take care of on her own. Once I have them cleared up, I'd like to run to the house for more clothes and a few other things I need, then we can return to the ranch."

Jacob parked the truck, his gaze moving around the busy loading dock and lumberyard. She'd bet he knew exactly how many people were moving about, what they were doing, and if there was anyone there that didn't belong.

Jacob nodded slowly. "I'll have a few men check the house and wait on us there. I don't like surprises."

"Can't say I've enjoyed them myself." She breathed out heavily, looking around again. "Did you know all your men from the agency?"

He looked at her, surprise flickering across his expression. "None of them were in the agency with me. Most are former military, though. Men I worked with at one time or another or who came to me through men I trusted."

"I was told the ranch wasn't really operating until a few years ago." She looked at him questioningly. "Tara said it was mostly deserted until then."

His lips quirked as he laid his wrists over the steering wheel and stared back at her. "Are you delaying going in, Sallie? We can go back to the ranch now."

"No, Jacob." Sallie shook her head, returning his smile. "I guess I just thought of it. I've heard quite a bit about you over the years. Gossip, you know?"

Gossip kept Deer Haven moving, Tara always claimed. Sallie tended to agree with her.

"There was some trouble here several years ago that a lot of people are unaware of." He stared around the busy loading area once again. "I was caught unaware and several friends nearly died. The sheriff, Justice, and I decided if we were going to keep our little area of the world safe, then we'd have to take care of it ourselves. I put the ranch in operation, hired men I knew I could trust, men who weren't ready to stop serving their country. And along with the sheriff's office, we keep our eyes opened, and our little corner as safe as possible."

"You left the agency, but you weren't ready to settle back and trust your country to take care of you or those you loved," she guessed.

Jacob nodded slowly. "The world is changing. The dangers we faced even twenty years ago have been surpassed by men who are far more evil than we imagined. Human trafficking, terrorists determined to destroy the lives and liberties we love. Drug cartels with more weapons and ammunition than most armies." He grimaced at the thought. "I lost my innocence long ago. I like the idea of preserving that innocence in others, and the safety of those untrained or unable to do so. And I love my home."

With an uncomfortable shrug of his shoulders he pushed open his door and walked around the truck to open hers and help her out.

Giving him her hand, Sallie felt the warmth of his grip, the strength in it. He wasn't like any other man she'd ever known. Hell, most of the men working on his and the Culpeppers' ranches were former military come to think about it, and the Culpeppers shared Jacob's arrogance and sense of responsibility.

They'd come together to protect Deer Haven and the surrounding towns, because it was their home, because they had the ability when others didn't.

A modern-day warrior, Sallie thought, her heart racing, filling with him as he walked next to her, protecting her as he rushed her through the loading entrance and into the supply store.

Jacob could feel that odd premonition of approaching danger, the watchfulness, all his senses heightened.

He covered Sallie's back, keeping himself between her and any danger that could be incoming, be it a bullet or a body.

Nothing could happen to her. Not now, not after he'd found her.

With one hand at the small of her back, his gaze moving constantly over the area, he hurried her into the store and up to her office. He wanted her to get what she had to do over with and to get her home to his ranch as quickly as possible. Only there could he be completely certain of her safety.

As they stepped into the outer office, Tara came out of her chair, an expression of relief racing over her face.

"Thank God you're here," she exclaimed as Jacob rushed Sallie across the room to the office door as Tara rushed behind them. "This place is going crazy, Sallie."

"I know, Tara," Sallie answered her as Jacob pushed open the office door and quickly checked the room before allowing her in.

He stood aside as she walked quickly to her desk as Tara headed to the coffee maker in the corner of the room.

"Davison is refusing to order extra supplies despite the fact that the numbers are severely low. Mr. Dillerman has already called twice today for you, and he's not happy at all for some reason. Every department head is going crazy and yelling at me because you're not here to hold their hands, wipe their noses, and tell them what good little assholes they are." She finished with a roll of her eyes and a lethal dose of sarcasm.

His cousin normally didn't get agitated easily.

Sallie was obviously smothering her laughter at Tara's agitation.

"Make the calls," she told her assistant. "Get the department heads up here in an hour and I'll address their problems. While you do that, I'll call Dillerman. I'll take care of Davison during the meeting with the others. It may be time to let him go and advance his assistant, Jim Allen."

Jacob knew both Roy Davison and Jim Allen. Davison had been given the position by Dillerman several years before Sallie took over the store. He was a superior ass who thought he should have had her position. Allen had been Sallie's choice as assistant just after she arrived, and she couldn't have made a better pick. The problem was, Jim Allen had no opportunity to do more than learn the ropes under Davison.

"I was talking to Rancor the other evening when I saw him in town." Tara took a seat in the chair next to Sallie's desk and crossed her legs as she leaned forward, resting her arms on her thighs. "Justice hesitates from moving his accounts from Prader's because of Davison, Sallie. I've heard several other ranchers are having the same reservations. Before you came in, we were always refunding accounts, making excuses, and dealing with irate customers because of him. He should have been replaced immediately."

"I promised Stanley Dillerman I'd wait the three years before replacing department heads." Sallie shook her head. "They were expecting a chance at the managerial position and it was jerked from them. That time is up now, so replacing him with Jim won't be a problem. I want to hear what he has to say first, though."

"You're being far more diplomatic than I would have been." Tara snorted. "That man is nothing but a bully with everyone but you and me." She flashed Jacob a smile as he propped himself next to the door, his coffee in hand. "He's too scared of my cousin to try to push me around."

Jacob lifted his coffee cup in a toast to her as a smile quirked his lips. Lily, Shay, and Tara were the only girls among his cousins; he was protective of them. And he made certain everyone knew just how protective he could be.

Those protective instincts that his father had always lamented were still rioting. He listened as Tara and Sallie discussed each department and Tara gave her opinions easily. Sallie listened to each point, a thoughtful expression on her face as she occasionally made notes on the tablet in front of her.

When they finished, Sallie went over the notes she'd made, typed in several more, then gave Tara the go-ahead to call the department heads together for a meeting within an hour.

Tara gave a quick nod, rose from the chair, and hurried to the door, her gaze flicking warily to Jacob as he reached for the lock on the door at her approach.

"Should I lock the outer door?" she asked softly as he opened it for her.

Jacob gave a subtle nod and after she left the room, closed and relocked the door.

"You don't have to stand there," Sallie told him, rising gracefully to her feet and moving to the file cabinet. "The couch is really comfortable."

She began pulling files, moving among the four

drawers until she had what he assumed were the files on each department head. She looked at him again when she returned to her chair, her gaze faintly quizzical.

"I'm not used to sitting around, baby," he reminded her with a slow, teasing grin. "Now, if you want to suggest something a little more energetic on that couch, we could discuss it."

He watched the faint flush that colored her face and neck but her expression showed definite interest. A second later she gave a little shake of her head and opened the first file.

"Davison is becoming a problem." She sighed. "He's one above normal order away from completely depleting our feed supplies. I had to make an emergency order last night."

"Good thing," he agreed. "Grange mentioned putting in our monthly supply order in a few days. And I know Justice intends to go through you when he orders for his own ranch."

"So both of them warned me by text yesterday evening." She was distracted now, her attention on the file she was going through. "Everything will be ready when they call. I made certain of it."

Remaining quiet, Jacob watched her as she worked, faintly surprised at how intent she was. Most people seemed to think she sat back and did little where actually overseeing the large business was concerned. And though Tara had denied the charge, Jacob had often wondered about it. Watching her now, he found himself agreeing with his cousin. The business may not be hers, but she was damned serious about ensuring its success. And very few people who knew her realized that.

She'd hid from the world in more ways than one. Along with hiding from the danger that followed her, other than a few friends, she hid from everyone else as well. She preferred loneliness to the fear that friends could be hurt if they tried to protect her . . .

At that thought, a memory, insidious and at first blurred, slipped into his head. One minute, his memories were still blank where that warehouse meeting was concerned, then suddenly, parts of it were there.

That moment in time when the final limo appeared in the warehouse six years ago, and an American couple stepped out. The woman, her features aristocratic, dark blonde hair pulled back from cool, composed features. Dressed in silk slacks, a pristine gray blouse, and black pumps she looked completely out of place among the rougher military wannabes she met with. Her partner had been a few inches taller, black hair, unassuming, almost plain. And Jacob had recognized both of them.

The couple had been at the American ambassador's party where Jacob had met Sallie, or Kyra as she'd been introduced. They were both part of the ambassador's staff. They'd seen him with Sallie, seen him dancing with her, walking with her in the garden. And the woman was CIA.

As the department heads were let into Sallie's office, the memories trickled back into his head, one piece at a time, like puzzle pieces. One part here, one part there. Faces, names, the knowledge that the investigation into Forefront hadn't gone anywhere because it had been betrayed from the inside, by a trusted source. By the same woman looking so cool and composed as she and her partner greeted Forefront's generals.

The agent could know who he was, probably did know. Using the camera feature on the phone he carried, Jacob had hurriedly snapped pictures. As he took the final one, it was in that moment that one of the men patrolling the building caught him. The battle to stay alive then had come with a single thought. If he didn't kill the traitor and he died instead, then Sallie would never be safe. She'd be taken, tortured, just on the off chance that she might know something.

The shoot-out that ensued had sent a bullet into one of the containers of chemicals positioned close to the couple and too damned close to him. When it went off, there was that moment that he saw that fragile, feminine body torn to pieces before he was thrown through the air like a child's forgotten toy.

His last conscious memory was thinking that the woman he'd fallen in love with wouldn't be safe if he didn't survive. And he'd been pretty damned certain he wasn't going to survive.

He focused on Sallie, every muscle in his body tensing to move into action. The phone he'd taken the pictures on hadn't been found, he knew that and he didn't trust the hope that it had been destroyed. Thankfully, he hadn't taken any pictures of Sallie on it, either. But, without the phone, there had been no evidence of the male half of that couple, and he knew that body hadn't been found. And the man had seen Jacob with the ambassador's lovely staff member. A woman he would have known was Ambassador Dougal's stepdaughter.

Revenge.

They'd come after Sallie, pushing her to find him, or

for him to find her. To bring them together and destroy them both.

They'd use her, torture her, kill her, all in the name of vengeance.

Watching her as she dealt with each of the eight department heads, his heart filled with so much emotion and savage determination that it was all he could do to keep from jerking her from that damned desk and rushing her out of the building and back to his ranch. He wanted her surrounded, protected from so much as stubbing her toe.

Nothing could happen to her. He couldn't lose her again.

He'd spent six years tormented by images of her, by the dreams he'd lost and the woman he'd given his heart to.

He'd be damned if he'd lose so much as another day with her.

chapter eighteen

Sallie worked her way through each department head, saving Roy Davison for last. Between the store, lumber, ranching materials, feed and granary, and hunting and fishing supplies, Dillerman's was a sprawling undertaking that sat right outside town. There were eight department heads as well as their assistants, and they were responsible for the running of each section of the business, under Sallie's direct supervision.

She'd tried to keep from restraining them, taking Stanley Dillerman's advice that the team he'd put together worked best when allowed to do their job without micromanagement. Which suited her fine. She'd been more concerned with surviving at the time. But the months had passed, she'd faced a Jacob that hadn't known her, Tara, Lily, and Shay had made their way past her defenses, and even those damned Culpeppers had managed to gain her affection.

Somehow, over the three years she'd been in Deer

Haven, the store had become important to her as well. She'd had no family, no lover, no children. Her future was iffy, and even her name wasn't completely her own. The store had become her focus instead.

She hadn't micromanaged, but that didn't mean she didn't keep her eye on everything going on in every part of the business. With Tara's help, she knew every strength and weakness of each department head as well as what was going on in their departments at any given time. Hence the knowledge that Davison seemed to be deliberately allowing the feed count to slip dangerously low as often as possible. The problem had been there before Sallie's arrival and only increased after she'd been given the position of manager.

Once she'd heard from the other department heads, she turned to him.

"Roy?" She arched her brow, keeping her expression cool, composed.

He was built like a bully, but managed for the most part to keep it contained at work. At the moment, the cautious glances he kept directing to Jacob assured her that he was only keeping it contained now out of fear.

"Yeah?" he answered, the tone just shy of belligerent.

"I had to make an emergency order of feed and other supplies last night because your counts were far below what's needed. This is the third time in the past six months," she pointed out, sitting back in her chair and watching him closely.

She was aware of Jacob, his body tense, prepared.

"My counts were fine." Davison's craggy face settled

into a sneer, his narrow gray eyes spiteful as he flexed his shoulders.

He was built like a pit bull with a shock of graying brown hair that always looked greasy and an expression that never failed to border on insolence.

"Your counts weren't fine," she told him, keeping her voice calm, even. "Three emergency orders in six months cut into profits for Dillerman. That makes me look bad and it just pisses him off."

Triumph shadowed Davison's face, accomplishment.

"I warned him you didn't have the balls to keep profits up." He grunted. "Maybe he'll listen next time."

It had been deliberate.

She'd wanted to give him the benefit of the doubt, but she'd known. She'd known since taking the job that he not only resented her, he hated her.

She nodded slowly. "I talked to Stanley Dillerman before coming in this morning. Collect your belongings when you leave here. You're fired." She nodded to Tara, who placed an envelope with his name on it on the table beside his chair.

Snatching it up, he tore it open and read the short note Dillerman had authorized Sallie to prepare for him. With it were all hours owed in the form of a check.

Davison's face went brick red and the sneer he'd been holding back curled at his lips as he turned to watch Jacob move in closer to her.

"Brave with him here, ain't ya?" A snarl pulled at his lips as he rose to his feet. "That's okay, bitch. Dillerman will screw you next."

With that, he stomped to the door, jerked it open, and

slammed it behind him with enough force that she wondered if the wood cracked. The entire room seemed to take a deep, collective breath.

"Well, it's just about time," Roger Oakley, the thin, bespectacled floor manager said in a deep bass voice that never failed to startle her. "Maybe the rest of us can get a little peace from his harping now." He stood and nodded to Sallie. "Good job, Ms. Hamblen. Damn good job."

The department heads followed him from the office, the door finally closing more quietly behind them and allowing Sallie to let out her own deep breath. Hell, she hadn't even known she'd been holding it until that moment.

"I'll catch the calls the department heads will be sending in after they're back downstairs," Tara announced, moving to the door herself.

Jacob followed her to it, opened it, spoke to her briefly, then let her out and locked the door once it was closed again.

"Damn good job, Ms. Hamblen." Jacob grinned at her, his expression approving as he stepped beside her once again, then bent to deliver a quick, hard kiss to her lips. "Are we done here now?"

The tension in his big body hadn't abated, nor had the hard gleam of intensity in his eyes softened in the least. He still looked like a warrior going into battle at any second.

"Done," she assured him. "Tara can take care of the rest of it. I just need to wait for confirmation that he's left the property."

She didn't trust Davison. Tara had the two security

guards waiting when Davison left, with orders to take the other man straight to his desk to clear out his belongings, then to his car and to watch him leave. Roy Davison was a known troublemaker when he was pissed off.

"I told Tara to contact Kenny. He's outside with two of the hands just in case. They'll make certain he leaves." He shrugged, stepping to the window to the side of her desk and looking out briefly. "They'll take care of it."

He was prepared, but he hadn't known she was firing Davison.

"What kind of trouble are you expecting, Jacob?" she asked worriedly, watching him as she felt panic begin to edge at her mind. "You have men at the house, here, and I know we were followed from the ranch."

"I have men in place just in case. That's what I do, baby, prepare for the worst." And that explanation sounded really logical, except his expression was tighter now, harder.

"And lie," she suggested, her tone low as she deliberate stilled the tremble in her fingers. "Now tell me the truth."

Jacob wasn't just prepared. As the morning had progressed, he'd become quieter, more intense, more watchful.

He paced around her desk again before turning to stare at her.

"The truth," he murmured. "The truth is, I just want you back at the ranch where I know for a fact you're safe, baby. I'm not comfortable right now with so many around. Once we find John, or Deverson's partner, then we'll know more. Until then, I don't know who the hell to watch for, or which direction danger might come from. These people aren't logical or sane. They're fanatics. And fanatics never do what you want or expect them to do."

She took a deep breath, let it out, then rose to her feet and slid her tablet back into her bag.

"I'm ready, then. I just have to stop at the house for a few more things, then I'll be good for a while at the ranch." Looping the straps of her bag over her shoulder, she faced him with what she hoped was a fearless expression. "Lead on."

As Jacob drove to the house, Sallie stared at the passing scenery as she fought back her fear and the edging panic. She tried to tell herself Deverson's death signaled the beginning of the end, and once John was found, it would be taken care of. Jacob wouldn't feel that he had to protect her every minute and she could finally live with the knowledge that she was safe.

But she knew finding John came with other risks. She had her own secrets, and the chances of her ex-husband revealing them were high. For all his faults, for all the secrets he'd kept from her, he'd never lied to her, unless the lie of omission counted. And he'd always warned her that secrets got more men killed than the truth ever had.

She should have gone to Jacob when she first realized he was in Deer Haven. When she had known beyond a shadow of a doubt that what she felt for him in Switzerland hadn't died. She hadn't done either of them any favors by remaining silent.

"You're too quiet." Jacob's voice was a dark rumble that stroked over her senses, caressed her even when he wasn't touching her. "I know you're frightened, but we'll get this taken care of."

She blinked back the tears that threatened to fall.

"I was just thinking," she assured him, hoping the smile she shot him was convincing before she stared in front of her again. "Davison gave in too easily, perhaps. I expected more of a fight." She latched on to the excuse.

It wasn't a lie. Roy Davison had capitulated a little too easily as far as she was concerned. He wasn't a man to step back, even when faced with someone stronger. He was a bully, true, and most were cowards. Davison was one of the rare few that had never shown cowardice. He'd fight as easily as he'd threaten, and just because his opponent was stronger, didn't mean he'd back down. He saw it more as a challenge, she'd always thought.

"Davison has his faults, but he's not a stupid man," Jacob mused. "I was surprised he was playing with his job that way, even to get back at you or Dillerman. Kenny knows Davison better than most. I'll talk to him, see if there's anything we should know about."

Sallie frowned over at him in surprise. "Why would you do that?"

He scratched at his cheek, his expression a bit sheepish. "Because he acted out of character." He shrugged. "That's what I do, Sallie. This is my home. I'm related to just about everyone here in one way or another, including Davison, and there was a time I would have trusted him to back me in a fight. So it concerns me that he let jealousy of a job get into his head like that."

Sallie watched him thoughtfully now, frowning.

"He's always been a bit confrontational with me," she

admitted. "Never to the point that I felt threatened, but I never knew what to expect from him."

"I saw that." He nodded. "He's a crusty bastard, I'm not denying that. I just want to make certain something besides the job isn't driving it."

She tilted her head, that undefined something that had always drawn her to him suddenly given definition. On the outside, Jacob might pretend otherwise, but he genuinely cared about people, especially those he knew.

"You're a softie, Jacob Donovan," she accused him with a sudden sense of lighthearted fun. "All scowls on the outside and melted butter on the inside."

He laughed at the description. "Keep tellin' yourself that, baby," he suggested, flashing her a teasing grin. "And when I get around to that spanking I owe you, I'll remind you of it."

She had little doubt that when that spanking came, she'd enjoy the hell out of it. He'd never hurt her. She knew that all the way to deepest part of her soul. He would never do anything, physically or emotionally, to hurt her.

The knowledge that she'd wasted the past three years avoiding him infuriated her. She'd lain alone, staring into the darkness, aching for him. She'd watched for him each time she left the house and dreamed of him when she slept.

"This will be over soon, Sallie," he suddenly promised her, reaching out to grip her hand where it laid on her lap, his fingers twining with hers. "And when it is, you have some big choices to make because I don't intend to let you go. Not this time. Not for a second."

She stared at where his larger, broader fingers held

hers, his grip gentle but firm. The ridged calluses and roughened flesh could bestow the greatest pleasure . . . or kill when needed.

The fact that he not only could but would kill in defense of her should have caused at least mild trepidation, instead, the thought of that protectiveness, that determination to keep her safe, wrapped her in reassurance.

"I don't want you to let me go, Jacob," she told him, staring at his profile and the rough handsomeness that had always drawn her. "Not ever again."

She loved him.

She loved him so much that she feared losing him again would be more than she'd ever be able to survive. But loving him meant the secrets she'd kept to herself and refused to share with him, would have to be told, soon. Before Jacob managed to find John and her ex-husband revealed them himself.

When they got back to the ranch, she'd tell him then. It wasn't a discussion she could have in the truck, and she didn't want to discuss at her house, not when Jacob felt it important to get back to where he felt she was most secure.

As he held her hand, she was aware of him talking in a low tone through the Bluetooth he wore, with the men he'd had watching her house. Evidently everything was secure because she heard him assure whoever he was talking to that they were minutes away.

Some clothes, the duffel bag she kept in her closet in case she had to run at a moment's notice. The bag held the pictures important to her. Those of her parents before her father's death, a few of friends, Sister Rebecca, and several of her with her father when she was an infant. Some jewelry passed down from her paternal grandmother, a baby blanket. A small snapshot she'd taken of Jacob in the hotel room in Switzerland when he hadn't known what she was doing.

His expression had been unguarded, and she'd always told herself what she saw there was love. She'd fallen in love with in those three days, surely he'd loved her just a little. Then, when he hadn't returned, she'd held on to the memories, to what he'd given her rather than the fact that he hadn't returned.

"Here we are." Jacob's announcement broke into her thoughts.

She lifted her head as he released her hand and watched as he drove the truck into her driveway and beneath the carport just outside the kitchen door. Once he parked, he talked to whoever was in the house again, letting them know he was there.

"Try to hurry, baby," he told her, his gaze going over the surroundings as he slid from the truck and motioned her out on his side.

Sallie nodded as she scooted across the seat and let him help her out. His arm went around her back and she noticed how he seemed to try to cover her at every possible angle before opening the door to the kitchen and pushing her inside.

Sallie paused after he closed the door, looking around the dimly lit house she'd bought when she learned Jacob lived in the area. She'd bought the furniture herself, decorated it, had begun to feel as though it was home.

"I bought the house just after I realized you lived here," she told him, walking slowly across the room, her fingers trailing over the back of a chair with its pretty pale blue chair pad. "I'd never considered buying a house before that."

It had nearly broken her the day she'd been introduced to him and realized he didn't remember her.

She realized then that as much as she still loved the house, she loved Jacob's house perhaps more, because he was there. Because she could feel him in every room even when he wasn't there.

"I knew you were mine when I first glimpsed you in town, weeks before that," he told her, following her as she moved through the house. "If other things hadn't been going on at the time, then I would have realized my familiarity with you had to have a reason. By time I could focus on it, I'd had you in my head for more than a month. You were a part of me."

He'd been dealing with terrorists and human traffickers and members of the town who had been involved in transporting both, she knew. The battle in the mountains outside Deer Haven hadn't been given news coverage, it had been kept quiet, but still, gossip and Deer Haven, as Tara was wont to say, were like the best of friends and the worst of enemies.

"I have my stuff in the bedroom," she told him, moving into the hall. "I keep it together, just in case I had to run fast I wouldn't lose any of it."

She went to the closet and pulled the duffel bag from inside, along with her suitcase. The suitcase wasn't a large one, but it would hold enough clothes for about five days. With those at Jacob's house, she'd be okay until she could come back to get the rest.

As she packed, she was aware of Jacob standing close

to the door, appearing relaxed, in no hurry. She swore she could feel the tension emanating from him, though. He didn't pace, or scowl, or look impatient. He looked as though he didn't have a care in the world other than waiting for her to pack.

Once her clothes were packed, she put hiking and riding boots in, just in case she needed them and closed the case. As she snapped the locks in place, she turned just in time to catch a glimpse of Jacob flying across the distance to slam into her.

They went to the floor. Hooking an arm around her waist, Jacob dragged her to the other side of the bed as a weapon exploded into the silence. Several shots, the feel of bullets digging into the floor as Jacob cursed furiously.

"Stay down," he hissed, returning fire as Sallie scrabbled along the floor as he kept pushing her toward the bed table and the window at the side of the room.

Where were the ranch hands he'd had in the house? She hadn't heard anything. No struggle, no warning.

Terror tore through her, nearly stealing her breath as she huddled at the corner of the bed and the table, suddenly thankful she'd picked a bed with drawers at its base, rather than a traditional one. At least there was some protection.

"Your men are down, Donovan," a familiar male voice called into the room. "They looked like good men too. Oh well."

Ray Masser?

Her stepfather's aide?

Sallie wanted to shake her head, to force it to make

sense. What was he doing there and why was he shooting at them?

Jacob didn't react. She watched as he reached to the
ear that held the Bluetooth in place.

"Phone's not working," Jacob said, barely a breath of
sound. "Jammed."

Lowering his hand, lying flat against the floor, he
glanced at her, and her breath caught at the predatory
purpose in his face.

"It's Ray?" She could barely breathe, let alone put
enough sound to her voice to even approach a whisper.

He gave a brief nod before motioning her to silence.

Sallie laid her face against the floor, fighting to hold
in her sobs, her fear. This wasn't supposed to happen.
She should have never stayed. Oh God, what if something happened to Jacob? What if they took him from
her forever?

What if she never again had a chance to tell him she
loved him?

"Come on, Donovan, surely your men mean something to you." Ray laughed. "I heard you were all about
your friends and family."

Jacob lay perfectly still, as though Ray wasn't dis-
cussing the murder of the men who worked for him.

"You know," Ray continued. "You're fast. I should
have been able to put a bullet in you before you got
behind that bed. But you know you're pinned down,
your men out of commission. Come on out, and we can
discuss this. I'll even let Kyra go now that I have you."

Kyra. She'd almost forgotten her mother's insis-
tence on calling her Kyra. Sallie had chosen her name

because she knew her father often called her Sallie before his death, so long ago. She'd been four when he died, but her mother had told her how he would sing to her, how much he loved her. For all her cold, unfeeling ways, Megan had her moments of softness.

Her mother had hired Ray though, Sallie knew. She'd often wondered how the weaselly bastard had managed to fool Megan Dougal as well as Rance.

"You're dead, Jacob. You know that. I'm not alone. You won't get out of here alive." Ray's voice was harder, colder.

Did he sound closer somehow?

She risked a glance at Jacob, uncertain what he was so focused on as he stared at the end of the bed.

Sallie felt silent tears fall from her eyes despite her determination not to shed them. She kept her head down on the floor, turned away from Jacob so he wouldn't see them.

"Tell him, Kyra." Ray's voice was a blade, sharp and cutting. "You know me well enough to hate me. You think he's going to survive this."

She didn't have a choice but to trust in Jacob, because she damned sure didn't trust Ray.

"I think I changed my mind about letting her go," Ray announced then. "I think after I shoot you a time or two, let you bleed some, I'll let you watch when I tie her to the bed and give her to my friends. They get inventive when it comes to their women. Especially when I give them permission to hurt the little bitches."

Sallie felt her stomach clench sickeningly but managed to keep her lips pressed together, her cries from escaping.

She was terrified Jacob would be hurt, killed. Dying herself didn't seem nearly so bad as the thought of losing Jacob.

She should have kept running. She should have never stayed here where she'd bring the danger to him. He was right, they wanted him and she'd been used to draw him out. Except she hadn't drawn him out, somehow, by coincidence or Rance, she'd ended up beneath his nose, endangering him.

What was he doing?

Looking up, Sallie watched as the muscles in his back shifted, flexed, though she couldn't see his hands or anything else. The motion beneath his shirt indicated he was doing something, though.

"Come on, Jacob." Ray was growing angry now. "If I have to risk my men to rush that bed, then she'll be the one that pays for it. I'll make her beg to die and I'll make you watch. You remember those women in Switzerland? What my people did to them? You really want to watch her hurt like that?"

Sallie could feel Jacob's tension now. The muscles had stopped moving in his back, he lay as still as death, waiting on what, she wasn't certain.

"That was my sister you killed in that warehouse, you fucker!" Ray suddenly snarled, fury erupting in his voice. "My only blood. You'll pay for it."

Still, Jacob didn't speak, he didn't move and Sallie made certain to follow his lead. She capped one hand over her mouth and fought against the tears, the sobs. She couldn't distract him, wouldn't distract him. Not when she could feel his focus like a heavy weight against her, urging her to caution.

"I thought for sure when I killed the bitch's mother, she'd run to you," Ray suddenly said, his voice gleeful as shock resounded through her. "Your momma cried for you, Kyra. Did you know that?"

Cried for her?

Megan would prefer torture to crying for anyone, Sallie thought. Her mother wouldn't have thought to cry for anyone, she would have cursed Ray, insulted, and reviled him until he killed her to shut her up.

Still, Jacob didn't move.

If she couldn't see he was breathing, she'd have thought him dead.

What was he doing?

Silence filled the house then, overwhelming and heavy, pushing at her, choking her with the insidious evil that seemed to move through it, searching, hungry for a victim.

A murmur of sound reached her then. Whispers, almost like the deadly hiss of a serpent from beyond her bedroom door.

Was he arguing with someone?

She looked at Jacob again. No movement. No sound.

He was waiting on something, she could feel it, certain that whatever it was, or whatever he had planned, would work.

The hissing sounds became more imperative, a sense of anger filling them before they stopped for long moments.

God, what were they doing? She would have never been able to wait like this on her own, to stay still and in place without Jacob there.

The room was darker on this side, the heavy curtains

closed over the window, whereas they were partially open on the other side, allowing a bit of sunlight in. It kept the side they were hiding on in deep shadow, lending a sense of security she knew wasn't really there.

The whispers began again, once again, softly at first, then with that sound of anger, like a cat denied a mouse that stayed just out of reach.

Jacob listened closely. He could hear two distinct whispers, one male, Ray Masser, the other female. He stayed perfectly still, his heartbeat steady, controlling the impulse to rush, to get Sallie out of there and safe.

For the moment, they were as safe as they could be. Masser and whoever his accomplice was evidently weren't certain of their location. The bathroom was on this side of the room, the door partially open, and he knew Sallie kept the shade closed on the small window there. Masser didn't want to take the chance that Jacob was behind the bed because to do so would leave him vulnerable if Jacob were in the bathroom instead.

The platform bed with its under drawers provided relative safety while keeping bullets from being fired from the doorway beneath the bed. It was darker here, shadowed. As long as they stayed still and silent, and waited, then Masser would mess up.

The furious whispers coming from beyond the doorway almost made him smile. The woman was more impatient, and she was making Masser impatient as well. The woman didn't have the sense of self-preservation Sallie seemed to have. Despite the tears he knew she was shedding, there weren't sobs, not a single cry. She was perfectly still and silent, following his lead. Just a little longer, he predicted. If they could ensure Masser didn't pinpoint their exact location, then he'd mess up. He'd let the woman convince him they were in the bathroom, or push him to make a move. And if he was lucky, real damned lucky, Justice would realize Jacob hadn't checked in when he arrived at the house as he was supposed to.

He'd nearly sent the text, had even reach for the phone, when he'd stopped. Staring at the door from the truck, he'd given into the impulse to wait. If the text didn't go through, Justice would call and when the call didn't connect, the other man would be on his way with reinforcements.

That was, if Justice hadn't become distracted. He couldn't depend on it, because the other man had the protection of Lily and Shay. If someone had gone for the girls, or made it appear as though they were, then the Culpeppers would ensure their safety before wondering if Jacob had checked in.

There were too many variables, too many ways Masser and whoever he was working with could have influenced the plans he and the Culpeppers had put in place. Ultimately, Sallie's protection was on his shoulders, and he'd never allowed himself to think otherwise. He didn't depend on the others to be in place to protect her. He'd seen that fail in too many operations with other agents and saw too many dangers associated it when the women in question belonged to him.

"Jacob, I know where you're hiding," Masser snapped. "Stop pissing me off and come on out. You're one man. You don't have the ammo to hold me off, or the firepower I have."

Yeah, he was just going to give himself and Sallie up like a twit with nothing better to do than die. And the little bastard might think he knew where they were hiding, but he wasn't certain. If he was certain, then he'd have already made his play.

Just a few more minutes, he predicted, holding his weapon steady, his body relaxed, prepared to move at a second's notice.

Another round of furious whispers, the feminine sound of it commanding, pushing Masser.

Yeah, that woman was going to get the bastard killed, Jacob was betting on it. He was lying there betting both his and Sallie's lives on the fact that she would force Masser to make a move.

A sudden round of automatic gunfire swept the room. Illegal, the rat-a-tat-tat of a small, handheld machine gun pistol by the sound of it. Hell of a lot more firepower than Jacob's Glock, but hell, it only took one bullet to kill.

The mirror on the wall at the end of the bed shattered, raining glass over his head. The rounds dug holes in the carpeting and sent cotton bedding in the air. The windows, so far, hadn't been hit.

He felt Sallie jerk behind him and tensed, wondering if she'd cry out. She didn't make a sound, but one hand gripped his ankle lightly over his boot, her fingers tightening then releasing.

Damn, she was smart. She let him know she was okay without a breath to give away their position.

"Bastard!" he heard Ray mutter.

Almost. He was almost there.

If they rushed the room, they'd come together, he

guessed. One would jump on the bed, the other would come across the room at the end of it, heading for the bathroom. That would be his plan if he was certain the enemy was in the bathroom, but wanted to be sure they weren't hiding beside the bed, and time was running out.

If Masser knew anything at all about Jacob, he'd know he'd have backup somewhere. And if nothing else, the sound of gunfire could be heard across the distance between Sallie's house and her nearest neighbor. Those neighbors were nosy as hell and didn't hesitate to call the sheriff if they felt it warranted. And hopefully, Masser wasn't aware of the neighbors' paranoid natures or the fact that someone was always home whether a vehicle was or not.

Another round of furious whispers. The change in tone and anger had him preparing himself.

Oh yeah, Masser's female partner wasn't happy. She might even suspect Jacob and Sallie had somehow escaped.

Keeping his shoulder to the bottom of the thick mattress to ensure he felt any pressure on the bed, he waited, watching that point where the shaft of light spilling from the other window fell across the floor just enough to alert him if anyone was moving in the room.

It didn't matter if they came in together or one waited behind as backup, both were dead. Male or female, once they targeted Sallie, they'd signed their own death warrants.

The whispers stopped and Masser wasn't speaking. They were gathering their courage now, he guessed, especially the aide. He'd be convincing himself that whatever argument the woman presented was logical and knowledgeable. A few deep breaths. Check his weapon, listen . . .

They rushed the room in a hail of gunfire that had him moving. He rolled to his back, catching the woman as she came across the bed and firing before he changed angle and fired again, hitting Dougal's aide in the chest and throwing him back.

Swinging back, his gaze locked on the woman as her fingers tangled in Sallie's hair and dragged it back, forcing her to sit up and provide cover for the woman.

Jacob knew her. The same woman Sallie had introduced as the head of Dillerman's pet department. Blonde hair, dark eyes, slender. She'd hidden her toned body with slouchy clothing and a shy demeanor and the fact she'd been in town nearly since Sallie had been.

Those eyes were narrowed on him, hatred gleaming in them as she placed her weapon at the side of Sallie's head.

Sallie stared back at him, tears filled her eyes, regret shimmering in the dim light of the room.

"Well, fuck," he said heavily, letting his wrist rest against his knee, his weapon lowered.

Cora smiled in triumph, her wrist shifting, the weapon turning in his direction.

And that was all he was waiting for.

Except someone beat him to it. Before he could fire his weapon, another exploded, driving a bullet in the center of the woman's forehead, flinging her back as brain matter exploded on the table behind her.

"Goddamn." He jerked Sallie to him, pushed her

to the floor and came around, weapon leveled on the older man standing in the doorway as three Culpeppers rushed around him and surveyed the room in surprise.

"Ambassador Dougal," Jacob greeted Sallie's stepfather as though blood and two dead bodies didn't lie between them. "What the fuck are you doing here?"

His arms tightened around Sallie, feeling the shuddering of her body, the sobs that began tearing from her as her hands held him, her fingers tight at his waist.

She was safe. That was all that mattered, he told himself, she was safe.

Justice, Pride, and Rancor looked around the room, their gazes heavy.

"We found John," Justice said quietly. "He's in bad shape but I think he'll live. From what we pieced together, he was trying to identify who sent Deverson. Masser caught him by surprise."

Sallie's head jerked, staring across the bed at the men gathered there, focusing on Dougal.

"Did he kill Mom?" Her voice was rough, filled with pain. "He said he killed her."

Grief flashed in Rance Dougal's eyes before he stared back at Sallie in surprise.

"Your mother had a stroke." He shook his head at the question. "I wouldn't have lied to you, Sallie."

Rance's dark face was creased, lined with worry, and for his age, he was in surprisingly good shape. The three-piece suit he wore looked a little out of place, but hell, he was a politician. They always looked out of place.

Pushing to his feet, Jacob helped Sallie, the sound of sirens in the distance assuring him that things were about to get decidedly uncomfortable.

Swinging Sallie up in his arms, Jacob stepped past Masser's body and the blood soaking the carpet. Cradling her against him, holding her tight, he carried her into the living room, where he placed her gently on the couch.

He was surprised that Rance was right behind them, his hands shoved into his pants pockets, his gaze on Sallie, his expression concerned.

Jacob jerked the throw from the back of the couch and put it around Sallie as Rancor sat a glass of water on the table beside her.

Crouching in front of her, Jacob framed her face with his hands, forcing her to meet his gaze.

"You okay, baby?" he whispered, her tearstained face breaking his heart. "Sheriff's almost here. I'll have to talk to him. Take care of this."

She nodded, obviously fighting to stop crying as she took several hard breaths.

"I'm okay." She nodded, those tears roughening her voice. "I promise. I'm not hurt."

"If you need me, send Rancor," he told her, leaning forward to kiss her gently before he pulled back and rose slowly to his feet.

He hated leaving her now. He wanted to rush her home, wrap her in his arms, shelter her, allow the tears and the cries to run their course before he filled her with all the love he felt for her.

"Rancor, stay with her," he ordered the youngest Culpepper before he turned to Rance. "You can come with me and explain what the fuck you're doing here."

Rance merely nodded, still watching Sallie with that heavy regret and grief before he turned and preceded

Jacob to where the sheriff rushed through the front door.

Just a little longer, he assured himself. A few more hours, then he could take her home, love her, and make damned sure nothing or no one ever threatened her again.

chapter nineteen

It was almost over. The threat to Jacob and herself was eliminated, but dealing with her stepfather came with complications, she knew. The next morning, he arrived not long after breakfast, his demeanor quiet, introspective, as she and Jacob sat in the living room facing him, waiting for him to speak.

"Sallie, I never agreed with your mother's decision to send you to boarding school so young. Hell, I didn't like the thought of it at any age." Rance pushed his fingers through his hair, his expression heavy with regret. "Your mother and I disagreed heavily over that."

Sallie watched him doubtfully. She'd been a child at the time, admittedly, but she couldn't remember a single time Rance and her mother had disagreed over anything. At least not in front of her.

"It doesn't matter, Rance . . ."

"Sister Rebecca was a close friend of mine while we

were growing up," he cut in. "I convinced your mother to send you to her school. Rebecca loved you, Sallie, more than she ever thought she would but I knew she would. You were a baby and so damned alone it gave me nightmares."

"Yet you still let her send Sallie away," Jacob pointed out, his tone hard.

Rance watched Sallie rather than Jacob, his expression growing heavier as weariness seemed to settle over his features.

"Megan liked to remind me often that Sallie wasn't my child and she brooked no interference in the decisions she made regarding her." Rance shook his head, rubbed at his neck, then sat forward on the couch and clasped his hands between his spread knees.

Sallie had never had a chance to really get to know her stepfather, but he'd never been cruel to her, and she'd always been thankful for everything he'd done for her.

"I chose to pick my battles with her," he continued, his voice resigned. "She was determined to send Sallie to boarding school, but I demanded she be sent to a school of my choice."

"I was happier with Sister Rebecca than I would have been with you and Mother anyway." She shrugged, but still, she could feel the regret that she hadn't had a family, or a home really. "I wasn't unhappy. I had what I needed."

Rance shook his head at the statement but apparently decided to let it go. "I've driven myself and the investigators crazy attempting to learn why you've been attacked." He glanced at Jacob. "At first, I thought John was the reason. Until Langley asked me to consult on an old case and the name Jake Rossiter came up. When I went to the director and called in a favor, he wouldn't give me the agent's identity, but he did help me to change my stepdaughter's name and instructed me to see Dillerman about placing her within one of his stores. And he made me swear not to reveal any of it to my investigators or anyone else. How Masser found out, I don't know."

"And Dillerman sent me here." Sallie turned to Jacob where he stood against the bar. "Why would he do that?"

"Because the case isn't closed. The agency would have someone watching you. And me," he stated thoughtfully.

"For three years?" She couldn't make sense of that. "Why would he do that? Why not just contact you?"

"After I lost my memories and came back to the States, I lost my security clearance as well due to the loss of memory. They couldn't be certain I hadn't somehow given away the operation. Our intel at the time identified that there was a high-ranking American releasing information on targets of interest to Forefront," Jacob revealed. "That's why I was at the warehouse that morning. John learned within hours of the meeting that the traitor would be at that meeting, turning over information involving our investigation of the group. Forefront's top generals as well as the head of the group were supposed to be there. From what the agency pieced together at the time, they learned I was there and a firefight ensued. Several containers of explosive chemicals detonated, killing everyone but myself, and according to John, two members of the meeting that showed up last survived as well. Unfortunately, they were unable to identify who it was, but it's speculated that I saw them."

"And according to the information I was given, there were no suspects," Rance stated. "That's why I was asked in to consult. My security clearance and the fact I was there at the time gave the director reason to believe I might be able to provide some information. According to the director, in the past few years Forefront had begun reforming."

"And to be taken seriously, killing the agent or agents involved in killing their generals would be their first order of business, suggesting one of the their leading members or even a general, survived the explosion," Jacob injected, his expression hardening, a flash of predatory calculation crossing his face.

"That's the director's belief." Rance nodded. "Somehow, he believes they identified John and when they came for him, they found Sallie instead. My own investigators believe somehow John was the target as well and they demanded Megan and I stay distant from Sallie and maintain the belief we were estranged from her. That impression Megan began when she and Sallie argued over the annulment John filed and served on Sallie. Megan blamed Sallie for the fact the marriage had been unconsummated. She knew Sallie had met and fallen in love with someone else and believed Sallie merely needed to assume her place as John's wife to get over it."

Sallie stared at the floor now and refused to look up as she silently cursed her stepfather. Heat rushed over her face and though she lifted her head moments later, she avoided Jacob's as well as Rance's gazes.

"Sallie." Jacob's voice was harder now, demanding.

"Would you like to look at me and tell me what the fuck he's talking about?"

Surprised flashed over Rance's face when she turned back to him accusingly.

"Sallie," he reproved gently. "Surely you told Jacob the truth of your marriage."

"It was no one else's business," she pushed out between gritted teeth.

Compassion and understanding filled Rance's expression then.

"I found the filing for the annulment," Jacob snapped. "It stated irreconcilable differences."

Rance sighed at the demand in his tone before a grimace of resignation crossed his expression. "Megan insisted I find a way to hide what she called Sallie's stubborn refusal to make her marriage work."

"Stop." Sallie glared back at Rance. "This discussion is pointless."

She didn't want Jacob to hear anything further where her so-called marriage was concerned. She couldn't afford it. Her heart couldn't afford it.

"That marriage was pointless," Rance snapped. "Had I known those two all but blackmailed you into accepting John's proposal, I would have fired his ass long before I did. John somehow managed to convince your mother that he loved you and she was desperate to find a way to make you forget whoever you met in Switzerland."

Jacob's expression was thunderous now, his gaze locked on her, burning with fury and demanding explanations.

"Let it go, Rance," she demanded, her voice low as

she gripped the arms of the chair with desperate fingers. "Stop this now."

"Like hell," Jacob snarled. "He can finish it, or you can. And I can promise you now, Sallie, I'll find out what happened. Now tell me what the hell happened."

Rance stared back at her as though confused. "Why didn't you tell me what they did, Sallie?"

He looked hurt, as though he had a reason to be.

"Why do you care?" she cried. "Don't pretend there was a single instance in my life that you gave me a reason to think you gave a damn, Rance. So why make it your business now? Just let it go."

He had to let it go. She couldn't bear it if it went any further. If Jacob learned the truth, she couldn't bear it.

"He can do that." Jacob's voice was a dangerous sound now, a warning of coming violence. "Doesn't mean I won't find out, Sallie."

She closed her eyes, aching to the point that she didn't know what to do with the pain.

Never in her life had Rance even hinted that he could be a friend, or that he was there if she needed him. She'd lived her life knowing she didn't have family, didn't have that support system that she had so needed.

"Sallie." The admonishment in Rance's voice was heavy now and no matter how gently it was delivered, she flinched.

"You need to leave." She came to her feet, adrenaline racing through her body.

She'd rather face an assassin than face this. She needed to run, to hide from it, just as she had been running and hiding for nearly five years from the memories and from the pain.

And she knew it was too late. As Rance came to his feet as well, she knew what was coming.

"Megan and John threatened to find the father of the child she lost after returning from Switzerland and destroy him." Regret and sorrow filled Rance's voice as Sallie turned to him, staring at him furiously. "I'm sorry, Sallie, he deserved to know."

"Did he?" she whispered painfully, fists clenching at her side. "Why, Rance? Why did he deserve to know something I hadn't told him? It was my business, not yours. It was my place to tell him, in my own time. I would have expected something like this from Mother, she was just that unfeeling. But not from someone who claimed to give a damn about me." She gave him a hard, cold smile. "You can leave now, Mr. Dougal. I don't think we need anything else from you."

And she wasn't staying, because she highly doubted he would leave.

She glared at Jacob. "I don't care much for threats and right now, I'll be damned if I want to talk to you either."

Pushing past Rance, she stormed from the living room to the guest room, closed the door quietly and locked it behind her. With her back to the door, she closed her eyes against the tears and let herself slide until she was sitting in the floor.

Laying her head against her knees, she knew she couldn't just make this go away now. There was no way to make Rance take his words back, or to make Jacob forget he'd heard them. And there wasn't a chance in hell he'd allow her to hold that agonizing event in her life inside, where she'd be safe from the pain and from the loss.

chapter twenty

Sallie pushed herself to her feet long minutes later, intent on washing her face, finding her composure. She'd no more than made it to the bed when the bedroom door pushed open then slammed closed.

Whirling around, she had a moment, a single moment to glimpse Jacob, the emotion, the hunger in his face before she was in his arms. Between one heartbeat and the next, Sallie found herself pinned against Jacob. One hand in her hair, pulling her head back, the other gripping her hip to hold her in place. And he was kissing her.

Wild, fueled by pure male lust, his lips covered hers, his tongue parting them and forging inside as a cry slipped from her throat.

She would have run from him, found a way to get her emotions under control first but once the greedy, ravenous kisses began, she couldn't force herself away from him. She became greedy herself. They'd nearly died, he could have died trying to protect her and all her dreams would have died with him.

The dominant sexual force she'd always sensed inside him came to the fore.

As his lips razed hers, caressed, nipped, his hand clenched in her hair, released, tugging sensually at the shortened strands and sending flames racing through her senses. The hand at her hip pushed beneath the snug camisole top she'd changed into, long, wicked fingers finding a sensitive, hardened nipple.

He didn't stroke it. He didn't just caress it. His thumb and forefinger gripped the hard peak, tugged at it, and sent the most incredible pleasure coursing straight to the hardened bud of her clit.

His head jerked back, his lips releasing hers, but only to nip the lower curve before his lips slid to her neck, the hand clenched in her hair tugging her head back farther.

"Oh God . . ." Strangled, torn with pleasure, her voice didn't even sound like her own. "Jacob . . ." His name was a sudden, shocked cry when he moved, his head lowering to her breasts, his lips surrounding the neglected nipple firmly.

"Yes . . . Oh yes . . . Jacob . . ." Arching to him, her fingers buried in his hair, the desperation to keep his lips in place the only thought she could manage.

Sizzling heat and rapid-fire pinpoints of ecstasy struck at her nipples, the tug and draw of his lips and fingers causing more of the slick heat to spill between her thighs. Her clit throbbed in need; each cell of her body begged for his touch.

Her senses were already in overload when she felt his hand move from her hair to her hip, then beneath the band of the leggings she wore. His fingers pushed past the thin pants, arrowing down until he was spearing through the slick folds between her thighs.

Sallie stilled, fighting to breathe, the tension amassing in her body tightened further, gathering. When his palm rasped her clit, she exploded.

Right there, her back to the wall, held in place by his harder body, his hand cupping her pussy, she came into his palm with a shattered cry of desperate, agonizing ecstasy. Shuddering, her hips pressing and rubbing the pulsing bud of her clit against his palm, she felt the rush of her juices spilling from her as her body shook in the grip of her release.

No sooner had she thought the violent sensations would ease and give her a chance to breathe than the sudden thrust of hard, broad male fingers into the clenching grip of her pussy only pushed her higher.

He stretched her, parted the tissue with pinching heat, with something she could only associate with painful sensuality, and sent another release of brutal sensation tearing through her. Heated, agonizing bursts of explosive release destroyed her.

Her thighs clenched on his hand, each shift of her hips intensifying the sensations sweeping through her. Her cries echoed around her, a sharp, male groan joining them as he worked his fingers against each clench and release of the muscles surrounding him.

Here was where she belonged, where she'd dreamed of being. Right here, in his arms.

His control was shot.

Jacob knew, the second he felt Sallie's release spill,

hot and silky into his palm, there wasn't a chance in hell he was going to ever let her go.

She was his.

As he felt the shudders racing through her body slow, the grip of her pussy on his fingers ease, the hunger ripping him apart rushed through his senses like a tidal wave and there was no waiting. He took her to the bed, jerking the tank top over her head, and as her back met the mattress, his hands went to the leggings.

In seconds, he had her naked. Sleek, soft flesh, swollen, hard-tipped breasts and one lush, bare, little pussy glistening with the slick, heavy spill of her release.

Tearing at his shirt as he went between her thighs, he shed the material, pushed her legs apart, and his lips went to the sweet honey waiting him. And the taste of her . . . Addictive, fucking sweet. Intoxicating.

He was undressed in seconds, one hand gripping the base of his furiously erect shaft as his lips and tongue licked, kissed, consumed the sweet essence of her. This was what he had walked away from six years ago, and if he had even suspected what had awaited him, he could have never walked away.

"Jacob," she gasped, her cry breathless, filled with wonder, with love.

Slender fingers slid into his hair, tangled in it as her hips arched to him. They rolled, lifted, and lowered to each stroke of his tongue and let the pleasure have her. She let him have her.

He was taking her. Taking it, loving it, by God, owning her pleasure as she owned his.

Pressing her thighs further apart, he pushed his hands beneath her rear, lifted her, and with a groan that was more a growl, sent his tongue tunneling hard and fast inside the sweet sheath and lush promise of ecstasy awaiting him.

Too much . . .

Sallie cried out at the fiery pleasure that tore through her, the feel of Jacob's tongue taking her, pushing inside her . . . oh God, licking at her inner flesh, destroying her.

She was sure she screamed, if she found enough breath to do so. She was fighting to breathe, to hold on, to anything, as the pleasure began to erupt inside her again. He was consuming her. Not just her flesh, but her senses. With his lips and tongue, he owned her, possessed her in ways she had no idea she could be possessed until she exploded to the hungry thrusts and licks of his tongue.

Dazed, perspiration slickening her flesh, she was only barely aware of him rising, moving between her thighs and coming over her.

"Jacob . . ." She stared up at him as he lifted her leg and pulled it to his hip.

A second later, a whimper left her lips, the feel of his shaft, iron hot and steel hard, pressing against the entrance to her body, stealing her breath.

Could she take more? Could her senses survive another wave of the brutal pleasure?

"I need you, Sallie," he groaned, his voice tight with emotion. "For so long I've ached for you."

Gasping, Sallie fought to drag in each breath at the slow, heated penetration of his cock inside her body. Each thrust sent him deeper, built each sensation until pleasure screamed through her senses. Digging her nails into his shoulders, she arched, taking more until he was fully embedded inside her. "Jacob." She whispered his name, shocked at the broken sound of her own voice.

Nothing mattered in that moment, in all the moments that would come after, but this. This man and the love and pleasure that filled her.

"Ah, baby." His tone was rough and filled with emotion as he pulled back, his cock stroking sensitized flesh as he nearly pulled free. A grimace pulled at his expression and he pushed deeper a second later, his shaft working deeper inside her. "God. Damn. Sallie, baby . . ." The harsh, graveled tone was followed by a short, sharp thrust that had her lifting closer with a shattered cry.

Her head thrashed against the mattress as sensation raced through her body.

"That's it, sweetheart," he crooned as her hips moved, fighting to push him deeper, harder inside her. "Take me. Work that sweet pussy on me just like that. Ah God, Sallie . . . Baby."

A hard, driving thrust buried him those final inches inside her. He filled her, overfilled her, the sensations dragging a breathless scream from her as her hands tightened on his arms, feeling the muscles bunch and flex beneath her palms.

"Sweet heaven, Sallie," he groaned as he came over her, his lips moving to her neck, stroking the sensitive flesh as his hips bunched, his muscles tightening as he pulled back, dragging the flared head of his cock over tender, nerve rich tissue. "So fucking sweet and tight . . . Fucking you is better than a dream . . . It's better than breathing . . ."

Heat surged through her, lashed at her. The erotic

words sank inside her senses and pushed her higher as more of her juices spilled to lubricate his way. Her inner muscles clenched around the retreat, hips arching to hold him inside her.

"Jacob, please . . ." she whimpered, she begged. "Oh God, please. It's not enough. Not enough . . ."

His groan sounded torn from his throat, ragged and in the next second, her pushed inside her harder, faster, burying several inches. He didn't stop. Each fierce impalement took him deeper, possessed her senses, as well as the unknown emotions beginning to tear through her.

His touch, his lips at her neck, hungry kisses, stinging little nips that she knew would mark her skin later, and she didn't care.

Her nails bit into his scalp, moved to his shoulders, and she fought to memorize every second of the incredible pleasure he was giving her. She wanted each moment branded into her brain, as vivid as it was now, to take out and remind herself that if only for a brief time once all this was over, Jacob held her.

She was lost in the almost painful ecstasy surging through her, a mix of pleasure and pain so extreme she had no idea how to process it.

As he thrust into her, pushed her deeper into the sensations amassing inside her, she fought just to hold on to enough of herself to survive without him. The pleasure was that extreme, that intense. She wanted it to last forever. To never lose it.

Holding tight to him, her lashes lifted and she stared up him, caught immediately by the savage hunger in his gaze. His eyes held her, locked her to him. Her breathing became harder, tighter, and she swore she felt a part of her open to him as her orgasm caught her so unaware that she had no time to prepare herself for it.

Ecstasy slammed inside her. Her eyes widened, a whimper passing her lips as Jacob's eyes narrowed and his thrusts increased, pushing her over that final edge and sending her flying.

The explosions of pleasure were cataclysmic, rapturous. Destructive.

With a final, desperate thrust, Jacob buried inside her a final time, his harsh groan vibrating around her. His hips pushed against her in several minute, hard jerks as she felt his shaft throb, pulse, his release pulling a hard grimace to his face before his eyes drifted closed.

"God help me, I love you," he whispered. "To the depths of my soul, Sallie. I love you."

Sallie collapsed beneath him, a final shudder working through her body before she felt the last of her strength ease from her limbs.

"To the depths of my soul," she repeated his words, something setting inside her, finally easing the pain she'd held on to for so long. "Forever, Jacob. I love you."

chapter twenty-one

That silence that filled the bedroom became nerve-racking, thick and heavy with unvoiced questions long minutes later.

Jacob lay on his side, her body tucked against him. He had one arm beneath her head, the other lying over her side, holding her in place. She knew what was coming. At least the bedroom was dark, her back to him, she didn't have to face him with the shameful knowledge that she hadn't been able to protect their child.

"I would have told you about the baby if I could have," she whispered into the darkness. "I wanted to tell you, but I had no idea how to find you and no one seemed to know who you were."

He was silent for long moments, but his hand moved, his fingers stroking over her stomach almost absently. Tears filled her eyes, the caressing touch, there, where their child had once laid, was ripping what was left of her heart into shreds.

"Why didn't you sleep with him?" It wasn't the question she expected.

"Because I didn't love him," she answered honestly. "I wasn't in the least attracted to him. Then he and mother threatened you . . ."

The tension rose quickly.

"What made you think I needed your protection?" Bleak, dark fury filled his voice despite the fact that it never rose. "You keep trying to shield me from what's going on with you. Do you think I'll continue to tolerate it?"

"It didn't matter," she whispered painfully. "I wasn't going to be the reason you were hurt then, any more than I want to be the reason now."

"But you let me be the reason you married that fucker?" he growled at her ear, his hold tightening when she tried to roll away from him. "Stay still, goddammit. Answer my question. I won't allow you to keep running."

She tried to fight her tears, but one slid free, making a long track down her cheek as he held her to him.

"It was my choice to make. I had to do what I thought was best, and that was what I did." She stared into the shadowed room, fighting the memories and the pain. "I can't go back and change it."

Just as she couldn't go back and the save the baby she'd lost.

"I should put you over my knee and paddle your ass. Goddammit, Sallie. Tell me why."

A sob escaped, despite her frantic attempt to halt it.

"Because I loved you." Her fingers gripped the sheet desperately as she fought to keep from screaming in anger. "Because I'd lost enough, and I couldn't bear to be responsible for hurting you."

She had to fight to keep from breaking down, to keep from screaming out her rage and pain. She'd been so overwhelmed with the loss of their child that she would have done anything to keep Jacob from knowing, on the chance that it would hurt him as deeply.

The man she had loved couldn't be so hard-hearted as to not grieve for his child, she'd told herself. Leaving her and not loving her didn't mean his child wouldn't matter.

She'd been so young, so naïve and alone, away from Sister Rebecca and her friends, terrified her mother would do as she threatened and find a way to destroy the man she loved. And she had been terrified of marrying someone she didn't know.

Jacob held her closer, tucked her head beneath his chin, and fought the black, vicious anger raging inside him.

Because she loved him.

She'd given him her virginity, loved him, lost their child, and married to protect him, and he'd been oblivious to it. He'd forgotten her. And the partner he'd trusted to have his back hadn't just lied to her, but blackmailed her into marriage.

"You can't save the world, baby," he told her, hating the knowledge that she'd loved him enough to try to protect him. "Sacrificing yourself is never an acceptable answer." But he knew he'd sacrifice himself for her, easily.

"I thought you didn't want me when you didn't come back." The vulnerability in her soft voice threatened to break him. "When I came here and we met again, you didn't remember me. Your name was different, you even moved and acted differently. I guessed then that you must have been an agent of some sort when you were in Switzerland."

"Why didn't you say something, Sallie?" he growled. "Why, baby? You've been here for three years and never said anything."

He felt a shudder work through her and the soft hitch of her breath, the sob she was hiding.

"I didn't know about the explosion," she said, those tears she refused to shed roughening her voice. "I thought you hadn't cared enough to remember me."

"You lived in my dreams nightly." He turned her to him, rising above her as he cupped her cheek in his palm and stared down at her, seeing the years of loss and pain in her expression as she stared up at him.

The room was dark, but there was enough moonlight peeking through the edge of the curtains to illuminate her face enough to read the emotions she normally kept hidden. "I was only existing until I had you in my arms again, baby."

Brain trauma and lost memories would have to be tricky. She was part of a week he'd lost that held information regarding a deadly group, a traitor, one that threatened him through her. And he was a good man. A loyal, fiercely protective man. He'd feel responsible for her, feel it was in his place to protect her. It wouldn't have to be emotional for him, not really personal, just a piece of the puzzle that he needed to figure out what happened that week.

She nearly lost the battle with her tears as his palm

moved from her face, caressing along her side then to her lower stomach, where he flattened his hand where their child had once lain.

"Protection didn't work the last time," he told her. "You left Switzerland carrying my baby. It won't work this time. I won't lose you again. And by God, you will not face carrying our baby, or raising it alone. You're mine, Sallie. Just as I'm yours."

"Always yours, Jacob." She touched his face, met the determination in his gaze, and knew, all the way to her soul, she'd finally come home. "Always . . ."